MAN OF MY WORD

A SAM POPE NOVEL

ROBERT ENRIGHT

In loving memory of Ellie Ceri Chandler,

CHAPTER ONE

As the brick-like fist collided with Sam's jaw, his head snapped to the left, rocking him against the tight binds of the wire. The chair wobbled, his limp weight threatening to topple him to the dirty concrete below. It was the third right hook Edinson had delivered, each one landing with the impact of a sledgehammer.

The man knew how to punch. That much Sam could still remember, despite the rattling of his brain.

Slouched over to the left, Sam drew the saliva back in his throat, before gobbing a mouthful of blood which splattered across the stone. Judging by the faded stains that peppered the floor, he wasn't the first person to be strapped to the chair.

Delicately, Sam moved his jaw from side to side, marvelling that it hadn't been broken yet. With a slight discomfort, he used his core strength to straighten himself in the chair, squinting at the uncovered bulb that shone down from the low ceiling. The barrage of punches had reopened the cut above his right eye, making a mockery of the fresh stitches. The wire binding his hands together pressed tightly against the cast of his fractured wrist.

Edinson circled him like a shark. His muscular, tattoo-covered forearms were exposed, the sleeves of his shirt rolled to the elbow. He stood over six feet three, and the sleeves were bulging under the bulk of his upper body. Sam knew the difference between a gym body and one built behind bars. Edinson had the same physique as numerous criminals he'd encountered in The Grid, the maximum-security prison he'd escaped from a little over two weeks ago.

It seemed like a lifetime.

'Again. Who are you?'

The question didn't emanate from Edinson. In fact, Sam was sure he'd never heard the monstrous man speak. Sitting on the other side of the room, wearing an expensive, beige three-piece suit, was José Vasquez. As one of the most powerful drug lords in the state of South Carolina, Vasquez was as rich as he was dangerous. With a reputation for eliminating his competition with brute force, Vasquez had sat opposite many a man, watching with silent pleasure as they were taken apart by his monstrous henchman. Despite his penchant for fancy clothes and exquisite etiquette, Vasquez had pulled himself up from the slums of Mexico City. Although he'd greased the palms of many officers to enable his expansion into America with manicured hands, Sam was sure there was plenty of blood on them.

In front of Vasquez was a metal table, littered with tools no doubt intended for Sam's torture. Beyond that, shadows engulfed the room, and Sam was certain it had taken Edinson thirteen strides to haul him from the door to the dimly lit chair he was now strapped to. A small detail, but one that Sam had registered in his mind.

It was habit.

Every little detail, no matter how inconsequential, could prove vital.

It was what had made him such a deadly sniper in a previous life.

A life he'd left long ago.

It had been a long and arduous road that had led to this point. From his motherless childhood following his father from military base to military base, being a soldier was in Sam's blood. His father, William Pope, had been a highly respected senior figure within the UK armed forces, known for his favouring of diplomacy over conflict. Sam's marksmanship soon saw him behind the scope of a rifle, but he'd tried to hold his father's principles dear.

Tried.

Sam's success rate soon caught the eye of General Ervin Wallace, a bullish man who had an unassailable position within the government. Called upon as the man to "fix" problems that the higher-ups wanted kept quiet, Wallace recruited Sam into his operation.

Project Hailstorm.

Countless covert missions, hundreds killed.

All off the books.

People eradicated from the world without explanation or mercy.

There were no questions asked.

No finer details.

Sam believed he was helping to protect the freedom of his country and the wider world. Then, on one fateful mission, Sam was sent home with two bullet holes in his chest and a slim chance of survival.

But that's what Sam was built for.

Survival.

Retiring from the armed forces, Sam settled into a life of normality with his wife, Lucy, helping to raise their son. Jamie had been everything to Sam. His incessant hunger for the written word had encouraged Sam himself to start reading more, and as his son grew, so did their bond. After

Jamie had turned five years old, he'd asked Sam for two promises.

One that he would read more and more.

And two, that he would never kill again.

Sam had intended to keep both.

Wanting to set a good example for his son, Sam enrolled in the Metropolitan Police, his impressive resume had him fast tracked to the training centre in Hendon in the London borough of Barnet, where he was excelling and on his way to becoming an officer of the law.

But then Jamie was killed.

On a summer's evening, while enjoying a few beers with his former comrade, Theo Walker, Sam noticed a drunk man entering his car and leaving the pub. Despite his intentions to stop him, Sam looked the other way. Minutes later, as he meandered down the road on his way back to his family, his life fell apart.

Lucy had brought Jamie along to surprise him on his walk home.

A car had skidded off the road, the drunk driver losing his bearings as he rounded a corner.

The image had been burnt into Sam's memory like a vile tattoo.

The flashing blue lights of the police cars.

The shocked faces of the onlooking crowd.

The man Sam had seen leaving woozily sat in the driving seat, tears streaming from his eyes and blood pouring from a gash on his head.

Lucy, on her knees, a guttural roar of anguish piercing the night sky.

And Jamie's body, lying broken and motionless in the road.

That moment changed everything.

Consumed by grief and guilt, Sam spiralled, and

despite her best efforts to bring him back, Lucy walked away from him after six months. The strength of her love for him made it impossible to stay, watching him torture himself for not doing the right thing for their son. When the driver, Miles Hillock, was given a short sentence and released early, Sam caved to his sadness.

The injustice for his son's death was too much to bear.

In his weakest moment, Sam was moments away from taking his own life, only for a fortunate visit from his commanding officer, Sergeant Carl Marsden, to bring him back from the brink.

Sam couldn't rewrite the past, nor could he bring Jamie back, but he could put some things right. Sam returned to the Metropolitan Police, applying for a position in the archives, and soon, he was scouring for criminals who beat the system. The people who were never bought to justice.

Sometimes the law was not enough.

Sam's fight against injustice went further than he could have imagined. A perceived terrorist attack at the London Marathon led to Sam bringing down one of the most feared criminals in London, along with uncovering ties to numerous high-ranking police officers.

All of them were now dead.

In the hunt for a missing girl, Sam toppled the Kovalenko human trafficking empire, saving four teenage girls destined for a horrific life of sex slavery. With the help of his former comrade, Paul Etheridge, Sam ventured to the Ukraine, burning down the last of the operation and putting the head of the Kovalenko family in the ground.

The echoes of his past soon resurfaced as Project Hailstorm, now named Blackridge, hunted his former mentor across Europe, a chase which Sam won but ultimately cost Marsden his life. Exposing the truth the horrors that General Wallace had sewn across the world, with

Etheridge's help, Sam, along with a rebellious Blackridge operative called Alex Stone, fought back.

Sam hadn't been saving the world. He'd been assassinating targets for one of the biggest global terrorist units in history. In his quest to end Wallace's tyrannical reign for good, Sam was imprisoned, sentenced to life in a maximum-security prison. Wallace had abducted DI Amara Singh, a plucky detective who Sam had heartbreakingly fallen for. To save her, Sam had killed Wallace and her captor and sacrificed his freedom.

While she walked away a hero, Sam was sent underground, left for the wolves. But it gave him a pathway to Harry Chapman, the man who pulled the strings behind most of the London Underworld, and after putting him down, Sam escaped from prison with the help of Singh and Etheridge. With his mission seemingly over, a fallen comrade, a man Sam had long thought dead, took his ex-wife hostage and threatened the destruction of a hospital in exchange for Sam's life. Sam confronted Mac, hoping he could restore a friendship that had been obliterated by a missile over a decade before.

It was to no avail.

Sam, once again with the help of Etheridge, evaded the police and finally found his freedom.

But there had been a cost.

Multiple people had been killed, either by his hand or by the violence that swirled around his life like a horrific tornado.

Theo Walker.

Sergeant Marsden.

Mac.

All dead.

Etheridge, through his acts of friendship, was now a wanted man and had disappeared wherever his fortune would take him.

DI Amara Singh had been recruited for a government agency, her career taking her even further from his arms than the one she had previously.

DI Adrian Pearce, who had investigated Sam during his original quest for justice, had retired from the force under a cloud of collusion. Despite his thirty years of service being embellished with his suspected deceit, Pearce had found happiness in helping under-privileged kids, carrying on the great work Theo had done before his murder.

For the first time since Jamie had died, Sam felt like his fight was over. There had been a toll-taking cost, but it was over.

There was just one final thing to do.

One more thing to make right.

A promise he'd made to Alex Stone after she'd saved his life. It was the promise that had brought him to America, and now that promise saw him strapped to the chair, at the mercy of a dangerous drug lord and his bloodthirsty henchman.

Sam had vowed to help Alex Stone get her family back.

And as Vasquez awaited the answer to his question, Sam knew the likelihood of fulfilling that promise was looking bleak. Vasquez sighed dramatically, sitting back in his chair, and lifting the passport from the desk. It was Sam's, a perfect counterfeit that Etheridge had provided during his venture to Ukraine.

'Jonathan Cooper?' Vasquez said. 'You have a strong jaw. My cousin, he was a boxer when he was younger. He used to tell me that you could tell a lot about a man by the way he took a punch. Now you. You can take a punch. That tells me you're a strong man. But are you a smart man?'

Vasquez stood, straightening his expensive blazer and running a hand through his dark hair. Like Sam, he was approaching forty, and a few flecks of grey dusted the temples. In contrast to Sam, however, he was clean shaven.

The man was worth a fair few million and definitely looked the part.

'I passed my exams if that helps?' Sam finally spoke, offering a bloody grin. Vasquez scowled and then nodded to Edinson.

Sam braced himself.

The fist crashed against his cheek, sending him lurching to the left once more, blood spraying out on impact.

It probably wasn't the smartest move to antagonise either man, but Sam needed time. Despite his ability to consume details, there didn't seem like a way out of this one. But the longer they kept him alive, and more importantly, kept Alex alive, the slimmest of chances remained.

'This is not working,' Vasquez said. 'See, you actually remind me of my cousin. He's a strong and resilient man but he used to ask the question…how do you hurt strong men? The same way you hurt every man.'

Vasquez strode across the room to the metal door and thumped his fist against it. Sam woozily straightened himself in the chair, blinking away the blur. Edinson stood to the side, and he gripped his powerful fingers into Sam's short brown hair and yanked his head up.

The door opened and Vasquez stepped to the side. Shuffled footsteps filled the darkness and Sam squinted, willing the pain and fuzziness away.

Two figures emerged through the darkness.

Sam's coolness faded.

Bound by her wrists and with a gag in her mouth was Alex Stone. Her immaculate brown skin showed signs of bruising on one side of her face, accompanied by a fresh cut that slashed her thin eyebrow. Beside her, a thin man, covered to the chin in tattoos, stood. His beady eyes locked on Sam and a sneer across his bearded face.

In his hand, he held a Glock 17 handgun, his finger looped around the trigger and the barrel pressed firmly against Alex's temple.

She stared at Sam, her fear shining through the tears.

Sam struggled against his restraints, but the metal bolts held the chair down.

'Let her go,' Sam demanded. His words laced with venom.

Footsteps slowly filled the darkness and Vasquez returned to view, a large cigar now hanging from the side of his mouth. He flicked a match, a small flame bathing his hands in an orange glow, and he lit the tip of his cigar. He took exaggerated puffs before a thick, grey cloud of smoke was thrust into the light.

Confidently, he stepped towards Sam, rattling his matches before pocketing them, and he took another puff. Sam tried to struggle again, but Edinson caught him with another hook, the man's fist crashing into Sam's jaw. The pain was excruciating, and Sam spat another pool of blood to join the rest, and he slowly raised his head to Vasquez with murderous intent in his eyes.

Vasquez smiled. A mixture of admiration and power spread across his face.

'You are a strong man, Mr Cooper.' Vasquez glanced back at Alex. 'But every man is weak when it comes to a woman. Now, tell me who you really are and what the fuck you're doing here, or I'll put a bullet in this bitch's skull.'

Alex squealed lightly in fear, and Sam looked to her for forgiveness.

He'd come to America to keep his promise to her.

To return her to her brother and sister.

But now, with a gun pressed to her head, a DEA agent

dead, and murderous drug lord on the brink of war, Sam's chances of keeping his word were less than none.

Their chances of survival, even less.

CHAPTER TWO

THREE DAYS EARLIER…

'Ladies and gentlemen, we will shortly begin our descent towards LaGuardia Airport. The weather is warm and sunny, and this flight has been exceptional.'

As the intercom crackled to signify the end of the message, Sam smirked at the well-spoken pilot's self-praise. The self-confidence of pilots had always impressed him, but he understood. Commanding a giant vessel and navigating it through the sky with hundreds of passengers required complete control along with expert knowledge. Sam appreciated the skill and dedication it took to sit in the cockpit of the plane, likening it to the similar requirements of staring down the scope of a rifle.

You needed to be trained.

Calm.

Emphatic.

Sam heard a few sniggers from fellow passengers who also enjoyed the light-hearted comment, and he looked around the aircraft. A multitude of people were sitting in their seats, entertaining themselves with a myriad of activities. Tablets were rested on tray tables; books were being read, and many passengers had taken the opportunity to grab some sleep. With roughly twenty minutes until landing, the dedicated cabin crew were making their way back through the aisle, holding open a plastic rubbish bag and encouraging their passengers to deposit. Sam looked down at his own tray table, picked up the bottle of water he'd purchased, and finished the last few gulps. It had been just over seven and a half hours since they'd departed London Gatwick Airport, and Sam had already helped himself to a hearty meal on the plane. Beside him, a young man named Eric was sleeping, a few empty crisp packets strewn on the table along with an iPad he'd switched off a few hours before. Sam kindly reached across, picked up the wrappers and, with a smile, dropped them along with the bottle into the bag.

The young air stewardess smiled at Sam, not for the first time on the flight, before she continued her way through the plane.

Her name was Emily, and she'd spoken with Sam as she'd served him pizza, questioning him about the light bruising that still littered his face.

Sam had lied, telling her he'd been in a minor traffic collision. Somehow, he didn't think telling her had fought his way out of a maximum-security prison and then faced off with a crazed soldier would have been the best idea.

Not since he was high on the UK's most wanted list.

But to Emily, Sam was Jonathan Cooper. The passport, a perfect replica sourced by Paul Etheridge, allowed Sam to leave the country undetected and was just another reason Sam was indebted to the man. There were few things in life that surprised Sam. Having seen the worst of humanity during his assault on organised crime, and having to say goodbye to his own son, Sam expected the worst.

But Etheridge had caught him off guard.

When they were comrades in the army many years ago, Etheridge was certainly a smart man, but he wasn't a soldier. A near fatal accident which broke his leg, almost cost him his life were it not for Sam's expert intervention. Lying prone at the bottom of a sharp incline, Etheridge was at the mercy of the approaching Taliban forces.

Sam dispatched them with ease.

After leaving the army, Etheridge had become a successful entrepreneur, developing a digital security platform used the world over. He had it all.

Money.

Mansion.

Trophy wife.

But he had no purpose. Despite his best efforts, the materialistic stop gaps only went so far.

Etheridge may not have had the skills of a soldier, but he certainly had the heart.

It was an act of desperation from Sam that brought a change in Etheridge's life. While hunting down a missing girl on the cusp of being lost to the sex trade, Sam had knocked on Etheridge's door, begging for his help to find her. What should have been a quick favour turned into a life-changing series of events.

Sam engaged the armed police in Etheridge's house.

Then, in his quest to find Sam, a furious enemy from his past tortured Etheridge and left him for dead.

That should have sent Etheridge running.

But it hadn't.

Etheridge had embraced it, selling his company and giving his wife a tidy divorce settlement. After carefully creating a financial narrative that saw him living a life of quiet retirement in Tenerife, Etheridge remained in his home, compiling information on some of the biggest crime syndicates in England.

To help Sam.

To join the fight.

After devising a plan that put Sam in The Grid to take down Harry Chapman, Etheridge hijacked Sam's transportation to another prison, freeing the vigilante and joining him on the government's most wanted list.

Now, like Sam, Etheridge had fled the country.

Moments before Sam boarded his flight, they'd said their goodbyes, with Etheridge heading wherever he fancied. Having sold his company for millions, Etheridge had the resources to go wherever he pleased. Sam didn't even want to comprehend how much Etheridge had placed in the account he'd given to him, but he was sure it was enough to see him through until Etheridge resurfaced.

Until he did, Sam was on his own.

Headed to America to do one final thing.

Make good on his promise to Alex.

A rumbling echoed from the plane as it slowly began its descent, the clouds fading to reveal a glorious view of the land below. A maze of roads sliced through large buildings, the busy city of New York in full flow. Sam had slept for a few hours during the flight, knowing the time shift would play havoc with him if he didn't try to rest a little.

It was fast approaching midday, and as the wheels touched down on the runway of LaGuardia Airport, Sam felt his stomach rumble slightly. Luckily for him, he'd travelled light, with just his phone, wallet, and passport, meaning there was no baggage collection to hold him up.

Unsurprisingly, everyone was out of their seat before the doors opened, and Sam calmly waited in his seat until the desperate masses made their way off the plan. Eric had woken groggily, and Sam wished him the best before making his way to the door. Emily smiled at Sam as he reached the door, handing him a sheet of paper which had her phone number on it.

Sam politely took it begrudgingly. A little twinge of guilt that he would shatter any expectations she had. Sam made his way through the terminal towards passport control, his eyes gazing at the armed security officers who patrolled the area. With the horrific history of terrorism that haunted the city of New York, Sam understood the need for them to be on high alert. Calmly, he approached the booth as he was called and handed his passport to a large woman who glared at him through her spectacles.

'Reason for travelling to New York, sir?' she asked with a heavy accent. Sam knew she was staring at his bruises, trying her best to guess their reason. With a smile, he obliged her.

'I was in a car accident.' He motioned to his face.

'I see,' she responded sceptically. 'Reason for travel?'

'I'm here to visit an old friend.'

The woman took a few more glances back and forth from passport to person before closing it and passing it back.

'Enjoy your stay, Mr Cooper.'

'Thank you.'

Sam offered her a smile which wasn't reciprocated and then marched through towards the baggage claim section of the airport. Already, throngs of agitated passengers were huddled around the conveyor belt, impatiently awaiting their luggage to continue their voyage. Sam strode past, walking through customs and out into the main terminal. Weaving his way through the throngs of waiting family members and drivers holding signs, Sam made his way to the food court area, choosing the booth with the smallest queue, and placed his order. A couple of minutes later, the young man behind the counter handed him his bagel and coffee and wished him a nice day. Sam nodded his thanks and walked through the terminal, stopping at a clothes shop. Having travelled with no luggage, Sam quickly demolished his snack and entered the store. Never one for fashion, Sam headed straight for the T-shirts, selecting five black T-shirts in his size and a navy bomber jacket. A few multipacks of underwear and socks, a pair of jeans and a rucksack, and Sam was good to go.

The young shop assistant helpfully bagged the new clothes into the rucksack, and Sam tapped in his pin number.

Four-four-four-four.

Silently, Sam cursed Etheridge for mockingly making the number so simple. Considering the incredible generosity of the man, Sam chuckled to himself as he agreed to let it slide.

Before heading to the taxi rank outside the airport, Sam stopped at the chemist, purchasing the necessary toiletries to see him through the next few days. With his rucksack over his shoulder, Sam took the final sip of his coffee and stepped outside the airport. The warm July afternoon greeted him with a cool breeze, and he held up his hand to block the sun from his eyes. Beyond the airport, Sam could see the East River, the sun shimmering off the water that separated the airport from Manhattan. The airport itself ran along the edge of Queens, with the busy streets already alive with activity. New York was the city that never slept, and Sam already felt the similarities to London. The roads were packed with slow-moving traffic, and the sidewalks were littered with civilians, scurrying among each other in their own internal rush.

Sam patiently waited in the queue at the taxi rank and eventually, he opened the back door of the vehicle and dropped into the seat.

'Where to my friend?' the driver asked enthusiastically, a thick Indian accent laced to his words. Sam peered through the screen and beyond the man's smile. Affixed to the dashboard was his identification, which Sam memorised instantly.

'Hello, Vikram.' Sam smiled politely. 'I need to go to Holland Avenue…'

'Ah, the Bronx.' Vikram cut in joyfully. 'We will get there in a jiffy.'

Sam sat back in the seat and chuckled. The driver's positivity was a welcome surprise, especially as the New York traffic was infamous. Sam fastened his seat belt and gazed out of the window, as Vikram pulled out of LaGuardia Airport and onto Grand Central Parkway, passing through Astoria Heights and onto the I-278 W. The drive was surprisingly pleasant, as the route took them through Astoria Park and across the Robert F. Kennedy Bridge. As they passed over the East River, Sam glanced across to Rikers Island, the isolated prison in the middle of the river. It reminded him of his experiences earlier that year, locked underground in the secret Ashcroft Maximum Security Prison.

Sam had incited a riot, killing a number of dangerous criminals, as well as exposing the staff who were on the take. He'd been saved by the warden, a good man fighting the system with the best intentions.

Ashcroft was no more.

And Sam, to the dismay of the British authorities, was a free man.

Cutting through Randalls Island, Vikram soon brought them off the freeway and onto Sheridan's Boulevard. As they travelled towards the Bronx, Sam watched the locals going about their lives, wondering how Alex Stone had been since he'd said his tearful goodbye to her.

It had been on a cold night in Naples, not too long after she'd saved his life. Having been lured into a trap as bait, Alex had been captured by her former Blackridge comrades in a desperate plot to pull Sam into the open.

Sam had fought back, and after a high-speed pursuit through the beautiful Italian city, Alex had led the final members of the team to an empty industrial estate.

Sam executed their pursuers before realising that his war with General Wallace would soon cost Alex her life if she stayed with him. Despite her remonstrations, Sam told her to leave, and he watched as she angrily entered the car and drove off into the night.

Sam went back to finish his fight.

It took him longer than he'd anticipated. But it was over.

Now all that was left was for him to keep his promise to Alex.

'Here we are, sir,' Vikram said cheerfully as he pulled onto Holland Avenue. 'Where should I stop?'

'Just here is fine.'

'Righty-oh.'

Sam smiled at his drivers' positive attitude and he reached into his pocket and pulled out the roll of dollars he'd exchanged at Gatwick.

'How much do I owe you?' Sam asked, his eyes flicking to the metre.

'Thirty-two dollars, sir?'

Sam poked two twenties through the screen.

'Keep the change.' Sam smiled as pushed open the door. 'Thanks for the ride.'

'Anytime, sir.' Vikram raised his thumb. 'Have a great day.'

Sam hoisted his rucksack over his shoulder and then closed the door. As Vikram signalled and pulled away, Sam wandered down the street, looking up at the large apartment blocks that lined it. The sun, blocked by the buildings, bathed the street in shadows, and Sam felt the cool breeze drifting through. The street was a residential block, littered with high-rise buildings. Scattered between were a few stores, a barber shop, and a pizzeria.

Eventually, Sam stopped at a small set of concrete steps that led up to the door.

This was the place.

Before Etheridge had fallen off the grid, he'd sourced Alex Stone's last known address. It was a shot in the dark, as Sam had no idea if Alex had returned home, although Etheridge had been able to confirm she'd returned to America. Blackridge had pulled her into a shady part of the world, and Sam hoped she'd made it back all right.

That she'd reunited with her family and that his trip would be nothing more than a few days of sightseeing.

But Sam knew the world wasn't so kind.

Whatever he could do, he would do without question.

Sam waited a few more moments until an elderly lady pushed open the locked door to the flats. Sam scaled the steps, holding the door for her and offering his best smile.

She nodded her thanks, and Sam entered the building in hope of finding Alex.

CHAPTER THREE

From the outside, the apartment block gave an impression of grandeur, the stone archway giving an undeserved sense of class. Once Sam had passed through the door, the ruse was revealed. As the auto locking door closed behind him, Sam was taken aback by the cheap, narrow corridor that presented itself. The wallpaper that was inexpertly slapped on the walls was peeling in certain areas, with a mucky corkboard affixed to one of the walls above a wobbly table. Piles of unopened letters were strewn across the furniture and Sam lifted them, gently thumbing through them.

Stone.

Apartment seventeen.

He was certainly in the right place.

And judging by the eviction notice stamp on the letter he held, he was piecing together that things still hadn't improved for Alex.

A resident turned the corner and stormed towards the front door, brushing past Sam and offering nothing more than a rude grunt. From the discussions Sam and Alex had shared during his recovery in Naples, he knew the situation. Alex's mother was a drug addict. With no father in the picture, Alex had taken on the responsibility of her two younger siblings, their freedom from the clutches of the child protection agency the carrot that was used to blackmail her in the first place. Alex wasn't squeaky clean herself, but the illegal street races she participated in kept the rent paid, her brother and sister in clothes, and food in the fridge.

She bent the rules to give them a better future.

To do the right thing.

Sam could relate.

Adjusting his backpack, Sam headed up the stairs to the fourth floor, a musky smell lingering in the stairwell. The Bronx wasn't the most affluent area of the state of New York, and Sam was certain a cleaner wasn't high on the landlord's list of priorities. As he arrived on the fourth floor, Sam followed the door numbers until he reached number seventeen. As he raised his hand to knock on the door, he realised he hadn't even rehearsed what he would say to Alex.

She had every right to slam the door in his face.

Behind him, he heard the opposite apartment door open, and as he turned, it slammed shut.

A nosy neighbour.

Sam took a breath and rapped his knuckles on the door.

Nothing.

'Alex?' Sam called out, rattling the door again with his knuckles. 'Alex?'

Again, nothing. Sam took a step back and then carefully reached out for the door handle. He turned it and the door clicked open, creaking gently as he pushed it. The putrid smell of waste seeped through the gap and Sam scowled as he eased his way into the miniscule hallway.

'Hello?' he called out again, trying his best to alert anyone to his presence. 'Alex?'

Cautiously, Sam shuffled towards the doorway to the kitchen, dipping his head in and scouting the place out. The smell of rotten food was unbearable, and he quickly withdrew, shaking the foul odour from his senses. But the quick glimpse was enough to count the number of dirty plates by the sink, the brand of coffee by the pot, and appreciate the poorly drawn artwork that was tacked to the fridge with a magnet.

Old habits die hard.

Sam took a few more steps and then crossed into the living room. A ripped sofa was pushed under the window, with a coffee table in front of it. Numerous shreds of tinfoil and empty plastic bags littered the top, along with over-flowing ashtrays and heat-stained spoons.

Sam had seen enough drug dens during his missions in Afghanistan to know when a place was occupied by a loser, but despite all the evidence of drug use, there were no signs of occupancy.

Alex was right.

Her mother was an addict.

The idea that Alex's mother indulged her addiction while living with her kids turned his stomach. Not only were they subjected to watching their mother seep away, but god knows the type of people they'd shared a flat with. The drug trade wasn't run by the nicest of people.

Sam could feel his fist clench in anger.

Just as he was about to walk across the room to the doors that lead to the bedroom, he heard a small clunk behind him and turned just in time to see the baseball bat raised high in the air.

Sam threw a hand up to protect himself.

'Who the hell are you?'

The bat didn't come down and Sam's eyes locked onto the old man who was wielding the weapon with shaking arms. From his height, complexion, and the grey hair, Sam would have pegged him for a man in his seventies, but he looked surprisingly sturdy. Sam slowly held both his hands up in form of surrender.

'I'm looking for Alex Stone,' Sam said calmly, trying his best to defuse the situation. 'Sorry, the door was open.'

'You a drug dealer?' The man spat coldly, looking Sam up and down with suspicion.

'No, sir.'

'A cop?'

'I'm a friend.' Sam spoke calmly, not wanting the situation to escalate. The man's dark eyes squinted as he assessed the stranger in his neighbour's home, and he lowered the bat slightly.

'You English?' the man asked, and Sam nodded.

'It's the accent, right?'

A smile threatened to break across the dark, wrinkled skin of the man's face, but he quickly shook it off.

'You're a long way from home, son.' The man looked around the room. 'I'm going to lower this bat now, okay? But you make any funny moves, I'll put a beating on your ass. You got that?'

The man smiled, and Sam reciprocated.

'Loud and clear.'

The man allowed the bat to swing down, giving his arms a rest. He looked Sam up and down once more.

'Ain't nobody here, son. Not for a few weeks, anyway.' The man sighed with sadness and then extended his hand. 'The name's Leon.'

'Jonathan,' Sam lied, reaching out and shaking it firmly. Despite the man's age, he had a solid grip. 'Where is everyone?'

With another sigh, the man turned to the door.

'What do you English boys drink again? Tea, isn't it?'

'Always.'

Leon chuckled and nodded for Sam to follow. As Leon

stepped out of the apartment, Sam took a final look around the small apartment. Something told him the truth wasn't going to be pretty, but he needed to find out. And right now, following Alex's neighbour was his best bet.

———

As Leon fumbled around in his kitchen, Sam took a moment to cast his eye around the elderly gentleman's apartment. Despite the austerity in the area and the general up-keep of the building itself, Sam was impressed by the décor. Leon clearly took pride in his home and the living room was a bright white, with a black trim around the skirting boards and windowsills. The shutters that crossed the window were open, bathing the room in a bright slash of sunlight and offering a view of the busy street below. A modest sofa was pushed against the far wall, underneath a large canvas of the New York skyline. Opposite, a large flat screen TV sat atop a neat stand, with rows of DVDs lined up beneath. Sam chuckled, as the dead technology was a sign that Leon wasn't too keen on the modern age of streaming services.

To his left, a well-used chair sat, with the latest Lee Child novel on the table beside it, along with what must have been a treasured photo of Leon and his wife on their wedding day. Judging by the lack of women's touch in the apartment, Sam felt a twinge of sadness for the man that she didn't seem to be a part of his life anymore.

Without thinking, Sam had lifted the photo, admiring the look of pure love the two shared. It made him think of Lucy, the love they'd held for each other, and the possible life he could have had if things had been different. Jamie would have been nine years old now, most likely heavily invested in hobbies that would have kept Sam and Lucy on their toes.

Sam would have been a police officer.

Maybe their family would have grown some more? Lucy had always spoken of her desire for a daughter.

Sam shook his head, struck by how life can take a turn at any moment. Leon's voice broke his train of thought.

'That's my Lizzy.'

Sam's focus snapped upwards, and he realised he was holding the photo. He smiled and carefully placed it back down.

'Your wife?' Sam offered as he gratefully accepted the warm mug.

'She was.' Leon glanced at the photo with sadness. 'She passed on over a decade ago. Cancer.'

'I'm sorry.'

'Don't be.' Leon smiled at the photo with pride. 'We had a wonderful life together.'

Sam shuffled awkwardly on the spot and then took a sip of his drink. The warm tea glided down his throat and he glanced around the room again. After a few awkward moments of silence, Leon spoke.

'So, what is Alex Stone doing hanging around with a British soldier?' Sam raised his eyebrow in surprise. 'Oh, come on. I may be old, but these peepers still work. The way you carry yourself, the glances around your surroundings. Either you're a soldier or a spy.'

'Here I thought I was fitting in.'

'Military?' Leon asked, sipping his mug.

'I was. Many years ago.' Sam tried to ignore the painful memories of the career he had. 'But I got out.'

'Don't blame ya.' Leon shook his head. 'Messy business, war. But you didn't answer my question.'

Sam smiled. He liked Leon and appreciated the man's hospitality and directness in equal measure.

'How much do you know about Alex?'

The question took Leon by surprise and with a smirk, he scratched his chin in contemplation.

'She's a good kid. I've lived across the hall from them for years. Since she was a little one. Smart. Bright. But with a mother like that, she never stood a chance. I used to let Alex study at the table in the kitchen because her mum had guests round.'

'Guests?'

'Her mother is a drug addict, Jonathan. And she wasn't exactly rolling in cash, if you get my drift. Soon, those visits lead to her shacking up with a drug dealer and she had two kids. Little Nattie and Joel. Nice kids. Smart, like Alex. Although their mum tried for a while to be a parent, she could never kick the habit. Once that scumbag left, she spiralled, and Alex stepped up. Working jobs. Doing what she could to give them a better chance than she ever did.'

'Did you ever think about calling the cops?'

Leon scowled at Sam; his eyes widened with offence.

'Of course, we did. Lizzy wanted to, but look around you. This isn't Manhattan. The police don't exactly put black drug addicts at the top of their priorities. No, they would take the kids away, shunt them off into care, and leave their mum to die in her den.' Leon took a breath to compose. 'While Lizzy was still alive, she would help Alex where she could. The kids would come round a lot. Alex would get the money somehow, but I always worried she was treading in dangerous waters to get it. Is that what this is? Is she in trouble?'

Sam finished his tea and offered Leon a warm smile. The man's selfless compassion for Alex's situation was heart-wrenching, and Sam knew he deserved the truth.

'You might want to sit down.'

With a degree of trepidation, Leon lowered himself gingerly into his seat. Sam took a seat on the sofa and sat forward. He laid out what had happened. How Alex had

26

been making ends meet by competing in illegal street races. That Trevor Sims, a shady government operative working for an off-the-books task force, had blackmailed her with threats of her siblings being carted off into separate care homes. The underground bunker in Rome, where Alex took a bullet to the leg but still came back for Sam.

That she saved his life.

As Sam concluded by explaining what happened a few months earlier in Naples and how she'd driven away from Sam when he decided to return home to put Blackridge in the ground, Leon was sitting with his head in his hands.

'Jesus,' he muttered under his breath.

'All I know is about a month or so ago, her passport record shows she was back in the country and this is her last known address.' Sam sighed. 'I just want to make good on my promise.'

A few moments of silence passed, and it was only when Leon wiped his eyes did Sam realise the man was crying.

'That poor girl,' Leon exclaimed. 'The world has dealt her a cruel hand, but she's not a bad person.'

'I know.' Sam stood. 'She saved my life. And I promised I would help her get her family back. If there's anything you can tell me, anything at all, it would be a big help.'

Leon shot a furious glance up at Sam and then hoisted himself to his feet.

'You promise me, Jonathan. You promise me you will help that girl and bring her back. God knows I don't have much, but I have enough.'

Sam smiled politely. He'd noticed the small pile of overdue payments that had been stacked on the windowsill in the corner. But despite it all, Leon was offering to help, and Sam knew the man had too much pride to admit he was facing financial ruin.

'I promise,' Sam said with determination. 'I'm a man of my word.'

'Lord, I hope so,' Leon said with a deep breath. 'She was back here about a month or so ago. The social services took her brother and sister not long after Christmas, and she was trying her best to get them back. Got herself a job, checked her mum into rehab. All to prove she could provide a steady environment.'

'That's brilliant. Where does she work?'

'The High Five Bar in Laconia. It ain't far from here. Couple of miles.'

'She working now?' Sam headed to the door.

'That's the thing. I ain't seen her or heard her for over a week.'

Sam stopped in his place. Something didn't feel right. Alex was a desperate woman, doing whatever she could to get her siblings back. But he had a lead, and that was enough. As he pulled open the door, he turned back to the worried old man who looked at him with hope.

'Thank you, Leon.' Sam offered him a smile. 'You're a good man.'

'One last thing.' Leon stepped towards Sam and extended his hand. 'The High Five, it's a biker bar. Not the nicest place in the world. You keep your wits about you.'

Sam took the man's hand, shook it firmly, and nodded.

'I always do.'

With that, Sam stepped out of the apartment and headed to the exit, following the next bread crumb.

CHAPTER FOUR

The High Five bar sat on the corner of Fenton Avenue, just off Gun Hill Road that ran through Laconia. The small district of the Bronx was on the rise, with the gentrification making it look considerably different to its surrounding parts. With the investment of money numerous businessmen had seen the opportunity to jump in with classy establishments and eateries popping up throughout the streets.

The High Five bar was not one of those.

With the rise in footfall and profits, other more nefarious projects had thrown their hat into the ring. The Death Riders, a notorious biker gang from the east coast had begun to venture further out and the High Five bar was seen as a hub within the city that never slept. The large bar didn't lack the polish of its competitors. The front had been decorated with faux wood panels, with a trendy sign affixed above the door. The front drinking space had been levelled off, replaced with parking spaces for the few welcome travellers to leave their bikes.

They were in no danger of being stolen.

Even in New York, the petty street criminals knew better than to tamper with Death Rider property.

Tony Mason was proud of how quickly he'd spread the reputation. Having been with the Riders for over a decade, Tony, known more commonly as Mason, had been tasked with expanding the Rider's operation into New York over two years ago. Based in South Carolina, the Riders were the unwritten law on the streets. While they ran a number of operations that should have seen the book thrown at them ten times over, their moral code had also ensured that street crime had fallen. By making the lives of the local sheriffs easier, it gave them far more scope to conduct their business.

A business that their leader, Trent Wyatt, had turned into an empire.

As with any midweek afternoon, Mason had arrived shortly after the bar had opened. The usual suspects were already in attendance, all decked out in their leather jackets and bandanas, all believing they were part of the crew. They weren't, and part of Wyatt's operation had been to commercialise the idea of the gang. While his core group were Riders till the end, the vast majority of patrons were middle-aged men, living out their crisis on the back of Harley Davidson bikes they could barely control, and listening to music they didn't like.

Mason didn't hate them. He pitied them. But as long as they kept showing up and emptying their wallets, he would greet them like his brothers and keep their pathetic dreams alive. As long as they didn't bother Kelly and Lacey, the two girls who worked the bar. While they would never force the women to do anything – that was one of Wyatt's strict rules – the girls were encouraged to flash a little flesh and flirt with the punters.

They didn't mind. The tips they received were more than generous.

Besides, on the rare occasion that one of the patrons got too aggressive with them, Donnie and Jay were on hand to bring them back down to reality. As the two other true members of the Riders, both men were more than happy to hurl a fraud face-first onto the sidewalk.

Jay greeted Mason with the usual handshake before returning to his bottle of beer. Leaning against the bar, Jay's hulking frame was turned to the TV that overlooked the pool table. A replay of yesterday's baseball match was in full swing, and Jay watched with mild interest. Behind the bar, Kelly was sorting through the glasses, and she greeted Mason with her million-dollar smile.

Lacey wasn't on shift until later, and with only four customers, Kelly was more than comfortable handling the shift. Mason waved back, entered his office, and as like most days, he told Donnie to get out of his chair. One day, Donnie would most likely sit in it. He had a little more brain than Jay, but Mason was always keen to remind him of the chain of command.

Wyatt was a stickler for hierarchy.

The Death Riders followed a strict code and seniority dictated it. Mason had never had an issue, but Wyatt's second in command, Eddie Sykes, struggled to fall in line. He had ambition.

A trait Wyatt admired. But one he had to control.

Mason took his seat and pulled his shoulder-length, grey hair back and affixed it into a loose ponytail. As he itched the beard that hung from his jaw with a tattooed hand, he flicked open his computer and readied himself for a day just like any other.

Then the door to the bar flew open.

———

As Sam stepped out of Alex Stone's apartment block, he turned and looked back up to the fourth floor. Ever since his son had been killed, Sam's world had changed. Through the following pain and suffering of losing his family, Sam had planned to end it all. It was his Sergeant, Carl Marsden, who brought him back from the brink, stopping him moments before he'd decided to end his own life.

Marsden had been a good man, built on solid principals and with a moral code that would eventually cost him his life. If he hadn't had interjected, Sam would be dead. It was Marsden's words, spoken to Sam as he sat in the dark with tears in his eyes that convinced him to fight back. That he had the power to channel the devastation of Jamie's death into something good.

While that set Sam on the path, it was meeting Miles Hillock face to face that set him on his path to fight for justice. The man, a vile drunk who had been released from prison on a technicality, was slowly drinking himself to death. Sam broke into Miles' house with every intention of killing him. The man had killed Sam's son.

He deserved no mercy.

But as he pummelled Miles in a blind rage, he realised that it would achieve nothing. Miles may have been behind the wheel, but it was the justice system that had failed to punish him for his crimes. The death of a young child had already dissolved the man's humanity, and Sam left him beaten and battered, begging for death.

When Miles committed suicide, Sam had felt no sense of closure.

Only the need to put things right.

For everyone.

That's what had spurned his fight and brick by brick, he'd torn down corruption within the police and the government, as well as removing some of the largest crime syndicates in Europe.

The world was a dirty place, and Sam knew he was in so deep that no amount of scrubbing would ever clean the blood on his hands.

It was people like Leon who reminded him why it was worth the fight. An elderly widower, struggling for money, who had done everything he could to help Alex through her tumultuous upbringing. How he'd opened his door to her and her siblings, when the world had dealt them a poor hand. There was no doubt in Sam's mind that had they asked, he would have given them the shirt off his back, too. There were good people in the world.

Leon was one of them.

That was worth fighting for.

With a nod, Sam turned from the building and tucked his hands into the pockets of his bomber jacket. The summer sun was shining, but a breeze ran through the city, sending a little chill through the air. Sam took out the mobile phone Etheridge had provided for him and tapped the screen a few times until he opened up his Maps app. A few clicks later, a thick blue line ran through the image of the Bronx, guiding him directly to the High Five bar in Laconia. It was a mile and a half walk, and Sam was keen to stretch his legs. Having spent years as a sniper, Sam was used to prolonged periods of consciousness. The lack of impact that jetlag had on him used to wind Lucy up, as he was usually full of energy despite the change in time zones. But after the last few weeks, he could feel a surge of tiredness echo through his body, and he stopped at a small coffee shop as he turned onto Boston Road. Moments later, he emerged with a double shot flat white and continued on his walk. He passed a number of outlets, from car parts to laundromats, weaving in and out of the locals. While not as enticing as Times Square or the more tourist centric parts of the state, Sam found the business of the community quite calming. Normal people, just trying to get by.

Alex Stone fit this town.

He picked up the pace and soon the phone beeped, encouraging him to turn off and head down Dewitt Place until he came to Gun Hill Road. Smiling at the name, Sam crossed the street, taking in the Eastchester Branch of the New York Public Library. The building itself had seen better days, and Sam couldn't help but compare it to a prison block. He turned down Fenton Avenue; the street lined with setback buildings behind metal fences. It was quaint, and Sam wondered why, of all places, a biker bar would pitch its flag here.

Still wondering, he approached the row of bikes parked outside and then glanced up at the sign.

High Five

This was the place.

Sam took a quick glance to either side, ensuring no one was paying any attention to his presence. In a city that busy, Sam knew he'd faded into obscurity, but it was an old habit that would be with him to the grave.

Without a plan, Sam pushed open the door and entered. The familiar smell of a bar hit Sam immediately. The last time he'd been in one, he was squaring off in a violent gun fight in the Ukraine. The High Five was considerably quieter, but judging by the heads that turned his way as he entered, the atmosphere was no more welcoming. A few middle-aged men sat around one of the tables sneered in his direction. Their obvious conclusions that he didn't belong drew an ironic smile from Sam. Another patron sat on his own – gloved hand wrapped around his pint glass – peered at Sam. They had all the correct gear on, but Sam knew the deal.

They were local men, playing biker.

The commercialisation leant on heavily by popular TV

shows and the media-driven idea of a midlife crisis meant that this bar was authentic as a politician's promise. The one person who did belong in the bar was sitting at it, turned away from the door, his eyes glued to the baseball match playing out on the screen above the pool table. With the lights above shimmering off his bald head, he casually lifted a beer bottle to his lips before wiping any residue from his thick beard with a tattooed forearm. As Sam's steps echoed, he swivelled on his seat and shot a look at Sam that instantly told him what he already knew.

He wasn't welcome here.

Despite the hostility, Sam approached the bar several feet from the hulking biker and offered a warm smile to the woman behind it. She glanced at the biker nervously, then back to Sam with a forced smile. She was pretty, and Sam was certain she was a factor in a number of men frequenting the bar.

'Hey, sugar,' she said cheerfully. 'What can I get you?'

Her accent was thick, clearly local.

'I'm looking for a friend,' Sam responded, aware the biker was listening.

'Hell, we all are.' She winked at him. 'What's her name?'

'Or his?' the biker interrupted, chuckling. Sam ignored him and kept his focus on the girl. She had a badge pinned to the cuff of her open shirt.

'Kelly, is it?' Sam said, and she glanced down at her exposed cleavage as if looking for confirmation. 'I'm looking for a girl named Alex Stone. Used to work here.'

The sudden flicker of worry in Kelly's blue eyes told Sam that he was in the right place. To his left, the biker turned on his bar stool and stood, making a grand show to display his height and sizeable bulk. Despite the paunch that dominated his midriff, the man was solid and was undoubtedly the doorman. Sam didn't even want to hazard a guess at how many letching wannabe bikers had seen his bad side. As the biker slowly stomped nearer to him, he spoke.

'You English?'

Sam turned; his face emotionless.

'What gave it away? The accent?'

'Nah, your smart-ass attitude.' The biker stopped a foot or two from him and leant on the bar. 'The name's Jay. Long way from home, aintcha?'

'I'm here to see a friend.' Sam turned from Jay and back to a nervous looking Kelly, who had her arms folded. 'Is she here?'

'You a cop?'

Sam shook his head. Jay sighed.

'This ain't a fucking tourist information booth. It's a bar.'

'Good point,' Sam said. 'I'll have a bottle of beer, please.'

Kelly shot a glance at Jay and half shrugged. She turned and opened the beer fridge and pulled out a bottle. She popped the cap and placed it on the bar, and Sam passed across a ten-dollar bill.

'Get one for yourself.' He smiled, and a flirtatious grin spread across her face. To break the seemingly friendly atmosphere, Jay finished his bottle and slammed it down hard on the counter, causing Kelly to jump.

Sam didn't flinch.

And Jay noticed.

'You sure you ain't a cop?'

'I'm sure,' Sam said casually, infuriating Jay further by casually sliding onto the bar stool and sipping his beer.

'FBI?'

Sam almost spat his drink out and then lifted his beer to Jay, as if congratulating him on a good joke. Jay pushed himself up from the bar and he arched his neck at Kelly, directing her to the door that was positioned at the far end of the bar. Sam assumed it was the door to the back office and whoever his questions were going to upset, they were most likely in there.

But something didn't feel right.

Leon had said he hadn't seen or heard from Alex in over a week. Sam was definitely in the right place. Despite Jay's attempts at unnerving him and diverting to conversation, the mere flicker in Kelly's eye had told him so.

Having spent a lifetime in the midst of multiple wars, Sam trusted his instincts.

His gut instinct told him he was in the right place.

It also told him it could be the wrong time.

Kelly slipped out from behind the bar and hurried to the door. She gently rapped on it, waited for the booming voice to welcome her in, and she disappeared inside.

Behind him, Sam heard Jay walk the seven required steps to the door, no doubt to block any chance of a swift exit. Ignoring the foreboding sense of dread that had filled the bar, Sam casually lifted the bottle again and enjoyed the cold, refreshing beer as it sloshed down his throat.

Sam had rattled a cage.

How badly? He was about to find out.

CHAPTER FIVE

When Tony Mason joined the Death Riders, he'd been enamoured with the lifestyle. The sense of camaraderie shared between the members was akin to a brotherhood, and they would cruise around South Carolina, their patches proudly emblazoned on the back of their vests. After a decade in an unhappy marriage and an even more miserable divorce, Mason had found a sense of purpose within the group. Every member was a lost soul, looking for meaning where there was none.

After a year or two, their adventures amounted to nothing more than a few excursions and drinks at their favourite watering hole. That was until Trent Wyatt seized control of the group. His predecessor, Wayland Birch, had been killed by a local drug gang and Wyatt saw not only the chance for revenge but for a new era for the group. None of the Riders knew much about Wyatt's past, apart from a long stint in prison, and his reaction was a defining moment in their history.

Wyatt systematically took apart the drug gang, even brutally beating the leader to a state of permanent disability. The Riders claimed their 'spot' and Wyatt's talent for persuasion saw him take control of the intake of drugs into the town. Soon, the Riders were the most prominent dealers in class A drugs in South Carolina and they evolved beyond a group of misfits just looking for companionship.

Those who couldn't handle it were exiled. Those who stepped up were rewarded. After a few months, Wyatt had struck up a deal with the local authorities to allow the Riders to operate in exchange for a share of the profits and for the Riders to act as an enforcement agency of their own. Not only did it nullify the competition, but it also kept the Riders out of the firing line. Their local bar, The Pit, was soon purchased and became their base of operations.

Then the expansion began.

As one of Wyatt's most loyal and trusted men, Mason was offered the chance to oversee the move into New York, one which he accepted with relish. Approaching his fiftieth birthday, Mason saw it as a semi-retirement. The chance to open a bar and begin the slow burn progression into the thriving drug culture in New York. Wyatt's code meant that they wouldn't launch an all-out assault on the other drug lords in the state. The plan was to establish a base, hopefully recruit a few loyal followers, and then slowly begin to turn the business towards the Riders. Provide assurances, along with clear repercussions, if people didn't fall in line. It was a two-year operation, and Mason enjoyed the slightly quieter life as he diligently worked to the plan. Donnie and Jay relocated with him and they'd found that while the appetite for drugs in the Bronx was vast, the potential for new recruits not so much.

The regulars could pump all the cash into his tills until the cows came home, but Mason hadn't met one who showed even the modicum of Rider potential.

It meant the expansion would need to wait.

Which suited him fine.

That afternoon, he was sitting at his desk, reviewing the takings for the previous week, while Donnie sat on the sofa opposite, clicking away on his phone. Less aggressive than Jay, Donnie was a smart man who Mason knew was being groomed as his successor. Either that, or another location. As both men went about their business, heavy metal music pumped out of the radio on the windowsill, bathed in the light that slashed through the plastic blind.

The tranquil afternoon was interrupted by a knock at the door. Mason raised his head, but before he could invite his guest in, the door opened, and an anxious Kelly slipped in. Donnie, a decade younger than Mason and with a sexual appetite of a college freshman, gave her a flirtatious grin.

It wasn't reciprocated and the worry on Kelly's face caused Mason to stand up, his meaty frame looming large over her.

'Everything okay?'

'Err, I think so,' Kelly said, shooting a glance back towards the door. 'There's a guy in the bar…'

'He giving you shit?' Donnie said, standing and puffing his broad chest. Mason rolled his eyes and motioned for him to sit back down.

'Look, Kelly. I've told you…Jay will handle any guys who step out of line.'

'Oh, he didn't do anything like that.' She shook her head. 'He's actually quite charming.'

'So, what's the problem?' Mason rested his hands on his hips in irritation. 'I'm pretty busy.'

'Jay sent me. I have no idea who he is, but he is asking for Alex.'

Mason's face contorted with confusion, and he stepped around the desk.

'He a cop?'

'I don't think so. Jay asked, and he said no.' Kelly shrugged. 'Did Alex ever mention a British guy?'

'British?' Mason's brow furrowed. Something didn't feel right.

'What's the matter, boss?' Donnie stood again.

'Wyatt has been emailing me about some grief he's been getting from the DEA. Couple of guys. Sinclair and Alan. Snooping around, trying to bring the Riders down.' Mason stroked his beard. 'Maybe they've sent someone to stir the shit here?'

'I don't know,' Kelly said, biting her lip nervously. 'He seemed like a decent guy. Said he was her friend.'

'Kelly, you stay here,' Mason said with authority. 'Donnie, come with me.'

A smile spread across Donnie's face, which drew a glare from Kelly.

'What are we going to do?' he asked enthusiastically.

'I want to find out what the fuck this guy wants.'

Mason returned to his desk and pulled open the top draw. He reached in, retrieving the Ruger Super Redhawk revolver from the stack of papers. It had been a long time since he'd needed it, but he couldn't be too careful. With a nod for Donnie to follow, Mason stomped to the door, yanked the handle, and stepped out into the bar.

————

Sam sat calmly on his stool, fingers wrapped around the cold, half empty bottle of beer, and he gazed up at the memorabilia above the bar. The décor had been designed to give the place the rustic appeal of a highway-side biker bar, but it was as fake as the patrons. Jay hadn't moved. The bulky man glaring at Sam in a failed attempt at intimidation. While the man carried sizeable muscle mass, Sam had already clocked the slight limp in his right leg, a clear sign of a bad knee. Undoubtedly, Jay was a scary figure to those passing through, but his considerable upper body, coupled with his age and proclivity to daytime drinking had caused his knees to weaken.

It wasn't obvious.

But Sam was trained.

Every detail, no matter how small, was noted and processed. It was a trait that had made him a valuable weapon and one that had saved his life on many occasions.

Casually, Sam lifted his bottle of beer, but before he could bring it to his lips, the door to the office opened and Sam was greeted with a deathly stare. The man who stepped out was almost as tall as Jay, but trimmer and slightly older. His grey hair was tied back and judging by the way he was adjusting the back of his jeans, was armed. He was followed by another leather clad man, younger, and with a hint of excitement glistening in his eyes. It was unlikely they had much trouble in this bar and the man who stomped towards Sam was clearly in charge. Kelly slid out of the office and closed the door, and she offered Sam an apologetic look.

Then she left.

Sam raised his eyebrows as if to say goodbye and calmly returned to his beer.

The man in charge stepped to within a few feet of Sam and pointed a finger at him. His arm was covered in tattoos.

'This the Brit?' he demanded in a gruff voice.

'Yup.' Jay responded with a smirk, pushing himself from the bar. The man in charge forced a smile at Sam and then turned his attention to the bar.

'Sorry, gentlemen, but the bar is closed. Please vacate the premises immediately.'

The few customers grumbled in annoyance, but they

obliged quickly. As they shuffled to the exits, none of them looked Jay in the eye as he smirked at them.

They weren't real Riders.

As the final customer left, Jay closed the door behind them and then stood, colossal arms folded across his barrel-like chest, and nodded to the boss. Sam put his bottle down and looked up at the man.

'I'm assuming you didn't want me to leave, right?'

The man ignored Sam's comment and coolly slid himself over the bar stool beside Sam, facing outwards. He leant back, propping both elbows on the bar, as if trying to calm the situation. It was a clear tactic, one that Sam was sure had worked a number of times. But from the corner of his eye, he noticed the other man move into position a few feet behind him.

They were strategically moving into position, like a chess player looking for checkmate.

The man in charge pulled a packet of cigarettes from his pocket, lit one, and then offered one to Sam. As Sam declined, the man shrugged, tossed the pack onto the bar, and exhaled a plume of smoke.

'I'm Mason. I run this bar. Now usually, it's a pretty easy gig, you know. Not hundreds of guys like us here in the Bronx.'

'Ain't that the fucking truth,' Donnie uttered, drawing a glare for interrupting.

'See, we might get a bad rep for what we believe in…' The man stopped and Sam turned to him.

'Jonathan,' Sam lied.

'…Jonathan, but we are fair. One of the things we value is our privacy. Our business is our business. It's the way it's always been and the way it will always be. So, I'm going to ask you nicely, who are you and what the fuck do you want?'

Sam turned to look at the man, who stared back with hatred.

'I'm looking for Alex Stone.'

'Who is Alex Stone?' Mason said, his gaze unwavering.

'Alex Stone. She worked here. I know that for a fact and when I mentioned her name, your attack dog butted in and just mentioning her name seems to have pissed you guys off. So, I think I'm in the right place.'

Sam shrugged and sipped his beer. During his early days as a soldier, he was told to never kick a hornet's nest. But over time, he'd found it was a good way to read the room.

This wasn't going to be pretty.

'Are all Brits this fucking smug?' Mason asked, drawing a chuckle from his gang. Sam turned to him.

'Look, I don't know you or what you guys do here. To be honest, I don't care. I'm just looking for Alex.'

'Bullshit,' Donnie called out.

'Fuck's sake, Donnie. Let me handle this.' Mason snapped, launching from his chair as if he were shooing away a pigeon. He turned back to Sam, who hadn't moved at all. The calmness of this mysterious Brit unsettled him, but he wasn't going to lose face in front of his crew. Especially Donnie. 'Who sent you here?'

'I did,' Sam said, swivelling on his chair. 'So just tell me where she is, and I'll be on my way.'

'See, I don't believe you.' Mason shunted a finger at Sam. 'And you're really starting to piss me off. Now, I could have my boys hold you down while I carve my name into your stomach with a knife, but I don't want the mess. So instead, you're going to tell me exactly who you are, or Donnie here is going to start breaking every bone in your right hand, followed by the left, and then we'll work up the arms systematically. Understand?'

'Loud and clear,' Sam replied, taking the final sip of his

beer. As he finished, he calmly laid the bottle on its side on the bar. 'Ready when you are.'

A flicker of caution passed between the bikers before Mason nodded at Donnie to begin. Sam listened to the footsteps approaching and leant forward, lifting his weight off the stool and placing one foot on the ground. Donnie reached forward to grab Sam by the collar of his jacket, but Sam shunted the stool back, driving it into Donnie's genitals. Before the man could even howl in pain, Sam dropped his shoulder, grabbed the hand that Donnie had now lazily flung in his direction, and twisted it by the wrist. Quickly, Sam stepped to the side, spun the pained Donnie around and with his other hand, drove the biker's skull down onto the bar, his forehead shattering the bottle.

Donnie slumped to the floor, unconscious, with glass and the last few drips of beer for company. Infuriated, Jay stormed forward. A guttural roar echoed from his foaming mouth. With nothing but hatred in his crazed eyes, he launched at Sam.

But he'd already given away his weakness.

Sam had clocked it the moment he'd approached.

With a swift kick, Sam connected directly into the man's right knee. The impact of the blow, combined with the velocity of the man's hulking upper body disconnected the kneecap instantly.

The crack was sickening.

The howl of pain that followed was just as haunting.

Scrambling to get to his feet, Jay collapsed down onto his other knee, lifting his head just in time to see Sam's knee driving towards his skull.

Jay collapsed, motionless from the blow.

Sam stood straight, turned to face Mason, only to be greeted by the barrel of a revolver. Behind the gun, Mason's eyes betrayed his confidence and to try to wrestle control of the situation, he pulled back of the hammer with his thumb.

Sam didn't move.

Trying his best to stem the gentle shake of nerves in his wrist, Mason snarled at Sam.

'You move, and I'll blow your fucking brains out. One last time, who the fuck are…'

Sam's hand shot up before Mason could finish his question, instantly gripping the pressure point on the back of the gun-wielding hand. The finger left the trigger and Sam twisted, loosening the man's grip before he slipped his own hand around it. He turned it, pointing it directly at the Mason's face.

It had taken him less than two seconds to disarm him.

The fear in Mason's expression outweighed his admiration, and he slowly held his hands up.

'Look, man. I'm sorry, but we can't be too careful.'

'Get on your knees,' Sam demanded. Mason did so, and Sam stepped forward, pressing the gun to the man's forehead. A bead of nervous sweat slid past the barrel. 'Now tell me, where can I find Alex Stone?'

'She's at HQ,' Mason stammered. 'Bar called The Pit. South Carolina. Just outside Dillon. You hit the I-95, and you'll come across it, eventually. Can't miss it. You wanna put the gun down?'

Sam took a look around the bar once more, at the two motionless men he'd shut down. There was no doubting that whoever was running The Pit would be warned of his impending arrival.

But he wasn't going to kill these men.

It wasn't why he was here.

Sam turned back to Mason and withdrew the gun, much to the man's relief. As he gathered himself, Mason looked up at Sam in confusion.

'Who the fuck are you?'

Sam looked down at him, emotionless.

'I'm just a guy who made a promise.' He turned the gun round in his hand, holding the barrel in his fingers. 'We both know I can't let you watch me leave, right?'

Before Mason could respond, Sam swung the gun like a club. The solid handle collided with Mason's skull, knocking him out cold. The owner of the bar sprawled across the bar room floor and Sam tucked the gun into the back of his jeans, straightened his jacket and headed to the door.

It was a long road to South Carolina, but as he stepped out of the High Five and into the sunshine, he found himself looking forward to the drive.

CHAPTER SIX

The longer the drive went on, the heavier the feeling of dread sat in Sam's stomach. After leaving the High Five, he'd quickly disappeared down a number of alleyways, doing his best to be swallowed up by the busy state of New York. Eventually, someone would walk through those doors and find the mess he'd made and would undoubtedly call the cops.

Or worse yet, one of the men would awaken sooner than expected and lead the charge to track Sam down, and quickly. Either way, Sam needed to move quickly, and after he'd cleared six blocks from the bar, he'd stopped at a small coffee shop just off Hammersley Avenue in the Valley. The adrenaline of dismantling the three bikers had subsided, and the first appearance of jet lag began to creep into his body.

Nothing a double shot coffee wouldn't fix.

As Sam knocked the caffeine back, he searched on his phone for the nearest car hire company and then, after ordering another coffee to go, he set off for through Haffen Park, allowing the sunshine to wash over him. The Motorcade Company was situated on Baychester Avenue, just outside of Edenwold and Sam was greeted by a cheesy grin and an abundance of hair product. The young salesman, whose name Sam didn't catch, clearly put a lot of stock into his appearance, the complete opposite of Sam. While the young man was groomed to the final strand of hair, Sam's short, brown hair was roughly brushed to the side, a few grey hairs beginning to sprout among the rest. His strong jaw was covered in a few days' worth of stubble, and the bruising around his eyes was hanging around like the final remnants of an echo.

Sam made it clear he wanted a powerful car for a long drive.

As the man showed him the forecourt, Sam threw the odd glance over his shoulder, ensuring he hadn't been tracked down or followed. Every time a motorcycle or siren echoed through the city, Sam's ears picked up. As the young salesman continued to babble on about the specs of a car, Sam stopped at a Ford Mustang.

It was a relatively new model; the sun shimmering off the black paintwork. Inside, the leather seats screamed comfort, and Sam cut the man off and made his choice. Despite the man's insistence on a higher priced car, Sam pushed through the rental agreement, providing the necessary documents, and ten minutes later, he pulled out on Baychester Avenue, the beast of an engine roaring with pride.

The satnav told him it was over six hundred miles to Dillon, which meant he would be driving through the night. With the jetlag slowly taking a hold of his body, Sam knew the nine-hour journey would involve an overnight stay, but he planned to get at least halfway through before he called it a night.

Now, four hours into the journey, it felt like his eyelids had been lined with lead and he rolled the window to allow the cool air to crash against his face as he hurtled down the

I-95. It would have been quicker to catch a flight, but after the damage he'd caused in the High Five, it was most likely the cops would have been looking for him, and he couldn't risk his freedom.

Not until he'd found Alex.

The sense of foreboding in his stomach rose, and Sam drummed his fingers on the leather steering wheel in a nervous pattern. After his run-in with the Death Riders, Sam had a bad feeling that Alex was in trouble. Sure, she was a street-smart woman who had fended for herself and her siblings in the absence of any parental protection.

But just like with Blackridge, she was in a dangerous place, and Sam had seen too many good people run out of luck.

What he'd expected to have been a pleasant drive down the east coast of America had been one of frustration, with every traffic jam only bolstering his anxiety. Part of him wanted to push through the impending tiredness and just get to Dillon, but he relented.

Even if he did the journey in one go, he would be too tired to do anything when he got there.

And the Death Riders didn't seem like the type of people who would just overlook the assault in the Bronx. After a painstaking crawl through New York, Sam soon found himself able to open up the impressive engine of his hire car as he cruised through Philadelphia. It was a city he'd always wanted to visit, but with the open road ahead of him, the engine growled impressively as he soon left it in his rear-view. As he crossed the Susquehanna River, Sam soon found himself passing through vast, open countryside, with the odd sign posting him off towards towns such as Emmorton and Bel Air. Sam stopped for gas at a roadside station, with a helpful old man filling his tank and thanking Sam for the generous tip. Sam stocked up on a few cans of energy drink and a sandwich, and he devoured all of it as he passed through Baltimore. The longer the drive went on, the more restless he became, and after passing through and into Washington, he felt himself begin to lag.

It was time to rest and as he passed through the state capital; he pulled into a motel just outside of the town of Fredericksburg. The Marsh Motel was as he'd expected. As cliché as anything seen on TV, the large parking lot was framed with an L-shaped building, comprised fourteen rooms, all of them identikit. At the far end, the reception office sat, and Sam parked the black Mustang in the space nearest to the reception. Then, with his body calling for any kind of bed, he turned the key and killed the ignition.

Alex would have to wait until the morning and Sam pushed open the car door, swung his legs out, and hauled himself up. Every muscle in his body was stiff, and Sam stretched the knots clear, his back thanking him with a slightly worrying crack. As Sam looked around at the motel, he saw a woman walk out from one of the rooms, marching with a purpose to the only other car parked in the lot. She was about thirty years old, pretty, although the bags under her eyes and her messy, mousy brown hair told Sam she hadn't slept in a while.

The tears streaming down her face told him the motel hadn't been in her plans. As she approached her car, she noticed Sam and wiped away the tears with the back of her arm. Sam offered her a smile.

'You okay?' Sam asked, raising his voice slightly to cover the ten feet between the cars.

'Don't worry about it.' She shrugged. 'You ain't from round here, are you?'

'I'm just passing through.'

'Lucky you.' She chuckled, pulling a packet of cigarettes from her jeans and popping one in her mouth. 'Want one?'

'No thanks.'

'Suit yourself. The name's Tammy.'

'Jonathan,' Sam lied, offering her a polite nod. As she lit the cigarette, the door to her room flew open and an irate man emerged. Dressed in jeans and a white vest, the man had an angry gaze fixed on the woman before noticing Sam. His eyes widened in fury, and Sam slammed his car door shut. The man, presumably her partner, stormed towards her.

'Who the fuck is that?' the man demanded, refusing to look at Sam. Tammy cowered, and Sam noticed her pull her hooded jumper up above her exposed arm.

But he'd seen the bruises on her arm the moment she'd turned around.

'I'm Jonathan,' Sam said protectively, stealing the man's intention.

'You got a problem?' the man asked, puffing out his chest in a pathetic act of intimidation. Sam shook his head.

'I'm just getting a room to get my head down.' Sam hauled his rucksack over his shoulder and headed towards the door of the reception and offered Tammy a reassuring smile. 'Nice to meet you, Tammy.'

'Get fucked,' the man spat in Sam's direction before aggressively turning back to his partner and as Sam approached the door, he could hear him accusing her of trying to sleep with him. Sam felt his fist clench, and every fibre of his being wanted to turn back.

But he was on his last legs, and the last thing he needed was to stumble into a domestic problem and risk the possibility of capture.

Although his forged identification was state-of-the-art, having the authorities look into his past and potentially connecting the dots would be a disaster.

With a heavy heart, he entered the reception and booked in for the night. The disinterested woman behind the counter was helpful enough, and when Sam emerged back into the parking lot, the couple was gone. Sam was under no illusion they were back in their room, no doubt engaged in an uncomfortable scenario.

But he had to step away from it.

He entered his mediocre room, dropped his rucksack on the floor, and didn't even bother looking at the furnishings as he collapsed on the surprisingly comfortable mattress and fell asleep before he could even crawl up to the pillows.

———

The bright sunshine cut through the gap in the curtains and eventually moved across the bed until it rested across Sam's face. The brightness caught him off guard, and Sam blinked himself awake, slightly startled by his surroundings. The feeling of panic was uncomfortable, as Sam's awareness of his surroundings had been in-built for years. But the long plane ride, coupled with the hours of driving had wiped him out. After a few moments, he mentally retraced his steps and sat up on the bed. Having slept without a pillow, his neck ached, and he cracked it gently to ease the stiffness. Still stretching out the stiffness of his body, he undressed, lifted his rucksack and stepped into the questionably clean bathroom. If Sam had any question as to why he ached, his body told him the answer.

The bruising on his face had subsided substantially, with just a little darkening beneath his left eye. The stitches in his eyebrow had dissolved, leaving a neat little line at the edge of his eyebrow. But his muscular body was a map of pain.

His shoulder bore the scar from a knife wound he'd suffered in his fight in the High Rise with the murderous 'Mitchell Brother'. His other, the bullet wound that he'd received in Rome.

The left side of his body was still scarred from the blast that had sent him tumbling off the cliff face in Chikari and on a long, drawn out collision with his comrade Mac. The very thought of Mac's story, the torture and pain he'd gone through caused Sam to grit his teeth with guilt, especially as Mac had laid it at Sam's feet.

Mac was responsible for the bullet wound in the shoulder and for the one that desecrated Sam's solid stomach. But the two white scars from the bullets that General Wallace had sent through his chest were the reminder of why he did what he did.

Why the world sometimes needed someone to fight back.

Sam stared at himself in the mirror, respected each scar for the fight he'd gone through to claim them as trophies, and he stepped into the shower. Five minutes later, he emerged from the bathroom, his hair freshly washed and combed into a rough side parting. As he'd brushed his teeth, he contemplated a shave, but the four-day growth wasn't too itchy just yet.

Sam finally checked the time as he lifted his phone.

It was just past one.

He'd slept for fifteen hours and he felt a twinge of guilt that his tiredness had delayed his reacquaintance with Alex. Even though she had no idea he was on his way, Sam still felt late, and he stuffed his worn clothes into his rucksack, dropped the key to the room on the bed, and stepped outside into the sunshine. The afternoon greeted him with a warm hug, and he carried his jacket and rucksack in his hand, the sleeve of his T-shirt wrapped tightly around his bicep. As he opened the passenger door of the car, he heard the click of a lighter behind him.

'Room for one more?'

Sam spun to see Tammy sitting on the bumper of her car, gently pulling the lighter away from her face and allowing a plume of smoke to dance gently into oblivion. She was sitting forward, her knotted hair draped over her face, obscuring her face. Sam looked around for her partner and then chuckled.

'Trust me, you wouldn't want to go where I'm going.'

'You could be going to hell and it would be a better place than this.'

Sam took a step towards her, but she recoiled slightly, refusing to look at him. The sleeve of her jumper drooped, and Sam could see the fresh bruising and a few cuts on her arm.

'Tammy,' he said softly. 'Look at me.'

She took another puff on her cigarette and then slowly turned to face him. Sam felt his heart drop. One of her eyes was swollen shut, the skin a terrifying shade of purple. Her lips were slashed with two cuts and there was a darkening of the skin around her nose.

Judging from the attack, the man was clearly out of control and Sam drew his lips together in anger and stared towards the door. He couldn't just walk away.

'Before you say anything, I can't just leave.' Tammy spat with anger. 'He'll just follow me.'

Sam shook his head and returned to his car. After a quick rummage through his rucksack, he returned to her and held out his hand. Her eyes widened in shock.

'Take this,' Sam said, his fingers offering the roll of dollars. 'It's five hundred dollars. Take your car, disappear and find your way to somewhere where you can be happy.'

Tammy looked up at Sam, her good eye watering. She stood up, glancing back with fear at the room.

'But he'll…'

'You got the keys to this car?' Sam asked. She nodded. 'Then get in and get gone. It doesn't have to be this way.'

Sam placed a reassuring hand on her shoulder, and then his eyes locked on the door of her room. As he started to walk towards the door, Tammy stared at the keys and then called out.

'What are you going to do?'

'I'm going to make sure he doesn't follow you,' Sam called back, not turning from his purposeful stride towards the door. Tammy stood in shock for a few seconds, but then a wave of self-worth hit her. She did deserve better than the hand she'd been dealt, and if a generous stranger was offering her a two-minute window to change her future, she couldn't turn it down. She tossed her cigarette, opened the car door, and dropped into the driver's seat. As she fumbled with the key in the ignition, she glanced at the rear-view mirror, watching as the door to her motel room opened and her partner's furious face was met with a vicious fist. She yelped in panic. The engine roared to life, and she pulled away, heading towards the exit of the parking lot, to a new sense of freedom as her saviour stepped into the room and shut the door behind him.

She turned onto the main road, put her foot down as hard as she could, and headed away from the life she was leaving behind.

Two minutes later, Sam calmly stepped out of the room and softly closed the door. He hung the 'Do Not Disturb' sign over the handle and walked towards his Mustang, shaking away the pain in his knuckles.

He got into the car, turned the key in the ignition, and set off on the rest of his journey, knowing there was another five or so hours before he would get to Dillon.

By the time the man was discovered or regained consciousness, Sam would be long gone.

CHAPTER SEVEN

'Happy New Year!'

Alex Stone sarcastically cheered in her New York accent and Sam smiled, then grimaced immediately. It had been nearly four weeks since Sam had been shot twice and the aftereffects were still in play. Whoever had fired the gun that had nearly ended his life was trained.

The shot through the shoulder had been during a deadly shoot-out, just outside an abandoned warehouse on the outskirts of Rome. The bullet that had ripped through his back, that had been precise.

A shot to wound.

Just trying to sit up caused Sam to wince, and his mind flooded back to that night. The wet, freezing Italian night, the cries of panic from the locals as Sam's car was sent spiralling into a lamppost. He had crawled through the broken glass in a pathetic attempt to escape when the gunshot echoed. The bullet ripped through his body, bringing him to his knees. The feeling of defeat as he heard the boots crunching across the glass behind him.

The sound of a coat sleeve shuffling as his attacker lifted the gun.

But it was the voice that had stayed with him.

'I've waited a long time for this.'

Sam didn't know if it was the blood loss, the pain, or just the devastation of his life over the past few years, but there was something haunting about it.

It sounded familiar.

Had Alex Stone not ignored his plea for her to leave, he would be dead. He'd rescued her from that abandoned factory and sent her on her way.

But she'd returned for him, slamming her car into Sam's attacker and diverting the bullet that was meant for his skull to slam off the pavement ahead of him. The hearing in his ear was still a little fuzzy, but he was alive. While the fact that she'd taken him to a veterinary student was now a source of hilarity between the two of them, he knew that without her, he would have died that night.

She didn't owe him anything. She had just done it.

Because she believed in his fight.

Because it was the right thing to do.

Now, as the obligatory fireworks began to light up the city of Naples to the soundtrack of a battleground, Sam glanced over to Alex who watched from the window. With her hair tied back in a ponytail, Sam could see the immaculate profile of her face. Her dark skin shimmered under the multicoloured glow of the fireworks and she lifted the rolled-up cigarette to her lips. At twenty-six years old, she was twelve years younger than Sam. But they'd formed a strong bond that went beyond the original attraction.

She'd been blackmailed into Blackridge the same way he was, although the carrot dangled before her was the safety of her siblings.

In the weeks since Sam's dance with death, Alex had opened up more about her life. Sam knew about her mother's drug habit and how Alex herself had refused to let her younger brother and sister's futures be ruined by it. She'd taken responsibility for them, worked several jobs, but it was her skill behind the wheel of the car that put food on the table. Soon, she was winning street races through her town in the Bronx, racking up a reputation and a criminal record.

That was when Trevor Sims had stepped in, preying on her desperation to keep her siblings out of the clutches of the children's services system.

Sam and Alex had found comfort with each other, spending a night together. But since then, that passion had morphed into a platonic friendship.

One that had saved Sam's life.

'Happy New Year,' Sam finally responded, glancing at the bandage over his shoulder. 'I'd cheers you if I could.'

Alex chuckled, blowing the smoke out of the open window.

'You probably shouldn't be drinking,' she said dryly, as she reached across to the side table and handed Sam his bottle of beer.

'Because of all the pain medication that I'm not on?'

'Hey, it was medication or beer.' Alex smirked, lifting her own beer. 'And I figured we could both enjoy these.'

Sam smiled again and felt the pain roar from his stomach. The bullet had missed his spine by millimetres, a small mercy considering the agony he was in. But he was determined to get better and with his teeth gritted, he pushed himself upwards, the crunch of his ab muscles causing him to hiss in discomfort. Alex quickly shot to his aid, readjusting the pillows behind his back to support him.

'Thanks,' Sam said helplessly.

'No problems, grandad.' Alex winked and returned to the windowsill, perching on the wooden ledge, and resuming her cigarette. After a few moments of comfortable silence, she spoke. 'So, what's the plan?'

'Stay alive,' Sam replied immediately. It was an in-built response, one that had been hard-wired into his mindset ever since he'd become a soldier all those years ago.

He was built for survival.

And they'd failed to kill him.

'I meant with my family,' Alex said. The mere mention of them caused her lip to tremble. Sam knew better than to ask her if she was okay. Alex was tough, he knew that, and she didn't need his sympathy.

She needed his help.

Trevor Sims may have been found dead in the lower levels of that warehouse, but he was an odious man who basked in the control he had. With him gone, and Blackridge most likely looking for both Alex and Sam, getting to New York would be nigh on impossible.

Getting her family back even harder.

But Sam had made her a promise.

Once they'd found Marsden, Sam had told her he would do whatever he could to help her return to her family. His shot in the dark was to contact Paul Etheridge, but Sam hadn't been able to. Alex had done some digging in a nearby Internet café, but the only information she could dig up was that his company had been sold.

Without Etheridge's expertise and finances, Sam was out of ideas.

But he'd made a promise to Alex, and as he watched her stare vacantly out over the city of Naples, he felt a renewed sense of purpose.

He hadn't been able to keep his promise to his son.

Hadn't been able to protect him.

Sam knew it wouldn't bring Jamie back, but by doing so, he would be able to fend off the pain of his loss a little longer. Ignoring the pain, Sam leant forward and gently wrapped his fingers around Alex's petite wrist.

She faced him, her eyes watering.

Sam looked her dead in the eye and said eight words that he would burn into his memory.

'I promise, I'll help you get them back.'

————

By the time Sam saw the signs for Dillon, it had already passed six that evening. After a much-needed sleep, he'd appreciated being able to stretch his muscles dealing with Tammy's husband. After the reception he'd received at the High Five, he was fairly sure a similar welcome awaited him at The Pit.

Word would have travelled fast, and Sam was surprised

that a fleet of motorcycles hadn't already caught up with him on the highway.

The drive had been relatively pain free, and he'd cruised down the I-95 just as Mason had told him, and sure enough, Dillon was on the horizon.

Despite the passing of six months, his shoulder still intermittently stiffened up, the eternal effects of the bullet wound that Alex Stone had nursed for him.

Just another reason he needed to make good on his promise.

The injustice of having her family used as blackmail was something he felt compelled to correct. A final middle finger to the legacy of Wallace's heinous Blackridge operation.

But above all that, she'd saved his life.

Now he would help her get hers back.

After leaving Fredericksburg, Sam had continued south down the east coast, the highway taking him through Richmond, Virginia, and then just over an hour later, after passing through Jarratt and Emporia, he crossed into North Carolina. Sam pulled over for a small, five-minute stretch and a snack and he stopped on the bridge looking over the Roanoke River, taking in the natural beauty that, despite humanity's best efforts, was still alive and well.

Two hours later, Sam was passing Fayetteville, a large city in North Carolina. But he kept his foot on the pedal, determined to make it to Dillon before the evening got away from him.

Just as the drive was beginning to aggravate him, he saw the Colossus of Dillon, an enormous landmark of a large man in a sombrero, holding a sign welcoming him south of the border. Sam chortled at the preposterous sign but welcomed the update on his journey.

Sam took the exit and continued down the 501 and sure enough, he soon embarked upon the small town of

Dillon. As he approached the first building, the unmistakable roar of a motorcycle piqued his interest, and he kept his eyes firmly on the rear-view mirror.

But the two motorcycles shot by, their riders' leather vests emblazoned with the Death Rider logo.

This was the place.

Before heading to the bar, Sam drove through the town, surprised by the gentrification it had clearly been through. In his mind, he was expecting to drive into an old Western, with derelict streets, wide roads, and abandoned shop fronts. The population of Dillon was small but the high street offered McDonalds, Pizza Hut, and a number of upmarket stores and banks. The footfall was relatively heavy, and Sam scorned his prejudice. He turned off onto Main Street and after passing a few eateries and a church, he crossed over the Little Pee Dee River and pulled into the Welcome Motel.

It was identikit to the one he'd stayed in the previous night, but the sight of it was a welcome one. Sam pulled into the parking lot, which had a few more guests than the one outside of Fredericksburg. He hopped out, entered the reception and was met by a friendly man with large glasses. The owner clearly took pride in his establishment, which was evident in the cleanliness of the room Sam was shown to. Sam dropped his backpack on the bed and locked the door. He then returned to his Mustang and headed back into town.

It was seven o'clock, and if Alex was working behind the bar of The Pit, as Mason had told him, then he wanted to make sure she was there when he arrived. If the welcome was to be as hostile as he expected, he needed to make sure he contacted her.

There wouldn't be a second chance.

Sam pulled his car into a space along the high street and ignored the chain restaurants in favour of a local deli.

The woman was as large as she was welcoming, and she told Sam he looked like he needed a good meal. At six feet tall and nearly fourteen stone of pure muscle, Sam didn't agree, but the rumbling in his stomach meant the woman knew a hungry man when she saw one.

Sam took his seat in a booth by the window and watched the town close down for the evening before a burger and a plate of chips were placed in front of him.

As Sam ate, he watched carefully and counted every time he heard the roar of a motorcycle.

As the sun began to set behind the shops, the frequency of the engines increased, polluting the air with its ferocious growl. He was definitely in the right place.

The owner of the deli gave Sam the check and as he paid, she warned him to not wander too far once the sun goes down. He didn't press her for more information, but Sam got the gist of what she meant.

He was under no illusion that under the control of the Death Riders, Dillon was an entirely different beast once the sun went down.

Sam thanked her for the meal, and then he caught her by surprise with his question.

'Where can I find The Pit?'

Her eyes widened with worry.

'Now, honey. You don't wanna be headin' there tonight.'

'Why's that?'

'You ain't from round here, are ya?'

'What gave it away?' Sam smiled, his handsome grin causing her to blush slightly.

'The Riders don't take kindly to strangers.'

'Oh, I'm pretty sure they're expecting me.'

The lady sighed and directed Sam to the bar. He thanked her for her help, handed her a generous tip, and stepped out into the cool evening. He slid his arms into the sleeves of his bomber jacket, checked his car was locked, and then headed on foot towards Lucius Road on the south side of town.

As he made his way down Patriot Street, the unmistakable sound of motorcycle engines and heavy metal music echoed through the night sky.

Turning onto the road, he saw The Pit.

In complete contrast to the store-bought aesthetic of the High Five, The Pit oozed authenticity. The large, wood-panelled bar sat on the side of the road, surrounded by rows of motorcycles. Scattered around the front, a few bikers drank and smoked, with many more inside. There was no one on the door, and Sam was sure that the incumbents didn't require assistance should anything kick off.

They made their own rules, and Sam felt a flutter of worry in his gut.

Not for himself.

He'd stared down the barrel of much worse in the hands of those more dangerous.

But he worried about how Alex had fallen into such a place. She was a long way from home, in a place that didn't take kindly to strangers.

As the large American flag fluttered in the cool evening breeze above the door, Sam took a deep breath and crossed the street. A few heads were already turning as he approached, and he felt a small semblance of calm from the gun pressed against the small of his back.

It had been a long journey.

A lot of people had died.

But Sam was ready to make good on his promise.

Ignoring the lazy protests of the biker nearest to the door, Sam stepped up the two wide wooden steps of the entrance, pushed open the door, and stepped inside.

CHAPTER EIGHT

The Pit had transformed since it had come under the ownership of the Death Riders. While it had revelled in being a bar frequented by motorcycle enthusiasts, once the Riders made it their home, it became as notorious as it had profitable. A beacon for lowlifes, all looking to move up in the world and wear the patch. It drew them in like a moth to a flame. The welcoming tavern changed completely, and outsiders were seized upon instantly.

If you couldn't step up, you stepped out.

If you could still walk.

It was an atmosphere that the regulars revelled in, with a number of disenchanted men and women soon falling in line, quivering in a cocktail of fear and adulation to the Riders, willing to do whatever they could to be 'in' with the Riders. For the select crew, those who wore the Rider's patch with pride, they were treated like celebrities. Their tales of crime and street justice spread through the bar like wildfire.

They had become as much a myth as they had a legend.

It was exactly what Trent Wyatt had wanted.

Sitting in his usual booth at the back of the bar, he watched as swathes of wannabe members and scantily dressed women surrounded members of his crew, hanging off every word that was spoken. The power of the Riders was magnetic, and sooner or later, those who were enthralled by the lifestyle would be given opportunities to please them.

It had made them untouchable to the law.

They had a number of lawyers in South Carolina who would represent them.

Enough bank managers to launder their money and fill their accounts.

Women, and men, who would fulfill any sexual desire they wanted.

The local sheriff's department gave them the necessary leeway, which was reimbursed by Wyatt's insistence that the Riders handle problems that the sheriff wanted kept 'private'.

Local gangs had been disbanded. Usually by the bloodied hands of Wyatt's number two, Eddie Sykes. When Wyatt emerged from prison after a stint for grievous bodily harm, Sykes was the first man he'd called upon. Previously a roadie for a semi-successful metal band, Sykes had met Wyatt a number of times at biker festivals and a few less than respectable bars.

Sykes was a smart man, but years of drug and drink abuse had uncoiled his mind, leaving him with an unbeatable addiction and a relentless urge to feed it. It made him a dangerous man, and Wyatt offered him an endless fix.

All he had to do was the dirty work.

Sykes had killed over fourteen men for Wyatt, the most recent just under two months ago.

While the Riders were stationed in Dillon, their legend

echoed through every street in South Carolina. The entire drug trade of the state went through them, and any attempt against their empire was met with brute force. Hidden beneath the facade of a brotherhood and street justice, the Death Riders were essentially a drug empire. But recently, a new batch of meth had hit the streets in Charleston, down by the south coast. Sykes had taken a crew to investigate, with the name Jose Vasquez being whispered. Sykes had eliminated the dealers, but Wyatt knew something else was coming. Vasquez was a name as synonymous with drugs as the Riders. Having built his empire in Mexico City, Vasquez had expanded into America, spreading like a plague across the coast.

Florida.

Georgia.

All of it was under his control.

Wyatt admired the man's ambition, a kindred spirit who wanted the world and was willing to take it. With Vasquez, there was no code.

No honour.

The police didn't go near Vasquez because of an unholy alliance. They stayed away because they were terrified. And with reports of Vasquez's product now filtering into Wyatt's state, the head of the Death Riders knew he was facing a test of his power.

Sykes knew this, too.

Occasionally, he'd even made thinly veiled threats to Wyatt about coming for the throne.

But Wyatt knew it would never happen.

As he looked around his bar, ignoring the beautiful women at either side of him, their hands stroking his thigh as they worked tirelessly for his attention, he knew that his gaze would stop any person in the room dead.

Wyatt was the Death Riders.

In his mind, and theirs. And while Sykes entertained a group of wide-eyed fans at the bar, describing in detail how he'd slit a rival drug dealer's throat and left him to bleed out on the ground, Wyatt knew their adulation wasn't just for Sykes.

It was for the lifestyle Wyatt had created for them.

A guitar riff kicked in through the speakers that were hanging from the wood-panelled walls, and the two women commented to Wyatt that they love the song. As they got up and began to dance together, a few other men turned to watch, cheering them on as they pressed their bodies together. Wyatt smiled to himself. The ease with which people were pleased amused him greatly, and he was careful to never show anything.

He was a closed book to them all, which only elevated his stature to them.

As he watched the two women dance with mild interest, a small commotion drew his attention. A number of his regulars had all turned to look at the door, their eyes wide with faux outrage, as if an outsider stepping into his bar somehow offended them. Wyatt saw Sykes' face contort to a scowl, and he slammed his bottle of beer on the bar before marching towards Wyatt, his gaze still affixed on the doorway. Wyatt waited patiently for Sykes to arrive, but he already knew what was happening.

He'd been expecting it ever since Mason had called him the previous evening.

The Brit who had dismantled all three of his men with relative ease had arrived. It was why Wyatt had insisted that Alex Stone work that night.

Like a moth to a flame.

Wyatt told Sykes to keep his calm for a few minutes. Then, once this British invader had flown too close to flame, Wyatt had every intention of roasting him alive.

———

As soon as Sam stepped into The Pit, he felt every gaze fall upon him. After the hostility he'd received from the few people out front, it wasn't unexpected, but never had Sam felt so out of place. The heavy metal music, combined with the copious amounts of leather and the clear violation of the indoor smoking laws, The Pit was every bit as authentic as the High Five was fake. Every member of the Death Riders who was in attendance legitimate, and despite having no real knowledge of their history, Sam was certain it wouldn't make for pleasant reading. A gruff man, bearded and with his hair pulled back in a ponytail stepped towards him, trying his best to intimidate him. Sam, noticing that he, like a few others, wore the Death Rider symbol he'd seen in New York, politely smiled and side-stepped the man, walking confidently towards the bar.

Heads turned.

Eyes bulged in anger.

Sam knew the clock was ticking, and he looked around the bar, ignoring the hateful stares of everyone inside. While the bar was packed, Sam quickly realised that there were only a handful of actual Riders among the group. Each one of them seemed to have acquired their own following, no doubt a bunch of misguided people looking for their own place among the elite. It was tantamount to a cult, but Sam knew the perception of bikers due to their representation within films and media.

They were cool.

They lived by their own rules.

But considering the panic of the local business owner, they brought nothing but fear to the community. Under-neath the hood, they were criminals, and Sam knew he was in a dangerous place.

More importantly, so was Alex.

As he ignored the venomous glares of the group surrounding the pool table, his eyes were drawn to the door to the side of the bar opening, and he felt his heart stop for a second.

Alex.

She stepped out, carrying a box of bottled beers, her dark hair pulled back into a ponytail. Wearing a tight, slightly ripped T-shirt that clung to her athletic frame, she smiled wryly at a passing comment and slid behind the bar, placing the box down. She crouched down and began stocking the near empty fridge. Two other women were keeping the drinks flowing, and Sam stepped confidently past a few people and leant across the bar.

'Can I have a beer, please?'

Alex looked up, went to respond but her jaw dropped. Sam, looking down from the bar, offered his best smile. Apprehensively, and with a few quick glances to the far corner of the bar, Alex leant forward.

'Sam?' She shook her head. 'What the fuck are you doing here?'

Her anger caught Sam slightly off guard and he reached out and clutched her hand.

'I told you, I'd be back to help you.'

'You need to go.'

'Alex?' Sam looked at her with confusion as she withdrew her hand. 'What's wrong?'

'Seriously. You're going to fuck things up.'

Out of the corner of his eye, Sam could see one of the Riders slam his drink down on the bar and begin to wade through the group towards them.

Time was running out. As Alex tried to step out from around the bar, Sam took a step towards her.

She was terrified.

'Alex, I didn't mean to leave you. I had to go back. You know I did.'

'And I'm doing what I have to do.' Alex glanced over Sam's shoulder at the incoming man. 'Look, you need to leave.'

'Okay. I'm staying at the Welcome Motel. Come and find me.'

Before Alex could respond, Sam felt a hand drop on his shoulder. With a sigh, he turned around, coming face to face with the crooked grin of Eddie Sykes. The man was taller than Sam by a few inches and was stocky. His arms, covered in ink, were well rounded and burst through the leather vest he wore. Around his neck, he wore dog tags, something that Sam would have respected if he weren't completely sure the man was a criminal.

'You lost, pal?' Sykes asked, a small threat underlining the question.

'No, I'm fairly sure this is The Pit, right?'

'Ah, so it is you.' Sykes removed his hand from Sam's shoulder, interlocked his fingers, and cracked them. 'Been waiting for you to show up.'

'Well, I'm going now so…'

'The fuck you are.' Sykes' eyes flared with fury. 'Now, as far as I'm concerned, I'd love to break every bone in your fucking body and then leave you in the fucking woods for the wolves. But Wyatt, he wants a word with you.'

'Who's Wyatt?'

Sykes didn't answer. Instead, he stepped to the side, ushering Sam through. Knowing full well one wrong move would probably be his last, Sam shrugged and obliged, stepping past Sykes, who then shoved him roughly in the direction of the back corner of the bar. All eyes were on them, but Sam noticed the heads turn away as he approached the far table. As they arrived, two scantily dressed women were sent away, and they scurried back across the bar. Sitting in the booth, keeping a watchful eye over the evening's proceedings, was Wyatt. His grey hair was cropped short, with most of it obscured by a bandana. His strong jaw, covered with a well-trimmed beard was dark, tinged with the same grey that blessed his head. His dark eyes pierced through Sam, regarding him with both intrigue and disgust.

'Sit,' the man commanded, his heavily tattooed hand gesturing to the seat opposite. Before Sam could respond, Sykes shoved him down by the shoulder. Sam glared back up at the henchman, who looked excited at the prospect of retaliation. Wyatt snapped shut his lighter, having lit a cigarette, and he let the smoke slowly filter from his slacked jaw.

'You know those things will kill you, right?' Sam offered.

'Trust me, son. This right here is the least dangerous thing at this table.' Wyatt took another puff and then pointed at Sam. 'Yourself included.'

'Excuse me?'

'The name's Wyatt. I run this place. The Death Riders. Pretty much this whole state. Nothing happens on these streets without my say so. So, now you know who I am…' Wyatt slammed his hand on the table, startling a number of watchers. Sam stayed calm. 'Who the fuck are you?'

'I'm just passing through.'

'Passing through, eh?' Wyatt clicked his fingers, and someone quickly handed him a laptop. He slid his finger across the mouse pad and then clicked. Quickly, he spun the screen round to face Sam. Sam watched the CCTV footage from the High Five as he systematically disabled the three men yesterday. As it finished, Sam looked back at Wyatt, who raised his eyebrows. 'So again…who the fuck are you and what do you want?'

'Those guys attacked me first.'

'I don't give a fuck about those guys.' Wyatt slammed

the laptop shut. 'What I want to know is who you are and why the fuck do you think you can mess with my business?'

'And why are you looking for Alex?' Sykes chimed in, drawing a side glance from Sam.

'She's a friend of mine. I was in the neighbourhood and just thought I'd check in.'

'Some neighbourhood,' Wyatt spat; his unblinking gaze locked on Sam's. 'New York to here. You working with Vasquez?'

'Who?'

'Don't play games with me, son.' Wyatt's drawl elongating the final word. 'If Vasquez has sent you to try to intimidate me, then I'll be more than happy to post you back to him, piece by piece, you hear me?'

'Sounds nice,' Sam said, leaning forward. 'But I don't know who Vasquez is. I don't want to. I came here to check up on an old friend, and I've done that. So, unless we are literally going to whip our dicks out onto the table, I think I'd like to leave.'

A smile crept across Wyatt's face. There was an unflappable courage to this British man, and Wyatt liked it. Although he was sceptical, he was sure the man was telling the truth about having no association with Vasquez. Wyatt stubbed out his cigarette and sat back in the booth.

'I'm intrigued. See a man who can do that to three men' – Wyatt tapped the laptop – 'is a skilled man. A dangerous man. Usually, men like you have a reason for turning up in places like this and trust me, it ain't for the girls. So let me make something truly clear to you…'

'Jonathan,' Sam answered.

'Jonny…I will be watching you. Like I said, nothing happens in this town without my say so. If it's Vasquez, those DEA fucks, or you're just here to try to fuck my shit up, I'll be watching. And the second, and I mean the very split second, you show me that reason and I don't like it,

I'll make you scream for god himself to kill you. Do you understand?'

'Loud and clear,' Sam replied.

'You're in an extremely dangerous place.' Wyatt finished, discarding Sam with a flick of the wrist. 'I'll be seeing you.'

Sykes stepped to the side, and Sam slid out of the booth. Wyatt had turned back to his drink and Sam offered a smile to Sykes who gritted his teeth in anger. With one final glance, Sam saw Alex watching in worry and as he marched towards the door, he gave her a wink to assure her he was okay. He hoped she'd come and see him, but he was well aware that he was already outstaying his welcome in the town. He pushed through the doors and marched through the rows of bikes, fully aware that Sykes had followed him to the door and was watching with violent intent as Sam made his way across the street and rounded the corner.

As the music began to die down behind him, Sam was half expecting the roar of motorcycles to follow him back to his motel. But there were none.

As he walked down the street, he began to worry just what Alex had got herself involved with. There was clearly a growing dissension between the Death Riders and this Vasquez, and she was a long way from home for it to just be a coincidence.

Why had she left the High Five for The Pit?

Judging from the state of the place and the people who frequented it, it wasn't for the money.

Something didn't feel right.

Lost in his own thoughts, Sam scolded himself for not noticing the van pull up alongside him, only realising as the side door flew open.

'Get in the van.'

Sam turned to see the barrel of a Glock 17 held by a

muscular man in a suit. Behind him, another man looked on with interest.

'What now?'

Sam's question was for no one in particular, and under the threat of the gun pointed at him, Sam stepped into the van and the door slammed shut.

CHAPTER NINE

Eddie Sykes was a hard man to please.

It had been that way ever since he was a child. He was a big kid from the outset, his stocky frame making him a target for numerous bullies to pick on with their quick wit and spiteful words. The only way Sykes knew how to deal with such problems was with his fists. As he ventured into puberty, the puppy fat shed from his body and he was soon a specimen that had people doubting his age.

Every coach at school wanted him on their team.

A number of girls wanted his attention.

All Sykes wanted was to fight.

For a while, competitive boxing satisfied that particular itch. But the rules and regulations would soon put to rest any chances he had of taking it further. There were only so many times he could headbutt an opponent or knee them in the gut before he was banned by the boxing authorities.

Sykes wanted to fight.

He just needed permission to do so.

As soon as he turned eighteen, he enlisted in the army, happy to be surrounded by like-minded men and women, all of whom wanted to face danger head on and throw up a middle finger. As the years rolled by, he excelled, only once having his knuckles wrapped for failing to follow orders. The man was a skilled fighter and was soon recruited into the Marine Corps. There, he was able to fight alongside the best.

But the rules were even stricter.

Eventually, they became his downfall.

On a covert mission in Istanbul, Sykes, on a quest to neutralise an arms deal, decided to open fire in a public area.

He gunned down three members of a terrorist cell.

Five civilians were also killed.

A further eight wounded.

His complete disregard for his orders also cost one of his team their life.

Before a media storm could hit, the United States Marine Corps dishonourably discharged Sykes at the age of twenty-eight, after a decade of service. The betrayal of his country still left a bitter taste in Sykes's mouth almost two decades later. It was why he decided to push back against the establishment, and why he thrived within the Riders.

For Sykes, there were no limits.

Despite Wyatt's insistence on a strict code, where they moulded the law to his whim, Sykes preferred the idea of striking terror into the hearts of everyone who lived within South Carolina. Sykes had been against an expansion to New York. The idea of selling out the Rider's logo under-mined everything they stood for.

They shouldn't be seen as a club.

Nor should they be the moral compass directing street justice.

The Death Riders should be a death sentence for anyone in their way.

Wyatt's failure to deal with the lingering threat of Jose

Vasquez and his refusal to fight back against the DEA had brought Sykes to his limit. It would only be a matter of time before Wyatt's carefully built empire collapsed around him and when the time came, and the Riders saw that Sykes had been right the whole time then things would change.

Sykes would take control.

And the Death Riders would handle their problems the only way Sykes knew how.

Standing at the bar, Sykes ignored the attention of the woman by his side and her clear attempts at seduction. On another night, he would probably have fulfilled her fantasy. There were plenty of girls who came through the bar, all of them wanting the thrill of being with a biker.

But tonight, Sykes's mind was pre-occupied.

After watching Jonathan Cooper leave The Pit, Sykes had demanded Wyatt explain why they were letting him live. The man had assaulted three of their guys, and despite his insistence he was just passing through, Sykes didn't trust him.

There was too much going on for a wildcard to disrupt everything.

How did he know Alex?

What did he want?

Wyatt had told him to stay calm. Let them handle it if it needs to be handled. Sykes had stormed to the bar, thrown back a few shots, and then ordered a whiskey. He watched as Wyatt beckoned Alex to his booth, and he felt nothing.

No guilt.

It was Sykes's insistence that Alex move from the High Five to The Pit. Wyatt had assumed it was because Sykes wanted to bed her. She was an attractive woman, but Sykes had made no such advance.

Everything was falling into place, and Sykes refused to

let some random British man turn up and turn it all upside down.

Sykes needed to know who he was.

And more importantly, what the fuck he wanted?

As Alex smiled at Wyatt and left the booth, Sykes finished his whisky. Completely ignoring the woman, he turned and headed to the door. Wyatt would be watching, and a little part of Sykes wanted Wyatt to challenge him.

He wouldn't.

Wyatt was too clever to allow everyone to witness a power struggle.

As Sykes stepped out into the night, he beckoned two men who were smoking, who were more than happy to get their names in his good books.

Sykes wanted his answers.

And he was more than willing to beat them out of that British bastard if he had to.

————

Sam gingerly lowered himself onto the leather bench that ran along the side of the van, glancing up at the screens that lined the opposite panel. A few grainy CCTV images from outside The Pit graced the screens, with Sam squinting to try to make out any of the faces.

He'd yet to engage with the two men who had demanded he step in, but judging from their suits, their haircuts and the myriad of high-tech equipment, they were government.

FBI.

CIA.

Whatever.

All Sam knew was he was on very thin ice. The only thing keeping it from breaking was a fake ID. They clearly weren't there for him specifically. The paperwork on the bench had mugshots of the bikers he'd just met. But as the most wanted man in the UK, being ushered into an undercover government van wasn't ideal.

The two agents couldn't have been more difficult. The man who had held him at gun point was mixed race, his light brown skin contrasting with the white shirt that clung to a muscular frame. He eyed Sam with suspicion, as if trying his best to place a memory in the correct mental folder.

The other was at least twenty years older. Approaching sixty at Sam's guess, and his grey hair was parted neatly at the side. His clean-shaven jaw was strong, and as he smiled, he revealed tobacco-stained teeth. When he spoke, his southern drawl made him sound like a cowboy.

'Sorry for my partner. Agent Alan can be a little more, shall we say, hasty when it comes to getting things done.'

'Who are you?' Sam asked, playing it as confused as he could.

'Bit late to be asking that?' The younger agent scoffed, folding his muscular arms across his chest as he leant against the back panel of the van. The older agent sighed and rubbed the bridge of his nose in frustration.

'Sorry.' Sam held his hands up. 'I would have asked before, but you had a gun in my face.'

'Enough.' The senior agent rose his voice, commanding the room. 'Son, I'm Special Agent Terry Sinclair. Behind me, that's Special Agent Joe Alan. We work for the Drug Enforcement Administration.'

'The DEA?' Sam asked, his eyebrows raised.

'Ding fucking ding.' Alan snorted sarcastically, much to Sinclair's annoyance.

'Again, let me apologise for my partner's behaviour. It's been a rough few months.'

'You guys need some counselling?' Sam shrugged. Alan

stepped past Sinclair and leant forward, going nose to nose with Sam.

'You got a smart mouth. I'll be happy to fix that for you.'

'Okay, let's calm down.' Sinclair reached forward and pulled Alan back by the shoulder. In the cramped environment, Alan looked double the size of Sinclair. Sam could feel the tension level rising. But again, he had no idea what was happening.

Alex was mixed up with a violent biker gang.

The DEA was snooping around.

What the hell was going on?

Sam kept his eyes on the irate Alan as he stepped back to the far end of the van and then turned to Sinclair.

'Am I under arrest?'

'Do you see any cuffs?' Sinclair smiled again, reaching into his jacket pocket and removing a small metal tin. He placed it on the side and opened it, revealing a number of pre-rolled cigarettes. 'Do you smoke?'

'Nope.'

'Fair enough.' Sinclair placed one in his lips. 'Joe, crack the door will you?'

As the furious Alan slid open the door slightly, Sinclair patted down his pockets, looking for a light. After a few moments, he began to search the pile of papers on the bench, turning a few over before locating a box of matches. He sparked one to life, lit his cigarette, and then shook the flame to extinction.

'Am I in trouble?' Sam finally asked.

'Define trouble?' Sinclair replied, taking another puff on his cigarette. 'Have a look at this, Jonathan. It is Jonathan, right?'

Sam's eyes raised in surprise and at the back of the van, Alan chuckled.

'You got an ID?' Alan spat, reaching out his hand.

Without taking his eyes off Sinclair, Sam slid the fake identification from his pocket and handed it to the burly agent. As it was taken, a twinge of discomfort echoed through his body.

'You have the place bugged?' Sam asked.

'We have people on the inside.' Sinclair smiled, before turning the laptop to Sam and pressing play. The same security video that Wyatt presented to him was on the screen, showing Sam handily taking apart the three Riders in the Bronx. Sam sighed as the video concluded with him pocketing the gun, and he then turned back to Sinclair, his face askew in a triumphant grin.

'So, I am in trouble?'

'That depends.' Sinclair extinguished his cigarette in the overflowing ashtray. 'See, that right there, looks like aggravated assault. And if my eyesight is correct, and it always is, you're now in possession of a firearm. Do you have a licence for that?'

Sam looked over Sinclair's shoulder to Alan, who was scrupulously checking his ID on a computer. Despite Etheridge's unparalleled skill, there was nothing but suspicion in his eyes. Sam turned back to Sinclair, the veteran agent's smugness beginning to wane.

'What do you want?' Sam sighed.

'Why are you looking for Alex Stone?' Sinclair asked, his smugness evaporating into a steely gaze that Sam knew would break a number of suspects.

'She's a friend.'

'A friend?'

'Yup. A friend. In fact, she saved my life last year, and I made her a promise to come back and help her. So here I am.'

'Help her how?'

'You're the super detective, you tell me?'

Behind Sinclair, Alan typed furiously away on his

keyboard. Then he rose from the uncomfortable looking chair and approached them, tossing the fake passport at Sam, who caught it instinctively. Outside the van, the street shook with the roar of a number of motorcycles as they shot past, their engines growling angrily into the night sky.

No doubt a few Riders hoping Sam was taking a late evening stroll.

Alan folded his arms, the white shirt pulling tight against his dark skin.

'It checks out.'

'Mr Cooper it is then,' Sinclair grumbled. 'A word of advice, Mr Cooper. Stay away from Alex Stone. Stay away from the Riders. We have been working on this case for months and we are this close to burying them under that godforsaken bar. This little incident in the Bronx, call it a freebie. You get involved again, and I'll bury you with them. Is that understood? We both have too much riding on it for some rogue wildcard to fuck things up. Is that understood?'

Sam looked up at Alan and then at Sinclair, and gave them a phony salute.

'Loud and clear.' He then nodded to Alan. 'Ex-military?'

'Excuse me?'

'Your arm.' Sam pointed to the right bicep as he stood. 'I can see your tattoo.'

'Marine Corps. Eleven years' service,' Alan said proudly. 'You?'

'Like I said, I'm just an old friend.'

Sam winked at Alan as he approached the door, and he stepped out into the cool evening. The echoes of The Pit hummed dimly in the distance, and Sam had no idea where they'd driven him. The car park was vast, yet empty, and at the far end, a large Walmart loomed, casting a shadow across the tarmac. Sam turned back to the van, where Sinclair stood, his hand on the door.

'Remember what I said, Mr Cooper,' Sinclair said as reached for the sliding door. 'I'm a man of my word.'

The door slammed shut, and the van rumbled before pulling away, a fake business name plastered across the side panel. As it sped towards the exit of the car park, Sam watched it, committing everything he'd seen inside to memory.

The files they had on the Riders, a few more on Vasquez, the man Wyatt had told him about.

The government issued Glock 17 that hung in the holster that was strapped to Alan's rib cage.

The name of the bar on the box of matches Sinclair had used.

All of it, no matter how irrelevant, would be stored away. Sam's mind was on the brink of being photographic, but his attention and absorption of detail was a skill that had made him such a deadly soldier.

The situation had escalated, with Alex now in the middle of either an impending drug war or a DEA bust.

Either way, her desperation to get her family back had her dangling too close to the edge for her to claw her way back.

Not without Sam.

Sam stuffed his hands in his pockets and began the walk back towards town, using pigeon's instinct to guide him to the high street and from there, he would remember the route back to the motel.

He needed to clear his head.

Plot his next move.

Figure out how to get Alex out of there.

As he strode purposefully across the parking lot, Sinclair's words echoed in his mind.

'*I'm a man of my word.*'

Sam chuckled.

'So am I.'

———

As the van pulled out of the Walmart parking lot and back onto the highway, Sinclair rolled down the passenger window and blew out a mouthful of smoke. With Alan behind the wheel, Sinclair watched with disdain as the small town of Dillon passed him by. Unlike his partner, Sinclair had never been to war. Had never fought for his country.

Not on the battlefields, at least.

His fight had been on the drugs that had ravaged his great nation, and despite fighting the good fight for over two decades, he felt no closer to winning.

All he had was a bleak acceptance of failure and a deep resentment for dedicating his life to a noble yet unwinnable cause.

He'd never had a family. Never been married. The job had consumed his life and with retirement looming in a few years, all he had to look forward to was a decent pension and no one to share his golden years with.

Bringing down the Riders would at least provide a modicum of comfort to him, and he was sure that once it was over, there would be no job left for him.

At the wheel, Alan signalled and turned the corner, heading back towards the hotel where they'd been holed up for months. He was a good man and Sinclair was envious of the honour with which he went about his work. Despite being honourably discharged by the marines, Joe Alan was still very much a soldier and Sinclair felt a pang of guilt for what their mission was doing to him.

When the Riders were no more, Alan would be a changed man.

But when you deal with the dirt, your hands get mucky.

Alan caught Sinclair looking at him out of the corner of his eye and turned to his partner.

'You okay?' Alan asked, his eyes returning to the road.

'Yeah, just peachy.' Sinclair flicked the cigarette out of the window. 'Just thinking.'

'About Cooper?'

'Do you believe him?'

Alan shook his head.

'I didn't believe a word he said.' A smile came across the burly agent's lips, his neatly trimmed goatee rising with the grin. 'His ID checks out. No criminal record. No military service. Nothing. But I know a soldier when I see one. So, whoever the fuck he is, it isn't an old friend just stopping by.'

'You think he's a mercenary? Working for Vasquez, maybe?'

Alan shrugged his broad shoulders and then slowed the van, guiding the wheel expertly with one hand and lining the van perfectly into the parking bay outside the hotel.

'I don't know. But I've got his photo being run through every database we have access to, and maybe a few we don't.' Alan's eyes glowed with menace. 'Whoever he is, you can bet your ass I'll find out.'

CHAPTER TEN

After Jonathan Cooper left the bar, Wyatt shot a glance towards Sykes, who was almost shaking with fury. With a stern shake of the head, Wyatt made it clear that there was no need for more action. Sykes, in his usual petulant way, grunted and stormed back to the bar, demanding another drink.

Wyatt sat back in his booth calmly, controlling the rage that was seething beneath. He was well aware of Sykes's ambition and that the idea of leading the Riders was one that he held dearly.

Unfortunately for Sykes, so did Wyatt.

He'd built the Riders into a criminal empire, untouched by the authorities and unrivalled by other operations. Their grasp on the state of South Carolina was unbreakable, and Wyatt knew his patience would outlast Sykes's desire for the throne.

What didn't sit well with him was the impending collision with Jose Vasquez.

It was part of the game to know who your competition was. Wyatt, while not as volatile as Sykes, was just as ruthless, and he kept tabs on several drug barons who skirted dangerously close to his turf. It was one of the benefits of building the Riders into what they were. Their loyalty to him and to the gang was undoubted, and whenever he needed someone to either investigate or shut down the competition, it was done without hesitation.

Vasquez had been on the radar for a long time.

From the first time his name was mentioned as a new, dangerous player in Mexico, to his brand of meth washing through Texas like a tidal wave, Wyatt knew the road they were on. It would only end one way.

Lighting another cigarette, Wyatt glanced back towards the bar, smirking as a young woman tried to speak to a clearly irate Sykes.

Beyond them both, he caught Alex Stone looking sheepishly in his direction. Wyatt liked Alex. She was a tough woman, who had clearly had a life as hard as his own, although hers hadn't included a long stretch in the pen. While he'd forged his way to power by fighting back against the system that worked against them, Alex had tried to balance on the edge of it.

It had landed her in trouble, of which he didn't know as much as he liked. Sykes had adamantly vouched for her and had practically begged Wyatt to bring her across from the High Five. It seemed strange to Wyatt at the time.

Why would a girl from the Bronx want to leave her hometown to live in fucking Dillon?

Wyatt had always assumed Sykes wanted to have his way with her, but from what he'd seen, there was nothing between them. She worked as many shifts as she could, lived in a crummy apartment a few streets away, and kept herself to herself.

That feeling of doubt was back.

Jonathan Cooper, which Wyatt doubted was his real name, was a monkey wrench. He clearly was trained; the video was all the evidence he and Sykes needed to agree he was a dangerous man. The clinical efficiency with which he took apart his men was as impressive as it was worrying.

How did Alex know him?

Two weeks ago, he had no idea who Alex Stone was. Now, with the pressure of an impending war with Vasquez and a DEA team sniffing around, the mysterious Cooper shows up looking for her?

Wyatt didn't sit on his throne by accident.

Nothing was left to chance.

As Alex offered him an awkward smile, Wyatt lifted his empty bottle of beer and wiggled it slightly, indicating he wanted another. The Pit didn't offer table service, but Wyatt was a different story. Quickly and obediently, Alex shuffled over with a fresh bottle of beer. Wyatt gratefully took it and took a swig.

'Thank you, Alex.'

'No worries, boss.' Alex offered her best smile and turned to leave.

'Hold on a second,' Wyatt said calmly, with just enough menace to assert his authority. 'You know I need to ask you a few questions, right?'

Alex nodded, shuffling awkwardly on her feet. A few interested patrons turned, excited to see the fallout of Cooper's visit. Wyatt's venomous glare soon sent them scurrying away. He took another sip of beer and then regarded Alex with a smile.

'Who is Jonathan Cooper?'

'Who?'

'So that's not his real name, then?'

A penny dropped in Alex's mind and she silently scolded herself.

'Oh, Johnny.' She tried to correct herself. 'He's just an old friend.'

'You have many ex-military British friends growing up in the Bronx?'

'Ex-military?'

Before Wyatt said a word, he spun the laptop to face Alex and clicked play. She instantly recognised the High Five, Mason, Donnie, and Jay. She watched as Sam systematically took them apart in a matter of seconds. She'd seen him do it before, months ago, when they'd both been blackmailed by Trevor Sims to join the now defunct Blackridge. She'd read about their dissolution after the death of General Ervin Wallace.

Alex was sure Sam had been responsible for it.

This confirmed it.

He'd won his fight and was back to keep his word.

With all her might, she stifled the smile that threatened to creep across her striking face, and she turned to Wyatt, whose face bore little emotion.

'Let me make something clear to you, Alex. I'm a careful man. I take steps, usually two or three, before they're needed. Sykes, he vouched for you. To me, it seemed a bit odd that you would want to move hundreds of miles from your home to work here.'

'I needed the job and…'

'Don't interrupt me.' Wyatt's tone seethed with anger. 'Now, I don't care whether you're sucking his cock or whether he just took pity on you. What I care about is my business. And right now, this man, he is an unknown entity. So, I'll give you one chance to tell him to get the fuck out of town, otherwise I will take steps. Is that understood?'

'Yes, boss.'

'And, Alex…you're on thin ice. Do you understand? And believe me, if that ice breaks, you will wish that the only thing beneath it was freezing water.' Wyatt stared deep into her eyes, hammering the message home. He then sat back, took a swig of beer, and turned from her. 'Get back to work.'

Alex nodded nervously and hurried away. Wyatt

smiled, knowing his threat had hit the mark. Every cautious bone in his body was urging him to just kill her and Cooper, but while the police were in his pocket, it would cost a lot to get them to turn away from two dead bodies.

He'd given her a chance.

A warning.

Alex seemed like a smart girl, so he was sure she'd take it.

Sykes slammed his drink down as Alex returned to the bar and stormed to the door, refusing to look back at Wyatt who watched with intent.

Wyatt sighed.

Sykes was obviously going to find Cooper.

Another flagrant disregard for his orders.

Sipping his beer, Wyatt made a mental note to put Sykes back in his place when he returned. But watching the video of Cooper assault his men, Wyatt was more than happy for Sykes to let the man know who was in charge.

Dillon belonged to the Death Riders.

Dillon and every person in it.

———

It was a surprisingly pleasant walk back through town. Although not warm enough to remove his jacket, Sam had enjoyed the cool breeze that flittered through the night sky. The entire town was empty, beyond the faint echo of The Pit, which hung over the town like a spectre. The residents of the town were clearly living in fear of the Death Riders, sacrificing any hope of a night life due to the bikers. Sam was under no illusion that they were dangerous.

With the DEA watching them like a hawk, Sam connected the dots as to what the Riders truly were.

Drug dealers.

With his war on organised crime over, Sam put his nobility to the side.

He wasn't here to bring them down.

He was here to help Alex get her family back.

Perhaps storming into their base and mouthing off to their leader wasn't the best tactic, after all. Sam regretted it, knowing he'd garnered their attention, which he hoped had little blow back on Alex, who was clearly in a dangerous position.

But why was she involved with the Riders?

How would that help her get back to her family?

As Sam rounded the corner and into the parking lot of the Welcome Motel, he immediately saw the motorcycles. Three large shimmering Harley Davidsons, all stood proudly, dotted strategically in a triangle. Two of the bikers stood, arms folded, a look of distaste across their bearded faces as Sam approached.

The biker stood nearest to the door Sam recognised.

Wyatt's right-hand man.

'Think we need a little chat, don't you?' Sykes asked rhetorically.

'Look, fellas, it's been a long day.'

'This won't take long.' Sykes smirked.

Sam heard the boots approaching him from behind and he squatted down, evading the tattooed arm of the biker who tried to grab him. Shifting his body weight, he drove his shoulder into the man's ribs, before reaching up and wrapping his arm around the man's throat.

Then a sickening clunk echoed.

Sam felt the pain and dizziness immediately and he stumbled forward, releasing his grip of the biker and dropped to his knees, his hands scraping across the tarmac. The other biker, gun in hand, nodded to Sykes who chuckled.

'That's for Mason,' Sykes said cockily, instructing his

henchmen to lift Sam to his feet. Sam's brain was scattered. The impact of being pistol-whipped had left him vulnerable. The two bikers hauled him to his feet, both of them wrenching his arms back behind him so he faced Sykes.

The burly biker patted down his leather vest and found his cigar, which he popped into his mouth before reaching into his jeans and pulling out a box of matches.

'You should always light a cigar with matches,' he mumbled through the teeth he had clenched on the cigar. 'It preserves the flavour.'

Despite the thunderous headache coursing through his skull, Sam tried to figure a way out. The two men were as big as Sykes, who towered over Sam and their grips were like a torture rack. Sykes arrogantly puffed on his cigar and arched his head back and puffed smoke into the air.

'Wyatt, he likes to sit back and watch. It's like a game of chess for him. He watches everything. Moves his pieces into position, usually two or three moves ahead of his opponent. But me, I'm the type of motherfucker who just flips the table over.'

Like a coiled snake, Sykes shot forward, his solid fist crashing into Sam's face, splitting his eyebrow and rocking him on his feet. Sam wobbled, but the two men held him up as Sykes swung an uppercut into his solid stomach, crushing his organs.

Sam hunched forward, gasping for air, and Sykes rocked him with another vicious hook, sending Sam spiralling to the ground with a spray of blood and saliva. Sam hit the tarmac hard, and Sykes squatted down beside him, cigar in hand.

'You tell Vasquez, if he wants a war with the Riders, he's got one. But if you really are just a dumb fucker in the wrong place at the wrong time, this is your only warning to get the fuck out of town.'

The sudden shooting burning pain shot through Sam's arm as Sykes knelt on Sam's wrist and pressed the cigar into the back of his hand. As the red-hot end scalded Sam's skin, Sykes shifted his weight onto his knee, the velocity cracking the bones in Sam's wrist. Sam gritted his teeth and as Sykes lifted himself up, Sam rolled onto his back, clutching his wrist, and concentrated on his breathing.

Deep breaths.

In and out.

Stifle the pain.

Sykes chuckled as he and his followers returned to their bikes and Sam stared up at the stars as the roar of engines echoed through the night, and he clutched his wrist. The fractured bone and the scalded skin of his hand was a cocktail of near unbearable pain.

But he'd been through worse.

Much worse.

Pain that no one should ever be able to come back from.

As he lay on the tarmac, he heard the friendly motel owner call out to him and he lifted his good hand to signal he was okay.

He offered to call the cops, but as Sam got to his feet, he told the owner that wouldn't be necessary. With Sam's arm swelling, the owner ran to grab him a bucket of ice. As he disappeared into his office, Sam stared out towards the road where Sykes and his men had made their exit.

Sam had had no reason to take down the Riders.

He did now.

CHAPTER ELEVEN

Sykes couldn't remember the woman's name. As she slid her dress back on over her toned body, he chuckled to himself at the things he'd made her do. Since becoming a prominent member of the Riders, getting laid was as easy as snapping his fingers. The local women wanted the infamy that came with being with a Rider.

Hell, even a few bored housewives were looking for some excitement.

As he lay on the bed, his naked body covered from the waist down, he reached over to his clothes that were dumped in a pile on the floor. He patted down his leather vest, pulling out the box of matches. Then he slid open the bedside drawer, reaching past the condoms to the packet of cigars. As he struck the match and held it up, the woman turned to him, playfully patting down her hair.

'That was fun,' she said sheepishly, as if embarrassed by their encounter. It had been pretty hardcore, and Sykes was pleased that the woman would no doubt be questioning her morals after the things he demanded.

'It was,' Sykes said through a plume of thick, grey smoke. When he'd returned from delivering his message to

Jonathan Cooper, he'd found his adrenaline pumping. News would soon spread through the Riders that he, not Wyatt, had acted against the man who had assaulted the High Five.

Sykes had defended the honour of the Riders.

It had sent his testosterone through the roof and after slamming back a few shots at the bar, he began regaling the other members of the crew with his colourful account of his attack on Cooper.

The intelligence of the attack.

How hard he hit him.

The snap of the man's arm.

As the crowd around him grew and grew, so did his insatiable need for a woman. A few had made it evidently clear they were his for the taking, and he'd invited one back to his flat. As soon as they'd stepped in, Sykes had pulled her dress down and within seconds of the door clos-ing, he was pushing himself inside her, thrust with the power of a conquering champion.

As she headed towards the door now, he looked up at the ceiling, lifting his cigar with a tattooed arm and heralding himself as the ruler of his own world.

The woman uttered a goodbye before the door opened and Sykes ignored her departure. It was only after a few moments that he realised the door hadn't closed and he turned to look across his apartment, to see none other than Wyatt standing against the door frame, his arms folded across his chest.

'Trent. What the fuck?' Sykes barked, pulling at the bed covers to ensure his genitals were covered. Despite his large frame and considerable bulk, Sykes also pathetically pulled the sheet over the paunch of his stomach. Unlike Wyatt, Sykes didn't do much to stem the effects of his increased affinity with alcohol. It was another log on the fire of their increasing tension.

Despite everything, Sykes still felt inferior to him. Sykes knew it.

And what pissed him off most was Wyatt knew it too.

With a forced smile, Wyatt stepped into Sykes's apartment, looking around at the minimal furniture with disinterest. Sykes's life was at The Pit, and his abode reflected years of neglect.

He slept and fucked here.

The rest of his life was at the bar.

'Fun night?' Wyatt asked, looking around nonchalantly.

'I'd say so,' Sykes replied, trying to stem his nerves.

'She was pretty.' Wyatt smiled again before taking a seat at the end of the bed. Sykes felt his grip tighten on the sheet. 'I imagine she was impressed with your story, huh?'

'Story?'

'The one you were telling at the bar. You know, how you taught that British piece of shit a lesson. How you upheld the dignity of the Riders. And so on.' Wyatt's smile hadn't faltered, and Sykes regarded him with a confused look.

'You heard it?'

'Well, yes, because it was said in *my* bar. I hear everything.' Wyatt reached into the inside of his leather jacket and returned with a bowie knife. Sykes's eyes lit up in fear, but Wyatt calmly rested it on his lap. 'See, Sykes, there is a reason I sit at the back of that bar. It's so I can watch every little thing that happens. Now get rid of the sheet.'

'What?' Sykes chuckled. 'You're fucking joking, right?'

'Have you ever heard me make a joke?'

Sykes looked at his boss, who returned a glare lacking in any emotion.

'Come on, Trent. Stop fooling around.'

'Remove the fucking sheet.'

After a small, awkward hesitation, Sykes sighed and tossed the sheet to the side. Splayed on the bed, his genitals no longer aroused, flopped limply between his thighs. Wyatt's eyes didn't waver from Sykes's.

'Like what you see?'

'How long have you worked for me, Eddie?' Wyatt asked calmly. Eddie blew his lips in exasperation.

'Years.'

'Yup. Years.' Wyatt launched forward, his gloved hand cupping around Sykes's testicles, and he tightened his grip. Sykes yelped in pain, and his eyes widened with fear as Wyatt lifted the knife with the other hand. He carefully lowered the blade, the edge a millimetre from the base of Sykes's penis. 'So, when I tell you to leave a fucking situation alone, what do you do?'

'Jesus, Trent.'

'You leave it the fuck alone. I know you don't agree with me at times, Sykes, but you disrespected my orders. And then you bragged about it in front of the entire bar. That took balls.' Wyatt smirked. 'So, I've decided to cut them off.'

'Fucking hell, Trent, I'm sorry.' Wyatt tightened his grip, and Sykes gasped in agony.

'Say that again.'

'I'm sorry. I'm fucking sorry, okay?'

Wyatt pulled the knife away and Sykes let out a sigh of relief. In one swift jerk of the arm, Wyatt crunched his fingers together and twisted, crushing Sykes's testicles in his hand. The big man heaved, turned to the side, and vomited across the dusty wooden floor. Wyatt stood, ignoring the howls of pain from his right-hand man, and pocketed the knife. Without looking back, he strode purposefully towards the door, stopping at the threshold to shoot a glance back at the incapacitated Sykes.

'Remember your place, Eddie. Remember your place.'

Wyatt slammed the door shut and disappeared into the

night, leaving Sykes curled over in pain, holding his damaged testicles and once again cursing Wyatt's name.

———

There was a long list of things that Etheridge had done that Sam was grateful for. Their relationship had begun years ago in the military, their friendship bound from the moment Sam rescued Etheridge from certain death from an inbound enemy unit as he lay crippled at the bottom of a steep drop. As Theo, a man who Sam would cherish for eternity, clambered down the cliff face to rescue Etheridge and later set his broken leg, Sam picked off the incoming attackers with the precision with which he built his legacy.

After that, Etheridge had left the army, built up a multi-million pound cyber security company, and lived a life of luxury.

But in Sam's time of need, with the clock ticking on his race to find Jasmine Hill, Etheridge had stepped up.

Broke the law.

Ruined his life.

Sam had always felt guilty for the effects his war on crime had had on those he held dearest. But Etheridge, he'd embraced it, as if witnessing Sam fight back had given him a purpose.

Since then, Etheridge had been as crucial to Sam's fight as the weapons in his hand.

Now a wanted man, Etheridge had disappeared, but not before providing Sam with a fake ID, building an entire history to keep him off the radar. He'd also put an eye watering amount of money in a bank account, effectively funding Sam's war.

But of all things Sam was grateful for, Etheridge setting him up with medical insurance upon his trip to the States ranked near the top.

After the assault from the Sykes and the Riders, Sam was helped into a car by the owner of the motel. Ben, who introduced himself formerly as he rushed Sam to the hospital, was a good man. He apologised to Sam for not calling the police once the Riders showed up, but both he and Sam knew that wouldn't have been any use.

The Riders were the law in Dillon.

Probably the entirety of South Carolina.

As they drove to McLeod Health on Jackson Avenue, Sam looked out over the town. He asked Ben about the Riders, about the grip they had over the town. Having grown up in Dillon himself, Ben was saddened by the reputation it had garnered as the beacon for bikers and criminal activity. Ever since Wyatt had showed up and took control, it was as if the town had evaporated from the map.

What Wyatt said, went.

But beyond the clear criminal dealings of the Riders themselves, crime was at an all-time low. There had been no muggings or robberies in over three years. The last time there was an incident, the Riders stepped in. As Sam pushed Ben for more information, he began to realise that the grip of fear he'd assumed existed was one of begrudging respect.

Wyatt had made the town safer.

Footfall into the local town had increased.

That incident that Ben alluded to had been at his very motel. A man had been seen beating his wife. Wyatt and Sykes had personally handled it, dragging the man from his room, stripping him naked and beating him into a coma. It had been excessive, but in the eyes of the locals, it was justice.

Street justice.

It was something Sam understood and would be hypocritical to target them for that. But they were clearly operating a drug empire. His accosting by the DEA told him that. Along with the broken wrist and third-degree burn on the back of his hand, he had more than enough to put them in his figurative crosshairs.

But he wasn't here for that.

He was here for Alex.

Sam held the ice pack to his swollen wrist as they exited the car, and Ben kindly sat and waited in the designated room while Sam was taken through by a nurse. The woman was kind, clearly overworked, and she lazily looked through his documentation before agreeing he had the necessary cover to have his wrist treated.

Had he not, Sam would have been looking at a sizeable bill.

The very notion that someone had to pay for treatment saddened him and he realised that no matter how hard he fought back, the world would always be an unjust place.

All he could do was his best.

Help where he could.

Set the things within his power right.

With a fresh stitch across his eyebrow, a bandage around his hand and a temporary wrist support, he emerged two hours later to find Ben asleep in the waiting room. They drove back quietly, and Ben even offered him a discount on his room due to the ordeal. Sam politely declined, apologising for bringing the incident to Ben's doorstep.

Then he returned to his room, popped a couple of painkillers, and collapsed on the bed. The pain interrupted Sam's sleep to the point where he felt like he'd been awake all night when he was abruptly woken by the thud on his door.

Knock knock.

Sam blinked awake, his body aching all over, his stomach throbbing from the well-placed fist that Sykes had drilled into him. He grunted as pushed himself up, his wrist sending a sharp pain to his brain which screamed for medication. Sam looked around the room, his blurred vision finding clarity as it zeroed in on the painkillers.

Knock knock.

'One sec,' Sam called out, as he popped the cap on the painkillers, knocked two back, and swallowed a mouthful of room temperature water. Stretching out his back, he pushed himself off the bed and he meandered towards the door. As he reached for the handle with his undamaged right hand, the knocking returned, and he pulled the door open with frustration.

Alex Stone greeted him.

Sam's eyebrows raised, putting the stitches to work.

With the sun shining behind her, Alex was dressed in shorts and a vest top, her dark hair pulled back in a pony-tail which poked through the back of her cap. Her face smiled with genuine happiness to see Sam but was quickly replaced with concern at the state of his injuries.

Injuries he didn't have when she'd seen him the night before.

'Hi, Sam.' She spoke. 'You look like shit.'

'Thanks. I feel worse.'

'Will this help?'

In her hand, she held a cardboard carrier, with two coffees lodged in it. In her other hand, she held a folded paper bag. The smell emanating from it promised Sam a tasty breakfast. Sam nodded and smiled.

Despite their fractured departure months ago in Naples, the love and friendship they'd forged still existed. Alex handed him the coffee and Sam took a swig, enjoying the hot caffeine as it rushed down his throat and awoke his senses.

He looked and felt like shit.

But he'd been through worse.

After an awkward few moments of silence, Sam looked at Alex.

'I think you need to tell me what the hell you've got yourself into.'

Alex nodded, turned on the heel of her trainers, and began to walk away, looking back at Sam for him to follow. Sam took another swig of his coffee, stretched his shoulder out, and stepped out of the motel and followed her across the parking lot, hoping to finally get some answers.

CHAPTER TWELVE

Two Months Earlier...

'God damn you, Sam!'

Alex slammed the palm of her hand against the steering wheel of the Alfa Romeo 4C Spider as she sped down the motorway, away from the industrial park. As the rain crashed down around the red sports car, she could hear the wailing of sirens behind her. Although they echoed through the night sky, she knew they weren't for her.

They would be swarming around the wreckage Sam had left behind.

The car wreck.

Matt's dead body.

But as the tears raced down her cheeks, they weren't in mourning. The man, masquerading as a race organiser named Matteo, had been sent to kill Sam. Alex was just collateral damage, and Sam had saved her. As she had saved him a few months before.

They had kept each other alive.

Forged a bond.

Become family.

In a world that had done nothing but push her down, Alex had finally found someone to help her up. Despite the initial attraction between the two of them, Alex had come to treat Sam like an older brother. He'd risked his life to save his former mentor and pulled her out of a war zone. It had seen him nearly executed on the streets of Rome, but Alex had intervened, steering a car into the masked assassin and fleeing with Sam's body.

She got him patched up.

Back on his feet.

The plan had been for her to make enough money to keep them going while Sam tried to get in touch with an old friend who would help them out. From what she knew, Sam had a contact who could forge them the required identifications to get to the States and who could help locate her siblings.

But now she was on her own.

The tears continued to flow, not just in mourning for her potential reunion being scuppered, but for Sam.

He was heading back to fight Wallace.

To take on Blackridge.

It would kill him.

As long as they were together, her life was in danger. She under-stood that, with the recent shoot-out with Matt and his crew all the evidence Sam needed to take the fight to them. It's what caused her heart to break. Despite the pain and turmoil Sam had been through, of which he'd tentatively divulged during their three months together, he was still fighting for others.

He was a good man.

But as she drove into the night, she knew her dreams of getting her siblings back were as aimless as her destination. Alex drove through the night, and as the rain softened and the sun rose, she could feel her eyelids starting to fall. She'd arrived in the city of Bari, and after weaving through the narrow backstreets, she pulled onto a side road, locked the doors, and shut her eyes.

She awoke a few hours later as the city sprang to life, the morning rush hour erupting like a thunderclap. With her passport and a few euros in her pocket, she took a long look in the mirror and thought of her sister and her brother.

Nattie and Joel.

With their mother's relentless drug addiction, there was no chance they would still be at home. Whisked off into care, she prayed that they at least had each other.

She'd promised them she'd be back.

It was that promise that made her choice for her.

Despite the criminal record, and her gap-filled recollection of the past few months, Alex walked into the American Embassy of Bari and asked for help. She gave a brief explanation of how she became effectively marooned in Italy and begged them to take her home.

They agreed, but she knew whatever was waiting for her in the Bronx wouldn't be a welcome home banner.

She was right.

Despite being interviewed by a few friendly government officials, it was a week later that the price of her return was set. At first, she thought the senior agent who'd visited her was there to help her find her siblings, but they were very quickly dangled in front of her.

The man never gave his name.

They never did.

Shady government officials making shady deals in darkened corners of the offices. The task was simple enough. She needed to ask for a job in the High Five bar, a recently opened biker bar in Laconia. He told her it wouldn't be a problem, and that she was to treat it like any other job.

All he asked in return was for her to feed him information, as the gang who ran it was being investigated by the DEA.

If she complied, then he would make the necessary calls and have her reunited with her siblings.

It was an easy ask, but after a few weeks, one of the senior members of the gang, Sykes, stayed for a week and demanded she relocate to The Pit. Seemingly impressed with her work, and with a clear infatuation with her, Alex turned it down.

But then the goalposts shifted.

The agent changed the deal.

Apparently, it would only be for a few weeks, as they were so close to finally nailing the Riders to the cross. With her inside the headquarters, it would give them the final strands of information they needed to bring them down.

And then it would be over.

Nattie and Joel would be home.

Her record would be expunged.

Desperation made her take the drive to South Carolina, where an eager Sykes showed her the ropes under the sceptical and terrifying eye of Wyatt. Rumours of an impending war with another drug lord circulated the bar frequently, and Alex absorbed as much as she could before relaying it back.

They were close.

Very close.

She knew she was playing a dangerous game, but she had done most of her life. Over the weeks since she'd left Sam, she'd kept her eyes on the news. She read about Wallace's death, how Sam had murdered him in cold blood. That Sam had been sentenced to life in prison. It had crushed her, knowing a good man had done the right thing but would pay for it with his freedom.

A selfish gut punch was that he would never keep his promise.

It birthed a determination in Alex to see this mission through, to play the game and get her family back.

All she had to do was keep out of Wyatt's suspicions, which she seemingly had done.

Up until Sam strode into The Pit and changed the game completely.

———

'Jesus,' Sam said, stepping forward towards the railing that boxed in Alex's balcony. Her story had been as gruelling as he had imagined and, heartbreakingly, had ended the same way as the last one.

With a government agent using her desperation as a tool to control her.

Alex had stopped off at a store on their walk, picking up some groceries and a few cold beers for them. While her apartment wasn't the biggest, it was tidy and organised. It took Sam back to their time together in Naples, where Alex had tended to him, nursing him back from the brink of death.

'I know, right?' Alex said through her chewing as she polished off the pizza she'd ordered for them. 'Pretty fucked up.'

'You need to walk away from this.' Sam turned to her, his beer hanging loosely through his fingers.

'Excuse me?'

'Alex, these people are dangerous. Look at what they did to me just for walking into their bar?'

'No, Sam. They did that to you because you decided to go all Liam Neeson on their boys back home.' Alex shook her head in despair and sat back in her chair. She pulled out her cigarettes and put one to her lips. 'And also, you don't have a fucking right to tell me what to do. You abandoned me. In Italy. Alone.'

'I had to go back…'

'Well, like you said, you got the job done. You set things right.' Alex lit her cigarette and exhaled an irritated cloud of smoke. Sam shook his head and looked out over the street. Alex's apartment was a few streets away from The Pit and was situated above a deli. Beneath them, Sam could hear the hustle and bustle of the afternoon footfall.

Alex's words cut him deep.

As she walked Sam through Dillon, she'd explained to him it was safe. The Riders weren't exactly early birds, and the message they'd sent him would be enough in their eyes. Sam winced, his fractured wrist humming in pain.

He'd explained to her how he'd got home, how he'd

found Etheridge, the man he'd pinned their hopes on, and how he'd been beaten, tortured, and left for dead in the hunt for Sam.

Another reiteration of how dangerous it was to be an unfortunate touch point of Sam's fight.

Sam explained to Alex how they'd lured Wallace into the open, only for the General to kidnap Amara Singh. Alex could tell from Sam's struggles that he'd cared for Singh, and she felt every ounce of anger as he explained to her how Wallace had died. That should have been it.

Sam would have been straight on the plane back to the States to help her.

But he had to stay. Singh would have gone to prison.

As Sam had explained his and Etheridge's plan that saw him infiltrate a maximum-security prison, Alex felt bad for being so mad at him.

Sam had made her a promise, one that she'd clung to every night as she'd slept on the sofa of that crummy apartment in Naples.

When he'd turned and walked away, abandoning her and her future, she'd cursed him.

Hated him.

Wished him dead.

But he'd fought, as always, for the right reason. He'd pushed back against the injustice held by high-powered people in privileged positions.

And now he was back.

To keep his promise.

She felt bad, watching him shift uncomfortably on the spot. Despite the split eyebrow, bruised eye, and broken wrist, Sam was looking in decent shape. His grey T-shirt clung to his muscular frame and his hair, neatly cut, moved gently in the breeze.

'Look, Sam. I'm sorry,' Alex said, stubbing out her cigarette. 'But I can't back out now. I'm so close.'

'Close to what?' Sam asked. 'To getting yourself killed?'

'To getting my family back.' Alex leant forward, tears in her eyes. 'I know you lost Jamie, Sam. And I can't imagine how hard that must have been. But I haven't lost them, not yet. And I need to hold on to that. You might not understand it, but it's just how it is. So, if I have to play these games, if I have to get my hands dirty, if I have to walk through the fucking gates of hell for just a sliver of a chance to see my brother and sister again, I'll do it.'

The silence hung between them like an unwanted third wheel.

'What do you need me to do?' Sam eventually responded. He swigged his beer, popping the empty bottle on the small table.

'I need you to leave.'

'No.'

'Sam, please.' Alex reached forward and her fingers clasped around his functioning hand. 'Please.'

Sam relinquished her hold and ran his hand across his stubbled jaw.

'Alex, if the Riders find out you played them in any way, they will kill you. That is a fact.' Sam angrily ruffled his hair, wrestling with his own train of thought. 'What's the deal? What do you have to do?'

'Just keep my guy informed.' Alex replied, lowering her voice to a whisper. 'Apparently, something is happening over the next few days. Something big. I just have to keep my ear out for the name of Vasquez and pass on what I know.'

'Vasquez?' Sam's eyebrows raised. 'I keep hearing that name.'

'He's a big deal, apparently. He's a threat to the Riders and Wyatt has encouraged Sykes to take steps to stop the rise.'

'Your guy told you this?'

'It's a working theory. Plus, you've seen what a good lap dog he is.' Alex lit another cigarette and swigged her beer. 'Sykes has been all over it. Seriously, Sykes says he hasn't been this taken with something, other than when he was begging Wyatt to move me to The Pit.'

'That was Sykes's idea, too?'

'Yup.' Alex shuddered.

'You didn't…you know?' Sam shrugged.

'Ew, no.' Alex chuckled. 'Christ, you were the limit for creepy old guys I've slept with.'

'Hey,' Sam said, faking offence. 'I'm not that old.'

Alex spat out her beer and for the first time since Sam had returned to her life, she felt that connection again. That brotherly bond and she felt guilty for trying to send him away. Every move he'd made was for her safety.

He went back to the UK to end Blackridge.

For himself, but for her as well.

To keep her safe.

And now he was back and had already spilt blood and broken bones to get to her.

She smiled at him and continued.

'Anyways, my guy wants to meet tonight, so I have to work. All I have to do is feed him any info. Then, if the deal happens, I'll go along to the bust. That's it.'

'Why do you have to go?' Sam asked sternly, folding his arms.

'Because they need a witness. Someone who can iden-tify the people involved.' Sam raised his eyebrows with concern. 'It's fine. My identity will be hidden the whole time.'

'I don't like it.'

'Tough shit.'

'At least let me come with you.'

'Why?' Alex asked, smiling.

'In case.'

With both of them understanding Sam's meaning, Alex looked out over the town once more.

'You know. This place isn't so bad. Take the Riders out of it and it would probably be a nice place to live.'

'Well, you can do your bit.' Sam reached over and rested his hand on her shoulder. 'I'll step back. Let you get on with it. You won't need to worry. I know how hard you've clung onto Nattie and Joel, and I understand. For the first few years after Jamie died, I had a voicemail on my phone of him telling me he couldn't wait to see me. I would listen to it every day, and for those wonderful forty seconds, it felt like he was alive, you know?'

Sam's eyes began to water, and he dabbed at them with the ball of his wrist. Alex could already feel the tears falling down her cheek.

'So, you understand why I need to do this?'

'Yes,' Sam said. 'You need to put it right. Do something that puts you at peace with the way things are. I get that. I've been able to delete that message, accept Jamie's death, and I use it every goddamn day to get out of bed. To fight back. To try to put this wrongful world right. So, you do what you have to do. I'll hang back and just make sure you're safe.'

'Thank you, Sam.' Alex looked at her watch and a realisation jolted her like a cattle prod. 'Fuck. I need to go.'

As Alex rushed to her feet and began to gather her things, Sam watched with interest as she shuffled through her apartment and out the door. Sam looked over the balcony, and a few moments later, Alex emerged, moving swiftly across the street. As she approached the van, Sam realised he recognised it.

It was the same van that had accosted Sam the night before.

Alex banged on the side of the van and then disappeared behind it.

Moments later, the van sped off, and Alex was gone.

Despite her explanation, despite her insistence, something didn't sit right with Sam. For her to be this close and involved in a potentially dangerous drugs bust seemed like a desperate play from a government agent in over his head.

Sam felt his fists clench in anger, his fury born out of the manipulation of Alex and how he hadn't been there to stop it from happening.

But he was more than happy to bring it to an end.

Sam turned and headed to the door, completely unaware that for his entire stay on Alex's balcony, Agent Joe Alan had been watching him from a few streets down, the binoculars pressed against his eyes and a cruel grin on his lips.

Sam had promised Alex he wouldn't cause her any more trouble.

Unbeknownst to Sam, Agent Alan was about to break that promise for him.

CHAPTER THIRTEEN

Sykes hated himself for his admission of fear.

In the early hours of the morning, Wyatt had invaded his home moments after Sykes's latest conquest had left, threatening to castrate him for his disobedience. Having left him with a twisted testicle, Sykes had been unable to sleep, finding himself throwing up a couple of times before throwing back a few painkillers.

Despite his pride at being a tough man, his actual manhood would have to wait.

Today was the day.

The day everything changed.

After trying to stomach some breakfast, Sykes limped his way to his bike, cocked his leg over the vehicle, and lowered himself onto the seat. The pain had been immediate, and his short drive to The Pit was excruciating.

But he couldn't let anyone see it.

Weakness wasn't permitted within the Riders. And just as he eyed Wyatt's seat at the top of the chain, he knew there were a number of guys hungrily waiting for Sykes to slip.

He knew who they were.

And he had plans on how to handle them once he ascended to the throne.

It was midday when Sykes pulled up outside the bar, and luckily, there was no one outside. Gingerly, he lifted himself from his bike, his testicle sending a sharp pain through his body. He took a few deep breaths, straightened his back, and walked powerfully to the front door, gritting his teeth to ignore the agony. With his powerful arm, he threw open the door and marched inside.

A few heads turned his way. A couple of the early rising Riders were gathered around the pool table partaking in some light gambling. They nodded a greeting, which Sykes reciprocated before he approached the bar. Becky, one of the barmaids, was already working, wiping down one of the counters.

'Mornin', Eddie.' She smiled, her Texan twang sending a little shudder of arousal through his body that peaked in a painful roar from his crotch.

'Becky.' He grunted. 'Beer.'

'Bit early, isn't it?'

'Just get me a beer.'

Becky smiled. She was used to worse from the Riders, but under Wyatt's careful watch, she and the rest of the girls were safe from anything too aggressive. Sykes himself had taken great pleasure in beating the hell out of a few outsiders who had got drunk and grabbed at her a few weeks ago. Sykes had broken both their arms before dumping them on the side of the freeway. He assumed they would have been picked up by an ambulance at some point, but he didn't care.

If they had died, then he would just chalk it up to another good night's work.

Becky slid the bottle of beer across the bar and Sykes swiftly raised it, necking half of it in one go.

'You okay?' Becky asked, her thin eyebrow raised. 'You look like shit.'

'Thanks.' Sykes smirked, his thick beard hanging from his jaw. 'Where's Wyatt?'

'Out back.' Becky arched her neck towards the door. 'Want me to get him.'

The thought of seeing Wyatt so soon after being emasculated by him sent a shudder through Sykes, and he shook his head.

'No, it's fine.' Wyatt finished his beer and put the bottle down on the counter. As Becky removed it, she gestured if he wanted another. Sykes shook his head and then marched towards the bathroom. As he entered, he checked to see if anyone was occupying a stall, but they were all empty.

He was alone.

Immediately, his guard went down, and he grabbed the sink and hunched over, the pain gripping him like a vice. He breathed through it and then reached into his leather vest, pulling out a few more painkillers and chucking them down his throat. He flicked on the tap and shoved his mouth under it, washing the tablets down in the faint hope of getting him through the day.

That's all he needed.

By this time tomorrow, it would be done.

Still hunched over, Sykes let the cold water wash over his hands, and he cupped them, before splashing the water back over his face. The sudden chill gave him a brief respite from the pain, and he glared at himself in the mirror.

He'd shown weakness.

Wyatt had caught him at his most vulnerable. Naked and tired, Sykes had been humiliated for an audience of one. But it was enough. Wyatt was a smart man, and by literally threatening to cut Sykes's nuts off, he'd neutered him. The palpable fear had been evident, and now Sykes knew that tonight had to happen.

If it didn't, things would still change, but not for the better.

Wyatt had little use for weakness, and chances were he would be pushed away from his side and eventually out the door. Given his proclivity for violence, Sykes knew he would react.

Which would most likely lead to his death.

He stuffed his hand into his back jean pocket and retrieved a small plastic bag filled with cocaine. Anxiously, he tipped a little out onto the edge of the sink, lazily lined it up with his finger and then inhaled it. The sudden shot hit his brain like a cold hose of water, and he shot up straight, arching his neck back and letting the buzz rush through his body.

The shame he felt dissipated.

The pain in his groin subsided.

Sykes felt himself again.

'Bit early for that, isn't it?'

Wyatt's voice echoed off the tiles, and Sykes spun on the spot to see his leader stood in the doorway, arms folded. A surge of fury joined the cocaine twirling through his body, and Sykes wrestled away his impulse to grab Wyatt's throat and choke him.

'Yeah, well, I didn't sleep too well,' Sykes barked back, turning away from Wyatt and staring at himself in the mirror.

'I won't apologise,' Wyatt said firmly. 'But I just want you to know I consider the matter over.'

Sykes grunted and shook his head. Wyatt watched him for a few moments before stepping back out of the bathroom. As the door swung shut, Sykes felt his grip tighten on the sides of the basin, his knuckles turning as white as the porcelain.

Sykes had done a lot of bad things in his life.

He'd disgraced the US Army.

He'd killed countless people.

One more bad thing was all it would take for him to get everything he wanted.

The Riders.

And after last night, after what Wyatt had done, his death would just be a nice cherry on top. Sykes pulled out his phone, opened his messages, and thumbed the keypad.

Time and place.

Within seconds, his phone buzzed with the required information and for the first time since Wyatt had crushed his testicles, Sykes smiled, thinking about how incredibly sweet his revenge would taste.

———

'Don't make promises you can't keep, son.'

William Pope afforded his usually stern jaw a wry smile while keeping his eyes on the road and his hands on the wheel. Sitting in the passenger seat of the Range Rover was Sam, slouched in his chair and his head pressed against the window. Despite the difficult conversation he'd just had with the teacher, William was proud of his son.

It had been a tough upbringing, one for which William scolded himself. But it was akin to his own, and it had turned him into the man he'd become. As a General within the UK Armed Forces, William Pope had built a legacy based on his authenticity and disgust for the political game.

He'd hoped it would create a steady path for his son, acting as a beacon of inspiration for him to be a good man.

As the rain lashed down against the windscreen, he registered the red brake lights on the car in front and applied pressure to the brake pedal, bringing the car to a stop.

'Are you listening to me, Samuel?'

William turned to his fifteen-year-old son. Sam unfastened his seat belt and flung his door open, stepping out into the rain. Panicked, William wrestled with his own belt before exiting the car as quickly as possible.

'Sam, what the hell are you doing?'

'Leave me alone.'

Sam stuffed his hands in his pockets and began to walk away, stomping down the small gap between the cars that were lodged in yet another traffic jam. William held up an apologetic hand to the car behind them, the woman offering him a nod of sympathy. Briskly, he jogged around the car and placed a hand on his son's shoulder.

'Samuel…'

'Let go of me.'

'What is wrong with you?'

'Nothing. Okay, Dad? Nothing is wrong with me.' With his wet hair pasted against his head, Sam looked up at his father who stood over six feet tall. Although he'd experienced a growth spurt during the complications of puberty, he still only measured up to his father's broad shoulders. Despite his insistence, Sam knew tears were rolling down his cheek.

'Let's get back in the car.'

'And go where? Back to another place we'll call home for a year or two?'

William felt his heart sink. He'd known that his job had impacted Sam, but ever since Sam's mother had left, they'd forged a bond. With his constant relocations, William knew Sam had struggled to make friends. It had brought them closer together, and while Sam was a diligent student, William knew his son wanted to follow in his footsteps.

The day he got to see his son in a military uniform would be the proudest day of his life.

But now, with a few impatient car horns blaring and the rain crashing around them, he looked into the pain-stricken eyes of his son and saw his child.

William stood a few feet from him and shrugged.

'I'm sorry, son. I am. I know it hasn't been easy. I know other *kids have their mums around, that they all have dinner together and their dad takes them to play football on Sundays.'*

'I don't give a shit about Mum!' Sam yelled, his voice croaking under the weight of his own sadness.

'Watch your language.' William snapped. 'Your mother made her choice to leave. It doesn't make her a bad person.'

'They said she was a whore…'

'Who? At school?' William frowned. 'Is that why you hit that boy?'

Sam's silence was more than enough to confirm it. William had been called to the school upon the news of Sam breaking another pupil's nose. It was why they were driving home through the rain and why he'd made Sam promise not to fight unless he had to. Sam suddenly looked embarrassed; his school uniform stuck to his scrawny body.

'I'm sorry, Dad,' he eventually uttered.

'It's okay, Samuel.' William stepped forward and wrapped his arms around his son. 'You're a good lad.'

After a few rain-soaked moments, the two of them turned and headed back to their car. With the road ahead of them cleared, the light green and a cacophony of car horns polluting the air behind them, William started the car up immediately and pulled away.

'Seat belt,' he ordered. Sam laughed and obliged before dabbing away the last of his tears. After a few minutes of comfortable silence, Sam looked up at his dad with admiration.

'How come you always see the good in people?'

'Because there is always good to be found,' William responded, not taking his eyes off the road. 'And if you can't find it, fight for it. It's the right thing to do.'

Sam sat back, absorbing his dad's words as gospel and looking out at the streets of the latest town they were living in. He knew his father was a good man.

A hero.

When he was old enough, he would enlist in the army and work his hardest to forge a career that he and his father could be proud of.

And when the time came for him to have his own child, Sam would do whatever it took to keep them safe.

Just like his father had to him.

'I promise I won't fight anyone again, Dad,' Sam said. His father pulled their car into their drive, killed the engine and turned to his son with a wry smile.

'Don't make promises you can't keep.'

CHAPTER FOURTEEN

With his dad's words echoing in his mind, Sam hunched over the sink of his motel room and cupped the water running from the tap with his right hand. He splashed it against his face, the chill a welcome feeling against the humidity of the heat. His left wrist was throbbing, the freshness of the fracture causing him to reach for the painkillers and throw two back.

It had been a hell of a few days and it was starting to catch-up with him.

His eyebrow, freshly stitched, had an accompanying bruise and his ribs ached from the clubbing blow from Sykes.

But the pain was bearable.

Sam had been through worse.

Much worse.

With his shirt lying on the bed of the motel room, he gazed over his naked torso in the mirror. It was an impressive memorial to the battles he'd been in. The scarring down his left side from the bomb blast that sent him spiralling down a cliff face a decade ago. The knife wound from his fight with one of the Mitchell Brothers on his quest to bring down Frank Jackson. The fresh scar down his spine as he fought The Hangman of Baghdad to the death. The bullet wounds that Mac had sent through his shoulder and his stomach, that should have killed him.

But they hadn't because Alex had saved his life.

Sam should have been dead by now, but Alex had pulled him from death's grip with both hands and kept him alive long enough to bring down Wallace. To bring down Chapman.

If she hadn't been there, who knows the damage those men would be doing. And now, she was moments away from being involved in a dangerous deal with a DEA agent who had dangled her family in front of her like a carrot.

'Don't make promises you can't keep, Son.'

Those words rattled around Sam's mind like a painful pinball. Sam had always strived to honour his father's legacy through every avenue of his life. From his exceptional career within the military, to his devotion to his own family.

But he'd failed to live up to that particular request.

He'd promised his son he would stop killing.

Since then, dozens of people had been put in the ground by Sam's hand.

He'd promised to keep his family safe.

Jamie was dead, and Lucy had removed herself from Sam's life.

Sam stared at himself in the mirror, knowing that despite the path he'd chosen, he wasn't a bad man. He'd broken the law, turning himself into legend with his war on crime. But along the way, he'd lost too many people for it to have been worth it.

Sam had done a lot of wrong things for the right reason.

Keeping his promise to Alex, and finally living up to his

father's request, would be the first right thing he'd done in a long time.

Sam stepped out of the bathroom and he immediately noticed the blue and red lights flashing through the net curtains that hung across the window. A fist pounded against his door and he swept up his T-shirt and slid it over his head, pulling it down over his war-torn body as he reached for the handle.

'Officers?' Sam raised his eyebrows, then his hands, as two guns were pointed in his direction.

'Sam Pope, you are under arrest.'

Hearing his real name caused Sam to freeze for a second. His identity had been discovered, and his mind immediately raced as to who could have tracked him down. Etheridge had built him an unbreachable electronic history, but somehow, someone had managed to see through it. Before his mind could run through the possible names, the first police officer reached forward, grabbed him by the arm, and spun him against the wall. Sam's face collided with the brick, and he shot a glance beyond the other officer. Another police car was waiting, with an officer proudly holding a shotgun.

A clear insurance policy if Sam proved as dangerous as his legacy.

Beyond them, he noticed the black Range Rover, and immediately recognised Agent Joe Alan leaning casually against it, his sunglasses protecting his front row view from the beaming sun.

Alan had sent in the cavalry. Clearly, he knew how big of a problem Sam could be.

Thinking about the immediate danger Alex was in, and the promise he'd made her, Sam was happy to prove Alan right. As the officer struggled to wrap the cuff around Sam's cast, Sam flung his head back, the top of his skull colliding with the bridge of the officer's nose, shattering it.

The officer howled in pain and clutched onto Sam's shoulder. The other officer, with his gun pointed squarely at Sam yelled something and pulled the trigger. Sam pressed one foot on the wall and pushed back, falling backwards onto the bloodied officer and dodging the bullet by a matter of milliseconds. Both men collapsed onto the bed and Sam rolled through, driving an elbow into the officer's temple and knocking him out cold. The dingy room worked to his benefit, as the other officer rushed forward with his gun at the ready, and Sam slammed himself into the door, crushing the officer's arm in the frame and loosening his grip on the gun. The officer grunted in pain, and Sam pulled the door open and hauled the officer in by his shirt before slamming it shut. He could hear Alan barking orders, and the incoming footsteps of the shotgun wielding officer. With his arm limp, the other officer tried to swing at Sam, but Sam lifted his left arm, catching the blow on his cast and gritting his teeth with pain. Sam rocked the officer with a brutal right hook, shutting his lights out before he even hit the rough carpet that lined the floor. Slumped against the door, the officer acted as a useful barricade, as the furious back-up tried desperately to shove the door open.

Sam scurried to the window in the bathroom, and shoved it upward, and began to push himself through the small gap to the unkept shrubbery below. He made his way through, just as he heard the other officer smash the window at the front of the room, to an anguished cry of dismay from the owner. Sam took off, running as fast as he could along the back of the motel, before submerging himself in the woodland that ran along the main road back into town.

As he ran, he glanced at his watch.

It was still early in the evening, meaning Alex would still be at The Pit. Somehow, he would need to stay off the grid for the next few hours, which, given his name was now known, would be harder than he thought. Taking deep breaths to keep the oxygen pumping, Sam continued his sprint through the woods, wondering how the hell he would lie low in a town so small. With every step, he heard his father's words, and he was adamant that this promise was one he wouldn't break.

———

Joe Alan was right.

When the email fell in his inbox and rattled his phone, he'd felt his stomach flip. Years spent as a marine had calmed his nerves to almost paralysis, but seeing the confirmation come through on his suspicions sent a bolt of excitement through his body like an electric shock.

After sending out the image of Jonathan Cooper's passport to a number of contacts, he'd seen it as a hail Mary. The nagging suspicion of the man's reasoning for being in Dillon, along with how handily he dismantled the Riders in New York had stoked a suspicion within him that he wasn't 'just an old friend.' Although there were guidelines and numerous hoops to dive through, Alan's standing within numerous agencies was high. As a highly decorated marine, he'd earnt a respect beyond his six years as an agent and the responses were almost instant. While nearly all of his contacts reiterated Cooper's backstory, it was a CIA contact, Jack Baker, who came through. After cross referencing the ID Alan had sent through, Baker was able to match it to an old, defunct file for Blackridge.

Cooper wasn't who he said he was.

He was far worse.

As soon as the files landed in his inbox, Alan was up, his phone drawing him from an anxious slumber, and a few cups of coffee later he was clear who he was dealing with.

A soldier with a terrifyingly efficient penchant for war.

A man who had single-handedly taken down numerous crime syndicates and shady government agencies.

Jonathan Cooper was Sam Pope.

And Sam Pope was a one-man army.

Alan had tried to contact Sinclair, but he couldn't get through. Although he trusted Sinclair completely, the man's obsession with bringing down the Riders had become all-encompassing. It even outweighed Alan's own quest to bring down Sykes for the deaths of his comrades. Although Sinclair had clear contact with someone within the Riders, he kept his cards close to his chest, so much so that Alan hadn't met them.

He didn't even know the name.

But they were close. Sinclair had assured him that within the next few days, they would have everything they needed to bring them down, and Alan would be able to look Sykes in the eye and take away his liberty.

Sam Pope arriving was the biggest wrench anyone could throw in their plans, and Alan knew he needed to take action. While Sinclair was meeting with his insider, Alan watched as Sam and Alex Stone went for a walk, keeping his distance as they caught up. Judging by the fresh markings on his face and the cast on his wrist, Sam had been visited by the Riders during the night.

But having read Sam's file, Alan knew that wouldn't be a deterrent.

It would be a reason.

A reason to stay and to fight back.

Watching the two of them sit on the balcony of Alex's apartment, he was slightly taken back by how casual they were. Perhaps his insistence on their friendship was legitimate, and he was just looking out for her? She was a long way from home, in one of the most dangerous places she could be. Maybe he was just a concerned friend?

But something told him it was more than that.

An escalating confrontation between two drug empires fit Sam's modus operandi, and Alan kept his eyes on Sam as Alex left.

He followed him back to the motel.

After a few hours, and with no movement, he made the call.

Two police cars arrived within minutes and three heavily armed officers lay siege to the room. Alan watched the door open and got out of the car as the first officer slammed an unsuspecting Sam Pope against the wall and slapped on the cuffs.

Only they didn't act quick enough.

Sam lashed back, falling back into the room with the officer and then dragging his covering partner in. The door closed and Alan yelled at the final officer to head inside. Even with a shotgun planted in his hands, the officer looked terrified, but no matter how hard he shoved, the door wouldn't open.

Alan didn't need to think twice, and he set off in a sprint, his athletic body barging through the guests who had gathered outside their rooms to witness the commotion.

He was in no doubt that Sam had incapacitated the officers. Alan had seen the video from the High Five and read the files.

Sam Pope was a dangerous man.

Trained.

Lethal.

And hell bent on keeping his promise, it would seem.

As he rounded the side of the motel, he could make out the figure of Sam in the distance, ducking into the bushes and trees of the woodland that backed onto the motel and spread like wildfire towards the town itself.

He was gone.

For now.

But Alan knew that Sam wouldn't go far. He would lie low, try to blend in. He'd spent a year as a sniper, so lying in wait in plain sight was his speciality.

Alan tried to call Sinclair once again, frowning as the call went to voicemail.

With a resigned sigh, Alan turned and headed back to his car, ignoring the recently arrived police who demanded an explanation. They hated having the DEA swarming over their town, especially when it threatened the profitable truce with the Riders.

But Alan didn't care.

He needed to get back to town and cut Sam off before he burnt all their good work to the ground.

CHAPTER FIFTEEN

After nearly three decades of pulling himself up from the dirt, José Vasquez wasn't surprised how numb he'd become at the sight of violence. From a fatherless home in the barrios of Mexico, he'd ignored his mother's good intentions and affiliated himself with the local gang. As a kid, he would act as a drop, an innocent child playing on the corner, who would receive and pass on drug deliveries for the local dealer.

It wasn't much, but he earnt enough to keep his stomach full, knowing his mother couldn't provide. Watching her health deteriorate before his tenth birthday, he never knew what killed her. Lost in the sea of poverty that made up his town, healthcare wasn't forthcoming. When he looked back now, he wondered if it had been cancer, but found his empathy missing.

She left him for the streets.

Left him for the only world he would ever know.

When one day, in broad daylight, he was thrown to the floor and beaten until his bones were broken by a rival drug dealer, nobody intervened. Twelve years old and not one person stopped as the boots rained down on him.

With no parents, and clearly no community to protect him, Vasquez knew then and there that the only way to ensure he would outgrow the favela was to push back.

To paint the streets red with blood and to command loyalty from those not smart enough or brave enough to do it themselves. On his sixteenth birthday, he was promoted to a drug runner by the local dealer.

Before his seventeenth birthday, he'd strangled the dealer to death and left his scorched corpse in an abandoned doctors' surgery five blocks from his home. With his reputation rising within the community, his cousin, Raul, begged him for work, and Vasquez had his first loyal soldier. By the age of twenty, he'd claimed the lives of three rival drug gangs and placed the first blocks into the foundation of his empire. Business boomed, with the cocaine and meth flooding the barrios like a plague and Vasquez watched, willing the despicable residents to rot.

They had turned their back on him when he was a lonely child, watched as he was beaten to the dirt, with no mother or father to protect him.

Just a young boy, trying to survive.

To them, he was as insignificant as a rat, flittering through the heaps of trash that lined the streets. Now all of them were the vermin, trapped in the maze that belonged to him, and he cared little for how many deaths his drugs caused.

Raul proved to be an exceptional right-hand man.

As cruel as Vasquez, Raul was a strapping man with a powerful voice, and he doled out Vasquez's demands with a venomous growl that terrified their drug runners.

Vasquez soon acquired a rivals' drug lab, confirming the deal by slitting the man's throat in front of the scientists and letting him bleed out, his fingers clutching desperately for life.

Vasquez had claimed it.

Just as he claimed everything.

But with fame came notoriety, and soon the police were sniffing around. Not to stop him, but to get their cut, and while their demands were outrageous, Vasquez soon forced them to lower their cut. Having their families dragged from their beds in the middle of the night and beaten will bend any dirty police officer to your will, and Vasquez realised then he was untouchable.

The barrios of Mexico City belonged to him.

When Raul introduced him to Edinson, a man who had recently been released from prison for manslaughter and several other charges, Vasquez kept him by his side as his own personal bodyguard. With Raul running the operation like clockwork, Vasquez decided to branch further north, infiltrating the United States and pumping the state of Texas with his own brand of poison.

Those who opposed him were introduced to Edinson.

Those who survived knelt before him.

The DEA were snooping around, but those agents were either bought or wiped off the face of the planet.

At one point, Vasquez had estimated he'd sanctioned the deaths of nearly hundred people.

By pushing his drugs further into the underbelly of Mexico, and now into the wealthier states of America, he'd been responsible for hundreds.

But it didn't matter to him.

People were insignificant. Addicts were like weeds. If one died, more would grow in their place, and as the economy tumbled, and the next generation pushed back against authority, his product became more appealing.

Louisiana, Oklahoma, and Florida all fell before him.

The empire grew, but branching into another country required patience and, more importantly, collaboration. With every drug lord he encountered, Vasquez gave them the choice to fall in line or face Edinson. Many offered empty threats, but after five minutes of Edinson's handiwork, they caved.

A few were defiant to the end, and Vasquez watched, unmoved, as Edinson stomped their skulls into nothing but a red paste.

It was when he began to filter into South Carolina that things became interesting. Despite the numerous palms he'd greased, the DEA and other agencies were swarming. South Carolina was a hotbed for drugs, manufactured and distributed by the reviled Death Riders. Vasquez had encountered a biker gang in Oklahoma, but found the entire notion pathetic.

He could spot 'fake tough' in an instant, and considering his own history, he smirked at the notion of intimidation.

But the Riders were different.

They were not a gang of middle-aged men, addicted to the idea that they needed to cling to their youth in some ridiculous notion of machismo.

The Riders were a drug empire.

Not as large or as vast as his own, but they were strong. As a unit and from the throne.

Trent Wyatt was a dangerous man, and Vasquez had come to respect him. Their similar paths to wealth made him a dangerous adversary, and despite his desire to bury the Riders, he knew that any action would provoke a reaction.

The Riders would fight back.

For the first time since he strangled that drug dealer over twenty-five years ago, Vasquez was on the verge of a drug war. Everyone else had been too scared or too artificial to fight back, as his power and drugs swept across city after city like a hurricane.

But this was different.

This time, things would have to be done a little

differently.

And with the end in sight, Vasquez was looking forward to the moment where he could look Trent Wyatt in the eyes, and let him know that he, José Vasquez, took everything from him.

Vasquez smiled, the anticipation of the evening's events distracting him from the torture being played in front of him. He turned, adjusted the lapels of his expensive suit, and he stared at the man who could no longer beg for help.

His tongue was on the floor.

Edinson had cut it out when the man refused to give up the others who had been involved in an unsuccessful raid on one of their labs.

Vasquez didn't remember the man's name, but he did know he was tiring of the situation. Dramatically, he stood from his chair, buttoning his blazer, before walking towards the violence. Edinson stepped back, his powerful frame stretching the T-shirt that clung to his muscles for dear life.

The man was a mess.

Blood dribbled from his split lips and one of his eyes was swollen shut. A few trickles of blood ran from his hair-line, and Vasquez could only imagine the bruising that was forming under the man's clothes. Vasquez calmly leant forward, the man shaking with fear.

'Your silence is not bravery. It is stupidity.' Vasquez patted him on the shoulder before turning to Edinson. 'Kill him.'

A faint roar of fear emanated from the man, which Edinson shut down with a brutal right hook. As the man hung by the binds of the chair, Vasquez stepped from the room, leaving Edinson to complete the task.

It wouldn't be pretty, but Vasquez felt numb to it.

Violence was just part of the world he lived in.

The three-storey apartment block was just one of many crack dens that Vasquez funded. The police stayed away for a slice of the profits, and it gave his customers a place to spend their money. No one would come looking for the man, nor would they have cared about the screams of pain. All the rooms were occupied, filled with the despicable vermin whose addictions had consumed them.

As Vasquez approached the ground floor, Raul was waiting, arms folded, resplendent in his black suit. Ever since they branched into the States, the two had decided their appearance mattered. In a materialistic country, it was best to play the part.

Raul pushed himself from the wall and nodded up the stairs.

'Did he talk?'

'He can't,' Vasquez stated coldly, ending the line of questioning. 'Any word?'

Raul smiled.

'Yes. Tonight. As agreed.'

The confirmation caused a slight tension to tighten Vasquez's body, and he shook it away quickly. He patted his cousin on the shoulder and smiled.

'I think that deserves a drink.'

The two men stepped out of the apartment block and into the warm, sunny afternoon, knowing they were hours away from winning a potential war before it had even begun.

———

Joe Alan sped back up the main road that led back towards Dillon, bypassing the police cars and ambulances headed in the other direction. The third officer had likely called in what had happened, and when police officers are hurt in the line of duty, the cavalry comes running. Although he'd never intended to put any officers in harm's way, he scolded himself for not being more careful.

He'd seen the files.

Read the reports.

Sam Pope was a dangerous man.

Trying to catch him off guard had been a mistake. The man was trained to hunt and kill people without detection, and undoubtedly, he was primed for anything. You don't rack up a military career such as his, and then go to war with the powers that be without keeping your wits about you.

Alan slammed his powerful fist on the leather steering wheel of his 4x4 in frustration. He tried to call Sinclair, but again, his partner was off the radar.

Perhaps he was meeting with his source?

The frustration Alan felt towards being kept out the loop was only exceeded by his focus on Sykes. It was the reason he'd requested his transfer to this case, and why he let Sinclair run it in such secrecy.

Bringing down Sykes was the only mission.

While the DEA would receive plaudits for their work, and he and Sinclair would be lauded as heroes, none of that would compare to the reward of seeing Sykes behind bars.

Or worse.

But Sam Pope was a spanner in the works.

Even if his story were true, and he was there for Alex, Alan couldn't afford to let a man like him loose. He'd already intervened. The video of his assault at the High Five was no doubt the reasoning for his broken wrist and fresh bruises.

But Sam was a soldier.

A fighter.

He was built to fight back and given the carnage he was on the run from in the UK, Alan was certain that Sam's response would be devastating.

Enough to ruin the case he and Sinclair had worked on.

Enough to stop Alan from getting his hands on Sykes.

As he approached the town, Alan peered out to the vast field that separated the town from the woods that Sam had disappeared into. He signalled and pulled his car to the side of the road, his eyes locked on the tree line.

'Come on, you son of a bitch.'

Alan's words were whispered beneath his breath, and just when he was about to give up, Sam burst through the woodland and sprinted across the field, throwing a few glances behind him. Realising he wasn't being tracked, his pace slowed, and he jogged casually the remaining distance.

Alan watched Sam enter the back of one of the establishments, and instantly, the key turned in the ignition and Alan slammed his foot to the floor, his car screeching and leaving a streak of burnt rubber across the tarmac.

———

Sam cautiously walked through the back area of the bar, grateful not to run into any members of staff. Despite The Pit's dominance of the town, the locals not affiliated with the Riders frequented the bar he'd snuck into it. It was nice enough; numerous booths lined the far wall, and an even number of stalls lined the bar which ran the length of the narrow drinking hole. As he emerged into the bar area, a few heads turned, some eyebrows raised, but as was such for the people of Dillon, not much was said.

The landlord, complete with a towel draped over his shoulder, moseyed casually towards Sam as he slid into a stall.

'Rough day, pal?' The owner chuckled. Sam smiled.

'You could say that. Can I grab a beer?'

'Coming right up.' The jovial owner turned to the fridge behind and retrieved a bottle, popping the cap on the opener affixed to the bar. 'English?'

'What gave it away?' Sam smiled, lifting his beer to his lips.

'You wouldn't happen to be the English guy that's caused a fuss with the Riders, would you?'

Sam raised his left arm, showing off the cast. Complete with his bruised and cut eye, he shrugged.

'Again. What gave it away?'

The owner chortled and popped a cap on another beer and held it up to Sam. Sam clinked his bottle and took another swig.

'On the house.' The owner smiled. 'Anyone who gives those pricks a hard time is welcome here.'

Sam nodded his appreciation and then returned to his drink, hoping his silence would end the conversation. He checked his wrist for the time, but the cast meant he'd removed his watch. Silently cursing, he looked around the bar for a clock, relieved to see one on the far wall.

It wasn't too late into the evening, meaning Alex would probably be starting her shift. She'd intimated that something was going down that night, but despite her dangerous game of espionage, she didn't know nearly enough to make Sam comfortable.

None of it did.

The US government had already leveraged her family against her once, but Alex was desperate. Too desperate to realise she was in too deep.

Adding to the anxiety, Sam didn't know when or where anything was happening. If he was going to help her, he would need to do it off the cuff. He had no weapon, and right now, no means of transport. Judging from the wailing sirens that echoed through the sky as he'd raced through the woods, the police were crawling all over his motel. His car would undoubtedly be impounded, a useless attempt to lure him out.

He finished his beer and asked for a food menu, which the owner handed to him with a tongue-in-cheek comment about his bravery. Sam needed to eat, and he'd decided that hunkering down in a corner booth hidden from the town would be a good place to lie low and formulate anything resembling a plan.

As he took a second beer and the menu across the bar to the booth, the door to the bar opened.

'Everyone out.'

Sam stopped and sighed in annoyance. He tossed the menu onto the table and turned towards the entrance. Joe Alan had his eyes locked on Sam, ignoring the few patrons who slid past his considerable frame and out of the door. The owner tried to remonstrate, but Alan lifted his badge, cutting him off.

'Stay or run, Sam,' Alan said, removing his jacket and unbuttoning the cuffs of his shirt, his intentions clear. 'Makes no difference to me.'

'I take it you're not in the mood to listen?' Sam asked, shooting an apologetic glance to the bar owner as the man slipped away and disappeared to the back. Alan didn't respond to his question. He finished rolling his sleeves up and then headed straight for Sam.

The time for talking was over.

CHAPTER SIXTEEN

Watching Alan rolling up the sleeves of his shirt filled Sam with apprehension. Throughout his fight against organised crime, he'd tried his hardest to make sure his skills were targeted at those who deserved it.

Drug lords

Sex traffickers.

Murderers.

Sure, there had been the odd scuffle with the law, but it was usually once he'd snuffed out those who were on the take. The only regrettable altercation had been at Etheridge's house, where his desperation to find Jasmine Hill fuelled him to open fire on an armed response unit. Shedding the blood of honest, good men was never his intention, but the ends justified the means.

He saved Jasmine Hill from a fate worse than death.

Besides, he'd aimed for their legs.

The same ill feeling sat heavy in his stomach at the inevitable fight with Alan. Despite the man's lack of manners, he was a former marine and an upstanding agent. What made Sam so uneasy was the gut feeling that was wrestling for space in his stomach alongside his apprehension.

Joe Alan was a good man.

A good man doing his job.

Sam was a wanted man and was sticking his nose into a situation that Alan and his partner had been investigating for months. If it were any other situation, Sam would walk away.

But he'd made a promise to Alex.

The woman who had saved his life.

And that promise far outweighed the need to do the right thing.

Alan took a few steps towards Sam, cracking his neck. Sam sighed.

'Look, Alan, we don't have to do this.'

'*We* don't.' Alan agreed. 'But *I* do.'

'Why?' Sam asked, but before the answer came, Alan lunged at Sam, his powerful arms latching around Sam like a straitjacket and locking his own arms in tight. Sam struggled violently, and Alan tried his best to position his foot behind Sam's legs, trying to sweep him to the floor. Sam kicked out, his foot cracking into Alan's shin, sending him off balance. As he teetered, Sam pulled his right arm free and drove the palm of his hand into the side of Alan's head, slamming his skull against the bar. The impact was enough for Alan to relinquish his hold, and Sam pushed him away and held up his hands.

'Look, I don't want to fight you.'

'You don't have a choice.'

Alan rushed forward again, driving his shoulder into Sam's gut and then using his momentum to lift Sam off his feet and drive him a few steps back before they collided into the wall. The whole bar shook, and a framed photo of a celebrated sports team fell from the wall, the glass shattering across the floor. With the wind knocked out of him,

Sam drove his elbow into Alan's spine, trying to free himself, but Alan slammed a hard right into Sam's ribs, reigniting the agony from Sykes's attack.

Arching over in pain, Sam dropped his guard, and Alan latched onto the cast wrapped around his left wrist and wrenched the arm back. Sam roared in pain and Alan twisted the arm, turning Sam to face the wall before slamming his cheek against it.

'Sam Pope, you're under arrest,' Alan spat venomously, a slight trickle of blood falling from his eyebrow on account of his introduction to the bar.

With the pain reaching an unbearable level, Sam needed to think. An arrest wouldn't just see him break his promise to Alex, but it would send him back to the United Kingdom in cuffs.

He'd escaped from prison once.

There was no chance they would let that happen again.

With every door slamming shut, Sam threw his head back, the top of his skull crashing into Alan's nose, the blow scattering both of their brains. In the painful daze that immediately followed, and with Alan still tightly grasping his arms, Sam shifted his weight back onto Alan and lifted both feet, planting them against the wall, and pushed as hard as he could.

The two men toppled backwards, with the base of Alan's spine connecting with a wooden table. With Sam's weight on top of him, Alan lost his balance, as well as his grip on Sam, and they crashed through the table. Sam ensured he landed on Alan, crushing the man between his considerable frame and the wood below. As they hit the ground, Sam rolled backwards, free of Alan's grasp, and stumbled lazily to his feet. He headed for the door, knowing he had a good ten seconds or so before a guy like Alan would be good to go again.

Was it enough to get away?

Unfortunately for Sam, the sound of a shotgun being cocked told him he wouldn't find out. Slowly, Sam raised his hands, his fractured wrist throbbing with agony, and he turned to the bar. The owner, who had been so welcoming, was now standing ten feet from him, the shotgun pulled to his shoulder, and his finger on the trigger.

'Sorry, son.' The owner spoke, his words laced with regret. 'You can give those Riders hell for all I care, but I can't sit by and let you assault a government official.'

'You don't understand…' Sam said, trying to catch his breath.

'I don't need to.' The owner nodded to Alan, who was pulling himself to his feet with a face like thunder. 'This man works for our country. I'll side with him every day of the week.'

Alan finally stood, stretching out his back, and then dusted down his suit trousers. With the back of his wrist, he wiped the blood from his eyebrow and then nodded at the owner.

'Thank you, sir.'

The owner nodded, proud to serve his country. Despite the inconvenience, Sam could understand the feeling. He'd fought for his country for over a decade, and he knew first-hand the respect that commanded. And despite his bullish nature, Joe Alan was a good man, fighting for what was right.

But something still felt wrong?

'We doing this again?' Alan asked with a smirk.

'I don't think you could handle another round,' Sam retorted. The owner shot a glance at both men, clearly perplexed. Despite the nature of the situation, and the commitment both men had to their own cause, neither man was the enemy.

They were just on other sides of the fight.

Recognising the respect that had grown between the

two of them, Sam shuffled to the nearest barstool and lifted himself onto it. Alan lowered his fists.

'Can I get a beer, please?'

The owner double took in surprise, and then turned to Alan who chuckled.

'Make that two,' Alan said, walking towards the neighbouring barstool. 'And I'll make sure we cover the damages.'

With the gun still locked firmly in his hands, the owner shot both men glances before shrugging and putting the weapon down on the back counter. He returned with two bottles of beer as Alan took his seat and Sam lifted his bottle to Alan.

'I'm not here to ruin your investigation,' Sam said firmly, as Alan clinked his bottle.

'I believe you,' Alan said. 'I ran a background check and I know you aren't affiliated with either the Riders or Vasquez.'

'Then why the hell are you trying to arrest me?'

Alan took a long swig of beer.

'Because despite whatever good intentions you think you have, you're still a wanted man. I read the files. Yeah, you took down a lot of bad people. Put a lot of them in the dirt. But this ain't the wild west, Pope. There's a way of doing things and I can't have you mess this up when we are so close.'

'We?'

'Sinclair and I.'

'And Alex?'

Alan raised his eyebrow.

'What about her?'

'She's your person on the inside.' Sam read the blank expression on Alan's face. 'He didn't tell you?'

Clearly seething, Alan took another sip of his beer.

'He said he had someone on the inside, but I figured it was a Rider.'

'Not an innocent woman, like Alex?' Sam shook his head. 'A woman he has manipulated into coming here?'

'What the fuck are you talking about?'

'The promise I made to Alex, the reason I'm here, is to help her get her brother and sister back. Sinclair has used that as leverage, and now he has her in that place, feeding him information and putting her life in danger.' Sam could see the anger and confusion bubbling within Alan. 'I promised I would help her, and I intend to.'

'This case…it's big.' Alan spoke, trying to convince himself. 'Whatever Sinclair has done, I'm sure it was necessary. But you being here, it's only going to put her in more danger.'

'Well, she said it will be over after tonight.'

'Tonight?' Alan sat up in surprise.

'How much do you actually know?'

Alan took the final swig of his bottle and slammed it down on the bar.

'Not fucking enough.' He stood, nodded a thank you to the owner, and made a mental note to ensure the man received ample compensation. 'So why don't we go and find out?'

'Now we're talking.' Sam smiled, finishing his beer and following Alan to the door. As he stepped through, Alan rested a hand on his shoulder.

'And if you try anything, and I mean *anything*, that will stop me bringing down the Riders, I will shoot you. Understood?'

Sam chuckled, nodded his understanding, and stepped out of the bar with Alan a step behind him.

———

Two Weeks Earlier…

'So, this is her, huh?'

Wyatt cast a seemingly unimpressed eye over Alex, his voice tinged with confusion. Alex nervously looked around the bar, intimidated by how real The Pit felt in contrast to the clearly fabricated aesthetic of the High Five. Wyatt wasn't as tall or as broad as Sykes, but he carried himself with such authority that he was twice as intimidating. With his bandana wrapped around his head and his strong jaw lined with a greying beard, Wyatt looked her dead in the eye.

'Why are you here?' The question caught Alex by surprise, and she shot a glance over Wyatt's shoulder to Sykes. 'Don't look at him, look at me.'

Wyatt's tone hardened, and Sykes spoke up.

'Jesus, Trent. Give the girl a break.'

Wyatt raised his hand in the air, silencing Sykes without even looking at him. His eyes were locked on Alex, who felt a bead of sweat trickle down her neck.

She now realised how dangerous the game she was playing actually was. It had been easy up until this point.

Sinclair, the DEA agent who had recruited her to infiltrate the Riders, had waxed lyrical about the risk involved. Mason, the man who ran the High Five was a cuddly bear in truth, despite a clear history of violence. The other Riders were harmless enough, unless one of the wannabe bikers got too friendly or aggressive with the bar staff.

Growing up in the Bronx, making her own way through life to keep food on her family's table had hardened Alex.

The trials with Sam in Italy, the bullet wound she'd suffered.

All of it had toughened her. Moulded her.

But as she stood before Wyatt with his unbreakable gaze Alex felt terrified to her very core.

'I wanted a job,' she eventually mumbled.

'You had a job,' Wyatt stated firmly. 'A pretty easy gig at the Five. Nice customers. Plus, close to home for you. So, tell me again, why the fuck would you leave New York to come and work in this shit-hole bar in this back road town?'

'Because Sykes asked me to.'

'So, you're here for him?' Wyatt threw a thumb in Sykes's direction. His right-hand man had gnawed his ear off about Alex Stone for a few weeks, and Wyatt had assumed he was attracted to her. Perhaps this was just a move for him to take her to bed.

It was a lot of effort, but Wyatt didn't care. He hadn't sat on the throne for so long by being courteous, or by letting his groin rule his head.

'No.' Alex smiled. 'I needed a fresh start. I had some trouble with the feds, and I needed to get away. Figured you boys might be a good start.'

'Ah, so you want to be a Rider?'

'Not really.' Alex shrugged, feeling her confidence. 'I'm more of a four-wheel kind of girl.'

A smile threatened to crack on Wyatt's face.

'Okay, fine. A few shifts. Let's see how you do.' Wyatt folded his arms across his chest. 'But I guess I don't have to reiterate that what happens in the bar, stays in the bar. My boys will keep you safe, but you might see a little more shit than you did in Yonkers.'

'Fine by me.' Alex dismissed it with a gentle shrug. 'Trust me, I've seen things that will make your boys look like they're running a crochet club.'

The smile eventually won the battle, and Wyatt nodded his appreciation.

'Well, we'll see. You've got the job. But it will take a little while for you to get my trust.'

With that, Wyatt turned and walked away, not even acknowledging Sykes as he did. The huge biker scowled in anger at his boss and then returned to Alex with a friendly grin. It sent a shudder through her body, and she was worried about the very real threat of having to rebuff his advances.

'Time to start your shift,' Sykes said, clasping his hands together. 'Let me give you the tour.'

Two weeks on, and Alex had been surprised that Sykes's advances never came.

She'd been convinced that he'd been attracted to her, instantly picking her out on his trip to the High Five and demanding she move to work at The Pit. It had seemed too good to be true.

Sinclair had planted her within the Riders, tasking her with working hard behind the bar of the High Five and relaying any information she could when it came to Wyatt or the Riders. For the first few days, Mason had been a closed shop, and even when he did let his mask slip, there was no slip of the tongue.

Nothing she could give as meaningful.

The Riders were a well drilled, well commanded outfit, and a senior figure like Mason knew the drill to the last-minute detail.

But Sykes dropped a golden opportunity on her lap, and at the behest of Sinclair, she'd accepted the opportunity. Hundreds of miles from home, dropped into one of the most dangerous bars in America.

Alex's desperation to pull her family back from the brink had pushed her closer to it.

But it was nearly over.

Over the few weeks, Wyatt had kept an eye on her, and she'd felt his impenetrable glare from the back of the bar on numerous occasions. She hoped that her explanation on Sam's assault of Mason and subsequent emergence in Dillon had done enough to keep him happy.

For one more night.

As Alex lifted the crate of empty beer bottles, she felt her arms shake with excitement, the glass clinking together and rattling like a maraca.

Sinclair had told her that evening he would collect her

at eleven. She didn't need to make any excuses, as she wouldn't be returning. It seemed a little peculiar to her, as there was no inkling of any deal or move being made by the Riders that evening. All the intel she'd provided had been useful in mapping out the operational structure of the Riders, but information of any major drug deal going down had been absent.

But Sinclair had it on good authority.

At eleven, she would leave the bar for the last time, and Sinclair would take her to her family.

He would ensure their reunion and their safety.

Not even Sinclair's partner, Special Agent Alan, knew anything about her. That was a slight disappointment for Alex, as she'd found herself attracted to him from the few sightings she'd managed to sneak.

But as the clock shifted another minute closer to her freedom, she recomposed herself, headed to the back and began sorting through the empties.

Ten minutes later. She snuck out of the back door, meandered through the parked motorcycles, and cut across a few back streets to where Sinclair had promised he'd be waiting.

As she approached the van, the engine kicked into life, and Sinclair pushed open the passenger door.

'Ready to get out of here?' he asked, a warm smile on his face.

'Like you wouldn't believe.' Alex sighed as she dropped into the seat. 'Get me out of here.'

'Will do,' Sinclair replied, pulling the van out into the road and putting his foot down, quickly heading towards the road that led out of Dillon. As the van raced down the highway, Joe Alan followed, his knuckles white with tension as he clung to the wheel.

In the back, Sam watched with confusion, with the feeling of uncertainty in the pit of his stomach that had been a useful weapon of his throughout his life.

It told him something wasn't right.

That something bad was about to happen.

In hot pursuit of the van, Alan and Sam rode in silence, heading towards whatever it was that Sam was dreading.

CHAPTER SEVENTEEN

As the van rumbled down the US-501, Alex could feel her muscles tightening with anxiety. Sinclair had kept his cards close to his chest, he always had, but now she was wondering what was actually going on. After picking her up from the Pit, they'd sped to the outskirts of Dillon, passing out the south side of the town and onto the highway, the wide roads vacant as always. The moon was bright, casting a wondrous glow over the terrain, which petered off into the shadows. Miles of fields, with no discernible signs of life anywhere, and Alex suddenly felt very vulnerable.

'Are you sure it's happening tonight?' she asked, flashing a glance towards Sinclair. The veteran agent stared out to the road ahead, his focus locked on the destination.

'I guarantee it.'

'But I didn't catch wind of anything.' Alex shrugged. 'I mean, they're worried about Vasquez and Wyatt questioned me about my friend, but that's it.'

'Your friend? You mean Jonathan Cooper?'

'Yes,' Alex lied.

'Is he going to be a problem?'

'Well, Wyatt wanted to know a little more, but I think that's as far as it went. Although Sykes and a few of them gave him an ass kicking.'

'Really?' Sinclair's eyebrows leapt up. 'When?'

'Last night.' Alex shook her head. 'Broke his wrist and everything.'

'You spoke with him today?'

'Yeah.' Alex could see Sinclair's irritation. 'The guy travelled all this way to see me.'

'Jesus, Alex.' Sinclair slammed his fist against the steering wheel in frustration. 'Not only could he compromise this entire case, but just associating with him could get you killed. You've seen the video, right? He has already proven to them he's a dangerous man and for what it's worth, Agent Alan is looking into him as we speak.'

'What do you mean?'

'Come on. A guy with that training and the balls to walk straight into hell itself with no fear isn't just a *concerned friend*, is he?'

Alex turned away from Sinclair, ending the conversation. She knew she'd done some regrettable things to try to keep her family together, but she wasn't going to give Sam up. Him turning up out of the blue was a shock. When she'd heard about Wallace's death and the dissolution of Blackridge, she'd assumed he'd either gone to prison or died trying.

She'd taken her family's fate into her own hands, and despite his best intentions, she hoped Sam was lying low. Wherever they were headed, Sinclair had promised her it would all be over. They would have enough to pin Wyatt to the cross, and she would be reunited with her family.

They would be kept safe, and everything would have been worth it.

She knew she trusted Sam.

She was doing her best to trust Sinclair, too.

An uneasy silence sat between the two of them as the van passed the sign welcoming them to Marion, a small town twenty miles south of Dillon. Alex had never visited. Her entire time in South Carolina had been spent exclusively on the few streets that separated her apartment from the Pit, and she looked at the buildings as they entered. It was identical to Dillon, with the wide roads lined with businesses, all of them closed with the shutters down. Foot traffic was completely absent, and beyond the odd lorry that meandered down the high street, the entire town was eerily silent. Sinclair guided the van through a few abandoned streets before pulling up opposite a large car park. A lone street light bathed the entrance to the car park in light, but the facility behind it was hidden in shadow. A large, chain-link fence ran around the sides, before they too were enveloped by the darkness.

'This is the place,' Sinclair said calmly, killing the engine. Alex shot him a puzzled look, and he calmly pulled a cigarette to his lips, struck a match, and set it alight. He rolled the window slightly and let the smoke drift through the gap and into the night sky. Alex followed suit, her nerves craving a calming nicotine fix, and the two of them smoked in silence. As the time passed, Alex felt her apprehension build and just as she was about to question Sinclair's intel, the roar of a motorcycle grew louder and sure enough, the hulking figure of Sykes appeared at the end of the road. Alex and Sinclair sat in the darkness, watching as the maniacal Death Rider slowed his powerful motorcycle to a crawl, before turning and disappearing into a side alley.

'What's he doing?' Alex asked, but before Sykes could answer, a black van rolled past them, turning sharply into the car park and disappearing into the dark.

Both of them sat in silence, staring at the shadows beyond.

A flash of light erupted somewhere within the car park, followed by the unmistakable roar of a gunshot.

'Fuck,' Sinclair exclaimed, unclipping his seat belt and throwing his door open. 'Stay here.'

Before Alex could remonstrate, Sinclair slammed his door shut and, keeping as low as he could, he rushed across the street to the entrance, his hand dipping into his jacket and returning with his pistol. As Alex watched on, Sinclair disappeared into the dark.

———

'What the fuck is going on?' Alan said to himself. Sam knew the question wasn't directed at him, so he ignored it and did his best to absorb as much as he could from the surroundings. The town of Marion was identikit to Dillon, and Sam hated his lack of preparedness. He knew coming to America, searching for Alex, was going to be risky. There was no plan of action, as he didn't know what to expect.

It certainly wasn't being elbow deep in a rising drug war between two dangerous empires and locked in the back of a DEA agent's car.

He had no weapon.

No back-up.

No plan.

All he had was his instincts, and although his burgeoning friendship with Alan meant he wasn't sitting in cuffs, his gut told him something was off.

Why had Sinclair kept the deal from Alan?

Why were they here if they were looking to bring down the Riders?

In the seat in front of him, Alan shuffled with discomfort, clearly irate at the unfolding situation. On the drive to Marion, they'd spoken a few words, but the agent's fury had kept the conversation to a minimum. Now, sitting in the darkness halfway down the street, Sam watched as Alan stared at the van as it came to a stop.

'He's stopped.' Sam pointed.

'But why?' Alan asked, not expecting an answer. Sam looked around the street. The roads were as abandoned as they were in Dillon. Although the Rider's influence was drastically reduced in the town, Sam had a feeling the group made the residents aware of who was in charge on a frequent basis. With the engine off, Alan sat back in his seat, puffing his cheeks in frustration before shooting a glance to the mirror. Sam made eye contact.

'Don't try anything stupid, okay?' Alan spoke firmly. 'If anything happens, I'll do my best to keep Alex safe. Once she's out of the way, we can discuss what we do with you.'

'As long as she's okay, and she gets back to her family, you can hand me over to the government for all I care.' Sam shrugged, turning to look out at the window. 'I know there is a price for the things I've done, and this is the last promise I need to keep before I'm willing to pay up.'

Alan huffed, trying his best to mask his admiration. But Sam could feel it. It was an in-built kinship that was shared by anyone who had served their country. Being a soldier wasn't just a job. To every man or woman who had worn their country's uniform and fought with pride, it was a vocation. The bond that was built between your comrades, the trust that you instilled in them and they in you, was what forged a link that surpassed any other.

There were soldiers who were closer to their brothers and sisters than they were to their own wives.

Sam had never felt a connection that strong, but he understood it. While Lucy and Jamie, when they were his family, were his reason for fighting, there had still been people he'd been willing to die for.

Willing to kill for.

It was what had compelled him to chase Marsden across Europe, inciting the war with Wallace and Blackridge.

That eternal bond created in the heat of battle when you trusted someone else with your life.

Along the way, he'd lost good men.

Marsden.

Theo.

Mac.

There were even soldiers he didn't know beyond their mission, such as Vargas, Bennett, and Connell, all of whom died in the middle of the Amazon, fighting bravely until the end.

Despite their shaky start, Alan and Sam knew the other had been through war and survived.

That was worthy of respect.

Whether it was worthy of trust was a different matter, and Sam couldn't blame Alan for treating him with suspicion. Alan was a man of the law, and Sam had been raging a war on the wrong side of it for a long time.

A roar of a motorcycle echoed down the empty street, and Alan shot forward as if someone had just zapped him with a cattle prod. Peering through the windscreen, his eyes squinted with fury.

'Sykes.' He uttered the name with the venom of a cursed word. Sam regarded Alan's disgust in the mirror.

'What's the deal with you and Sykes?'

'What?' Alan snapped back, his eyes shooting up and meeting Sam's in the reflection.

'You seem hell bent on taking down Sykes, rather than the Riders.' Sam leant forward. 'I may not be Sherlock Holmes, but I'm not an idiot.'

Alan turned away, his focus on the street ahead as the large figure of Sykes pulled into an alleyway and disappeared into the shadow. His powerful jaw tightened, and Sam could see Alan's knuckles whiten as he gripped the steering wheel.

'My older brother, Peter, was a hell of a marine. He was older than me, so he'd been fighting for a few years before I even made the grade. He was a good man, you know. Strong, brave, and he gave a shit. Loved his family, had two beautiful little girls with his wife. Hell, he even did charity work.'

Sam smiled. It was the first time he'd seen vulnerability in Alan, a trait the man was trained to keep shielded.

'He sounds like a great guy.'

'He was.' Alan's tight jaw shook slightly. Enough for Sam to notice the pain. 'He was promoted, commanded his own squadron. I was a fresh jarhead, finding my way, but he was a hell of a man to look up to. Nearly twenty years ago, he took a team to Istanbul to intercept an arms trade between a couple of known terrorist cells. The mission was clear as day. Neutralise the men in play and safely claim the weaponry. It should have been in and out.'

Alan snapped his fingers to emphasise the point. Sam waited, letting the man continue.

'One of my brother's men decided that was the moment he was going to take a piss on the flag, and he opened fire just as the deal was beginning. In an open, public market, he took his M16 rifle, and he unloaded it. He killed three members of the terrorist cell. Five innocent members of the public' – Alan took a deep breath – 'and he killed my brother when he tried to stop him.'

Sam sat back in his chair, exasperated. He didn't need Alan to connect the dots for him. Alan's reason for hunting Sykes was clear as day.

'When the dust settled, to avoid a shitstorm of investigations, Sykes was dishonourably discharged, and he disappeared. Can you believe that?' Alan shook his head. 'The man should have been rotting in a military prison, but due to the rising wave of discourse in this country against our armed forces, they swept him under the rug. Maybe they were planning on something after the fact, but the man disappeared. Vanished. So, I honoured my brother, I served for a decade and when I was discharged, I tracked him down and every bit of me wanted to put a bullet between his eyes.'

'I know that feeling,' Sam offered.

'No, you don't. Because you don't have the restraint.' Alan kept his eyes firmly on Sinclair's truck and the neighbouring car park. 'I found the person responsible for killing the person I held dearest in the world, but I knew killing him would make me no different. So, I went to work, I worked my way to this position and now we are this fucking close to bringing him down and I'll be damned if I let you or anyone stop me.'

A silent tension filled the car like it was taking on water, and before Sam could answer, a black van rolled past their car. Both of them watched as it drove past Sinclair's van and turned into the car park.

Alan's hand instinctively gripped the door handle, the other sliding into his jacket, his fingers wrapping around his pistol.

'You're wrong.' Sam spoke quietly. 'I found the man responsible for killing my little boy, and I beat him near to death. I had every intention of killing him. I mean, this guy took away my boy. But I didn't. I realised that if I did that, I couldn't make a difference. I couldn't fight back against those who break the law and those who let them get away with it.'

'You're a vigilante.' Alan spun his head round. 'You

may have good intentions, Sam. But you still chose your path.'

'I did.' Sam sat up with pride. 'And I'd walk it again.'

A gunshot exploded from the car park, and both men snapped to attention. From the van ahead of them, Sinclair emerged, gun in hand, and keeping low to the ground, scurried across the street and into the darkness.

'Shit.' Alan threw the door open. 'Stay here.'

Before Sam could remonstrate, Alan sprung from the car, slammed the door and ensured it was locked. With his own gun in hand, he jogged briskly down the street, keeping close to the buildings and the shadows they bathed the street in. Sam pulled at the door handle in frustration.

Alex was in the van, a sitting duck in the very real threat of a drug deal gone wrong.

As Sam pondered his next move, and Agent Alan approached the car park, another gunshot echoed loudly into the night.

CHAPTER EIGHTEEN

The gunshot acted like the start of an Olympic race, the terrifying, unmistakable sound instinctively spurring Sam into action. Whatever was going down, Sam knew that he needed to get to Alex, and they both needed to get out of there. He watched as Alan approached the car park, his gun held still in a firm grip.

The man was a trained marine.

Despite the danger, Sam knew he could handle himself.

Swivelling on the plush leather seats of the car, Sam rolled onto his back and planted the base of his Chelsea boots on the window. He drew his legs back, and in one powerful thrust, he slammed his feet against the glass.

The glass cracked.

Another thunderous lunge and his feet smashed through the glass, the shards exploding across the road and clattering to the concrete. Quickly, he sat up, reached through the broken panel, and unlocked the door. As the door swung open, he saw Alan shoot a glance back at him. But they both knew that this was bigger than Sam's incarceration.

Keeping low, and on the opposite side of the street, Sam scurried towards Sinclair's van, dipping in and out of the lights that overhung the street and bathing patches in a yellow glow. As he moved, he could see a few curtains twitching, the terrified locals peeking out from their sanctuaries, hoping they were mistaken.

Marion was as peaceful as Dillon.

But just as dangerous.

There were no sirens filling the air, nor did Sam expect any. Towns like this left the Riders to their business, knowing that whatever mess they created they would likely clean up themselves. Whatever the hell Sykes was doing here, and whoever was in that van, Sam was sure the police would sit this one out.

He approached the back of the van, and looked over to Alan who was pressed against the railing of the fence, gun in hand, shielded by a parked Range Rover. Alan held his hand up to Sam, asking him to stop.

Sam responded by raising his, then he pointed to the van, before slowly backing away, intimating that he was going to check on Alex. With his partner lost in the darkness, and a potential shoot-out, Alan nodded and then spun from the gate and approached the entrance to the car park. Sam shuffled up to the door of the van and peeked in, only for the door to swing open and crack him straight in the side of the face. The metal made a hard clunk, and the striking pain rattled his brain and he stumbled back, blinking through it.

'Stay the fuck awa…SAM!?' Alex cried out, her defiance quickly shifting to concern. 'Jesus.'

'Nice to see you, too,' he whispered, shaking the blow and gritting his teeth. 'Are you okay?'

'What the fuck are you doing here?' Alex hissed.

'I'd ask you the same question.' Sam looked over the

hood of the van, watching as Alan took measured steps into the parking lot, his gun at the ready. 'You told me this wasn't going to be dangerous.'

Despite her best efforts, Sam could see the fear in Alex's eyes. She was in deep, and whatever the reason Sinclair had brought her out here, it had gone south. Before she could answer, the sound of stumbled footsteps came from the parking lot and she turned to look, a sharp gasp escaping from her dropped jaw. Sam peered over the hood, and he felt every muscle in his body tighten.

Alan had already sprung into action.

Sam's voice was as stern as it had ever been.

'We need to go. Now.'

————

As Alan had approached the chain-link fence that surrounded the parking lot, he'd heard the back window of his car burst open and he glared back as Sam pulled his feet back through the empty window. It was a government car, so there would be no financial cost, but Alan still sighed with frustration.

Despite the man's criminal past, there was a side to Sam Alan admired.

Possibly even liked.

Although Alan would never condone the course of action Sam had taken to avenge those he lost, he understood. They may have ventured down vastly different paths to get there, but they were both soldiers who were looking to put things right. Alan did his by the book and behind a badge.

Sam, on the other hand, had fought back against the system in a way that hadn't blurred the line of right and wrong, but completely erased it.

But despite now being free of the clutches of the DEA, who would hand him back to the UK government to spend the rest of his life in prison, Sam wasn't running.

Alan knew why.

Sam hadn't broken out of the car for his own protection.

He was there to make good on his promise to Alex.

And despite the man's defiance, Alan respected it.

On the other side of the fence, Alan could hear the slow, lazy footsteps of a person. The foot scraped across the concrete as if struggling to walk. Whoever it was, they were headed for the exit and Alan wanted to cut them off at the pass. His partner was somewhere in there, along with whoever was driving the black van.

And Sykes.

Despite not seeing the man's face, Alan's obsession over the years had meant he could spot the man from a mile away. Sykes was a tall, imposing man, and Alan knew it was him the moment they'd heard the bike.

But if this deal was going down tonight, and Sinclair knew about it, why had he not told Alan?

Sinclair was a veteran, less than a year away from a pat on the back and a glorious pension. He'd been a mentor to Alan for a number of years and knew how deep his vengeance ran.

Sam approached the van and Alan held up his hand, a silent order for him to stop. It was a pointless act of authority, but it was instinctive. Sam held up his hands in surrender, pointed to the front of Sinclair's van, and slowly slid to the side of it. Whatever Alan ordered; he knew Sam wouldn't listen.

Not until he knew Alex was safe.

Alan needed to know the same about Sinclair, and he rounded the fence and stepped into the sliver of light that illuminated the entrance. His nerves were steady, the gun unmoving in his dangerous grip.

The sloppy footsteps grew louder, and Alan lowered his gun, his eyes widening with terror.

Behind him, he heard the unmistakable sound of a door colliding with something, but he was unmoved.

Through the darkness, the figure of Special Agent Terry Sinclair emerged, the shadow sliding away from him as he stumbled into the light. Weak and wounded, his eyes cried out for help from Alan, with his arm loosely swinging from his side, the gun hanging sloppily in his feeble grip.

His other hand was pressed firmly against his stomach, his white shirt now completely stained with the terrifying shade of blood. His hand was bathed in it to, and he stumbled into Alan's arms, almost collapsing to his knees.

'Jesus, Terry,' Alan yelped, catching his partner before he fell and holding him up. 'Stay with me.'

From the darkness, two headlights burst into existence, blinding Alan temporarily as he raised a hand to shield the brightness. The van engine roared to life, and the tyres screeched like a banshee as they spun on the concrete.

'We gotta go, Terry,' Alan yelled, and with impressive strength, he hoisted his injured partner over his shoulder. The man moaning in pain. Alan shuffled quickly to the entrance, knowing that whoever had done this was likely to be behind the wheel of the van.

As he moved to the exit, Alan tried his best to collect his thoughts.

Sinclair had clearly been shot in the stomach.

But there had been two gunshots.

Where was Sykes?

As he stepped to the outside of the parking lot, he lowered Sinclair onto the ground, squatting beside his friend to try to take a look at the wound. Sinclair clutched his stomach tightly, his bloodied hand covering the bullet wound and before Alan could get a decent look, Sam's voice distracted him.

'Alan, look out.'

Alan's head lifted, noticing a worried Sam rushing towards him. Despite the warning, Alan was too late, and as he turned around, he saw Sykes's heavily tattooed arm falling violently towards him.

Something metal collided with the side of his skull.

Everything went black.

————

Alex had shifted along to the driver's seat of the van and turned the key as instructed when Sam had stopped. As soon as they'd seen the wounded Sinclair stumble into Alan's arms, Sam realised that unarmed, the two of them were sitting ducks. Just as he was about to climb into the passenger seat, two headlights illuminated the entire car park, bathing Alan and his partner in its glow, and Alan showed great strength and loyalty to lift his partner up and race to the exit.

But the light also gave Sam a glimpse of the alleyway that ran down the side of the car park, and he'd noticed something.

A figure moving at speed.

'Keep the engine running.' Sam nodded to Alex and then stepped back onto the street. As he stepped around the front of the van, he saw the looming figure of Sykes emerge from behind the fence, a mere foot or two behind Alan who had crouched to tend to Sinclair.

In Sykes's hand was a gun.

'Alan, look out,' Sam yelled, rushing a few feet in a useless attempt to intervene. Alan looked up at Sam, registering his worry, and before he could turn to face his nemesis, Sykes swung the gun, the butt of it making a sickening thud as it cracked against the side of his skull.

Alan was out before he slumped to the ground.

Sam stopped in his tracks as Sykes looked up, a twisted grin etched across his cruel face. Recognising Sam from their altercation the night before, he raised his arm, the gun pointing at Sam, who ducked to the ground.

Sykes pulled the trigger.

And again.

Sam opened his eyes, baffled that the bullets had missed. Despite the anarchy, his ears were tuned perfectly, and he failed to hear the errant shots hit the van behind him. Before he could register his own survival, the black van that had illuminated the car park sped towards the entrance and despite the guilt of leaving Alan at the mercy of Sykes, Sam's promise to Alex drew him to her like a magnet. With Sykes stepping coldly over Alan's limp body and approaching the dying Sinclair, Sam rushed to the passenger door and jumped in.

'Reverse.' Sam commanded, and Alex shifted the gear stick and slammed her foot on the pedal. As they distanced themselves from the chaos, Sam watched helplessly as Sykes stood over Sinclair, casually straightened his arm so the gun was pointed at the agent's head.

The black van turned sharply out of the car park, the driver lining the vehicle up with theirs, and it sped towards them.

Just before it collided with them, Sam saw a flash of light from Sykes's gun.

Another crack echoed. The gunshot the exclamation point on Sinclair's mortality.

The distant sound of sirens filled the air, but Sam knew they would be too late. Alex was angrily groaning as she tried to speed up. The black van's headlights growing bigger as their impending crash became a reality.

'Hold on to something,' Sam yelled.

Then everything shook.

Blasted front on by the van, Alex tried her best to keep control of the wheel, and as she wrenched it upon impact, the van spun to the side, the back wheel clipping the curb and sending it sprawling. Rattled among the interior and broken glass, Sam felt the world spin, his skull colliding with the dashboard.

Alex let out a scream of pain.

Things went blurry.

After a few rolls, the van eventually slowed, tipping slightly before resting on its roof. With no seat belt holding him in place, Sam opened his eyes, lying front down inside the roof, shards of glass embedded in his forearm. He could taste the blood dripping from his lip, and his left wrist was throbbing in pain.

Strapped to the seat, and hanging upside down, Alex was unconscious, a trickle of blood dripping from her skull.

Outside the van, Sam could hear the faint crunch of boots on glass, but they were muffled by the ringing in his ears.

'Alex?' he mumbled, his voice cracking in fear at their impending death.

He'd promised to help her.

To save her.

He'd failed.

The driver's side door was wrenched open, and through his blurred vision, Sam saw two arms reach in, unclip Alex's belt and wrench her from the car. He tried his best to call out, to remonstrate with their attackers.

He would offer himself in her place.

But it didn't matter. The passenger door behind him opened, and as he felt the hands wrap around his legs, he tried to muster the energy to fight back.

To survive.

But this time, they hauled him across the glass with little effort, and before Sam could get a look at their faces, a solid fist slammed against his jaw, sending a spray of blood across the panel of the van and everything went black.

CHAPTER NINETEEN

THREE YEARS AGO...

It had been a year to the day that Jamie had died.

Every single moment of that year had been one of unrelenting torture. Each second that ticked by was a painful reminder that everything Sam had ever fought for was a memory. Not only did the world cruelly take his son from him, but the agony that coiled around his life like a hungry snake soon relieved him of his marriage.

Lucy had been his world.

When his father had died, Sam found his home in the military. The brother he never had, he found. His bond with Theo thicker than most bound by blood. Although his father had passed, Sam pushed himself to fill the large shoes his legacy had left behind, and for a long time, those were the only two things that mattered.

He didn't feel alone.

He felt like he had a purpose.

Then that one night where he met Lucy in a nightclub changed it all.

His entire fight became for her.

Every mission. Every fight to the death.

169

Every desperate attempt for survival.

All of it for her.

There were times, whether he was hiding in the wall of a generous local doctor in an abandoned Afghan town, or fighting for his life in the middle of the Amazon, where Lucy's face had been his beacon.

The thought of not returning to her, of not seeing her face again, pushed him to survive the most thankless of odds.

When Jamie arrived, that instinct doubled.

All of it snatched away by one drunk driver, and Sam's hesitation in stopping him from getting behind the wheel.

Miles Hillock was only twenty years old when he lost control of his car, swerving into his son and ending his life. That moment changed everything, tearing apart Sam's life at the seams, and for it all, he spent nine months behind bars.

Nine months.

The same time it had taken Lucy to carry their son into the world.

Sam had hit a low ebb when Jamie died, his mental state evaporating as he fell into a deep depression. Six months of trying to pull him back from the brink had taken its toll on Lucy, and she left their broken marriage with a shattered heart.

Sam no longer had anything to live for.

His reason to survive had gone.

Had it not been for the timely interception of Sergeant Carl Marsden, Sam would have taken his life.

But Marsden's words had hit home, and in the intervening months, Sam had built up the courage to not only face what had happened, but the man responsible.

Miles Hillock.

Drinking himself to death in a grotty flat, Miles was already circling the drain by the time Sam had broken in, assaulted the man with a flurry of vicious blows and a clear intent to kill him. Placing a knife to Hillock's throat, Sam wanted the justice that the system had failed to deliver. But as the man, battered, bleeding, and barely

170

conscious had feebly tried to apologise, Sam had a moment of clarity.

The instances of the system failing were growing by the day, with violent and dangerous criminals destroying thousands of lives. The police, despite their best efforts, were fighting a losing battle, and their hands were being tied tighter and tighter by the constraints of the very law they were trying to uphold.

Sam was trained.

Capable.

Ready to fight back.

Leaving Hillock in a pool of his own blood, Sam walked away. The young man took his own life that night, the guilt of ending such a young life too heavy to continue his own.

Sam shed no tears.

There were some crimes you couldn't come back from, and a year on from Jamie's death, he was sure that his journey would probably end with him joining his son in the afterlife.

But he had to do something.

Someone had to fight back.

The graveyard where they'd buried Jamie's ashes was immaculate as always, the groundsmen taking pride in offering those grieving a place of tranquillity to do so. The summer sun was shining down, bathing the morbid atmosphere in a warm glow, and Sam watched from the shade of a tree as Lucy crouched down in front of the plaque, which stood on a metal stand that was embedded in the earth. Behind it, the shoots of a tree, planted in their son's honour, had begun to reach towards the heavens, its leafy fingers reaching upwards for the clouds. Lucy's body was shaking, her crying audible even from the distance Sam had put between them.

A small gathering of her family had joined her to celebrate their son's life, with her parents huddled together, sharing their grief. A few of Lucy's friends were there also, one of them holding a beautiful bouquet of flowers.

Heartbreakingly for Sam, he could see Theo, dressed in his Sunday best, standing proudly as only a soldier can.

All of them bound together by their grief for his young boy.

A few feet to the side of Lucy's parents, a handsome man stood patiently before stepping forward and sliding his arm around Lucy's shoulder. As he squatted beside her, he planted a firm kiss on her head and she fell into him, overcome with her loss.

Sam knew she'd found someone else.

It should have been him, holding her tightly as they dealt with the devastation.

But Sam had pushed her away, and while it cracked the last remaining fragment of his heart to watch, he was happy that she'd found the love that he couldn't show her.

But love he would always hold for her.

Slowly, Lucy got to her feet and turned to the group, thanking them for coming with her. Sam couldn't hear the words, but he was certain they would have provided her with some comfort. Even Theo offered her a hug, which drew a deep breath from Sam as he shook.

He'd made his decision.

Decided the path he would take and although it was the right thing to do, he knew it was in the opposite direction to them.

As he turned to walk away, the entire graveyard shook, glitching like a broken TV aerial, and when it returned, he was no longer standing in the graveyard.

He was in the charred remains of Theo's house; the interior devastated by the blast of a grenade. The walls were stained black; the furniture scattered in numerous pieces. The windows were blasted into a million fragments, and the smell of burnt flesh filled the air.

The rain leathered down outside, the wind sweeping it through the empty windows, crashing against him with a cold selfishness.

Slumped against the wall, Theo's mutilated body rested. The attack on his house had been to eliminate Amy Devereaux by a powerful criminal, Frank Jackson.

The walls began to flicker, as Sam's memories were being jolted, as if some external force was slamming itself against his brain.

Just before he was snapped back from his thoughts, Theo's eyes shot open, the lifeless gaze burning a hole through Sam deeper than the one that had blown Theo's chest open.

Sam could feel a tear roll down his face as he stared at his dead friend, knowing none of it was real.

Moments before Sam awoke, Theo spoke.

'You can't save everyone.'

Sam closed his eyes, and the cocktail of memories ended.

―――――

Edinson's solid fist collided with Sam's cheek and rocked him against the chair, the cable ties binding him to his seat and holding him upright. In the abandoned warehouse, Jose Vasquez had risen from his chair on the other side of the room and approached, seemingly frustrated with Sam's resolve.

He'd been through worse.

But Sam was a long way from home, the numbing ache of the car accident still echoing inside his body.

It had all gone wrong. So very wrong.

Agent Sinclair was dead.

Alan too, most likely.

But most importantly, all Sam could recall was Alex's unconscious body, hanging from her seat in the upturned van, blood trickling from her head, before she was wrenched through the door. Sam had been pulled from the wreckage too, before a clubbing blow had knocked him unconscious. When he'd awoken, he was strapped to the very chair he sat in, the dim lighting showing him just enough to know he was far enough from civilisation that screaming for help would be redundant.

Vasquez has been questioning him on his true identity. Edinson had been rejecting his quips with his pounding fists. Despite the pain, all Sam could think of was Alex.

Vasquez, resplendent in his suit, wore the expression of a man not used to flippancy. Or a lack of fear.

'This is not working,' Vasquez snarled. 'See, you actually remind me of my cousin. He's a strong and resilient man but he used to ask…how do you hurt strong men? The same way you hurt every man.'

Right on cue, the door opened, and Sam could hear the scuffled footsteps before Alex shuffled into shot. A scrawny, tattooed man held her firmly by the hair with one hand, a gun pointed to her head with the other. Alex's eyes were wide with fear, begging Sam for help. Her face was covered in cuts and bruises, but Sam didn't know if they were the result of the crash, or the despicable man's handiwork. Sam lunged against his restraints, the cable tie digging into the cast and caused his fractured wrist to throb in agony. The sharp edges of the plastic tie shaved into the cast, slicing a thin layer and thinning its bulk.

The hold loosened.

The pain increased.

Sam ignored it.

'Let her go.'

Sam's words carried an empty threat, drawing a smirk from Vasquez. Nonchalantly, Vasquez lit a match and cupped his hand, lifting it to his cigar before waving it into extinction. As the thick, grey smoke filled the atmosphere, he shook his matches at Sam before nodding to Edinson. A meaty right hook sent Sam back into the chair, reminding him of the hopeless situation before him.

'You are a strong man, Mr Cooper.' Vasquez glanced back at Alex. 'But every man is weak when it comes to a woman. Now, tell me who you really are and what the fuck you're doing here, or I'll put a bullet in this bitch's skull.'

Alex gasped in fear, shooting another terrified glance at Sam. There was no comfort he could offer her, and Sam sighed. All he'd wanted was to make good on one promise he'd made her. That was all.

Keep his word this one last time and the fight was over.

The truth of Project Hailstorm.

The downfall of Blackridge.

All of it had meant that the deaths of Theo, Marsden, and Mac had not been in vain. Even the death of Helal Miah, which hung heavy on his conscience, wasn't for nothing. The unfortunate journalist may have lost his life, but in exposing Blackridge for what it truly was, he helped save thousands more.

Sam's fight was over.

But now, with Alex's life hanging by the thinnest of threads, he could feel that pure, visceral rage that had spawned his war on crime ebbing through his veins.

His muscles tightened.

'My name is Sam Pope,' he blurted out, not taking his eyes off Alex. 'I've killed a lot of people for a lot less. Now I made that woman a promise, one I intend to keep. So, either you let us go, or mark my words, I will burn everything you have to the ground.'

Sam turned to face Vasquez as he spoke his final warning, his eyes locking onto the drug lord's gaze like a shark smelling blood. Unperturbed, Vasquez took two confident puffs on his cigar and let the smoke pour from his mouth. The silence hung in the room thicker than the grey fog, before Vasquez adjusted the lapels of his jacket and nodded to Edinson.

Another rocket of a right fist launched at Sam, this time connecting in the centre of his solid abdomen, driving the air from his body and causing him to slump forward. With Sam gasping for air, Vasquez took a few more steps towards him before squatting down.

The smell of the cigar was overpowering.

'Nobody threatens me.' Vasquez spoke calmly.

'Nobody. Now she, she will live. We need her. But you, my friend, you are just in the way.'

Vasquez stood once more. Sam, trying to regulate his breathing, stared at the dirty concrete floor and the man's expensive shoes. The door opened to the room and Raul strode in, flanked by two more men. Vasquez didn't know their names. He didn't need to.

All that mattered was that they knew his.

Alex watched on, tears flooding down her cheeks as Sam struggled to sit back straight. Edinson, with his hulking frame looming over him, shoved him back, allowing Sam one final glance at Alex before she was ushered away. With the air slowly refilling his lungs, Sam watched helplessly as she disappeared into the shadows.

They needed her?

What the hell was going on?

With his mind racing, Sam tried to direct it through the memories of his time in America. Throughout his career and his assault on organised crime, he'd trusted his instincts.

His training.

There was never a situation where he hadn't memorised his surroundings or committed as many details as possible into his memory bank.

He had to be missing something.

As he frantically shuffled through the details he'd collected, his trail of thought was cut off by the clear instruction he heard behind him.

'Kill him.'

Vasquez had given the order, and Sam struggled against his restraints, knowing that if this was the end, he would at least deny them the satisfaction of a bargaining plea. As footsteps approached behind him, he could hear the familiar sound of a gun being removed from a holster.

The footsteps stopped.

The cold steel of the gun pressed against his head.

Sam closed his eyes.

He saw Jamie. His beautiful boy, smiling and giggling.

Vasquez's voice interrupted his final goodbye.

'Not here, Raul.' The irritation clear in his voice. 'Take him back to Dillon. Make his death a problem for the Riders. It will make tomorrow easier.'

Sam tried his best to piece together what was happening, when he noticed the hammer like fist entering his periphery. Before he could even register Edinson's strike, the fist connected with the side of his face, and it was all he could remember before everything went blurry, and then to black.

CHAPTER TWENTY

Losing someone in the line of duty was always a bitter pill to swallow. As a former marine, Joe Alan had never expected to go into battle with the expectancy to return. It was part of his training, knowing he would likely stare death in the face and if it was his time, then he would accept it with the nobility the crest that was tattooed to his arm deserved.

But losing a comrade.

A friend.

It always hurt and was a timely reminder to Alan just how deadly the games they played ultimately were.

By the time he'd come to on the cool concrete of the Marion streets, the place was already swarming with cops. A few paramedics had been attending to him, but he shook them off, demanding the officers tell him the whereabouts of his partner.

The blank faces and shrugs he received had caused his already throbbing skull to ache further. As he rushed to the overturned wreckage of Sinclair's van, he pushed the few attending officers aside. He already knew he would find nothing, but with his brain rattled from the clubbing blow from Sykes, Alan was running on autopilot.

A few officers tried to ask him for further information, but eventually, he walked to his car and dropped into the driver's seat. The rear window lay in shards across the concrete and Alan started the engine and headed back to the sheriff's office on West Hampton Street in Dillon.

As he arrived, the few deputies on duty turned in shock. With a cold compress pressed to the side of his skull, and Sinclair's blood splattered across his shirt, Alan looked like he'd been in the wars.

When he stumbled into the office where he and Sinclair had met upon their arrival, he realised he was heading into another.

Sheriff David Cobb was staring at their white board, his eyes fixed on the multitude of photographs, maps, and statements that adorned it. A shrine to their hard work, all of it connected with crudely drawn arrows.

'You shouldn't be in here,' Alan mumbled, heading straight for the side cabinet, which was topped with a jug of water.

'You know I said the same damn thing to your boss when he told me you boys were coming here.' Cobb didn't turn, but the anger laced within his tone was clear. 'Told him we didn't need anythin' cleaned up by the DEA.'

As Cobb spat the initials as if they were a curse word, Alan popped two painkillers from the orange plastic bottle and downed them with a cup of water.

'This room has been repurposed as a DEA office. So please, Sheriff Cobb. I'd like you to leave.'

'Likewise.'

Cobb turned, unfolding his meaty arms and taking a step towards Alan. In his late fifties, Cobb had served his hometown with pride for over thirty years. Time hadn't been kind to the man. Reducing his hair to a thin, grey

179

crescent around the side of his skull and expanding his gut until it pulled his shirt tight.

He drew his jaw tight, his thick, grey moustache lying across his upper lip like a slug.

'Tough shit,' Alan said through gritted teeth, trying to mask the pain. Cobb could sense the vulnerability and took another step closer.

'This is a nice town, son. The people here are happy and there is next to no crime. Hell, me and the boys often wonder why the hell we're even needed. When Wyatt came here with the Riders, we were nervous at first. Of course we were. This little town didn't need that kind of business. But Wyatt and the Riders, they ain't no trouble. Sure, they might do a little deal here or there, but they keep it off our streets. That's the deal. Dillon may be their home, but they don't do no business here. In fact, them being here has caused a decline in all crime and a major boost for tourism. A lot of folk who come to see Charlotte, they make their way here just to catch a glimpse at one of those boys riding a motorcycle.' Cobb arrogantly chuckled. 'Hell, my granddaughter says she wants to marry a Rider when she grows up. So having you and your boss here, trying to fuck up the good thing we got going on, it's pissed a few people off. Now, I've been accommodating up till this point, but I think in light of what's happened, it might be best for you to be on your way.'

Alan finished the rest of his water and then calmly put the glass on the table. Slowly, he eased out of his jacket. Cobb's eyes widened in horror at the amount of blood on Alan's shirt as he turned to him. Without speaking a word, Alan unbuttoned the shirt, the bloodstain having also seeped through to the white vest he wore beneath. Without saying a word, he tossed the bloodstained rag at Cobb, who caught it and then grimaced.

'That there, that's my boss's blood,' Alan spat angrily.

'He died tonight. Shot in the stomach by Eddie Sykes. The name ring any bells?'

Cobb put the shirt on the table and tried to recompose himself.

'Yes, Sykes can be volatile, but I don't think…'

'Think what?' Alan strode forward, going nose to nose with the burly sheriff. The power dynamic had shifted, and Alan noticed the slight flinch in the man's movement. Despite his best efforts, Cobb had shown his fear. While he'd done a somewhat admirable job as Sherriff over the years, he paled in stature to the ex-marine before him. 'It doesn't matter what you think, or how much *"good"* the Riders have done for this town. They have built a drug empire worth millions. They have sold drugs throughout this state and many others, wrecking thousands of lives and ending just as many. And tonight, Sykes put a bullet in my friend. Not just my boss, my friend. A good man, who had dedicated everything to bring Wyatt, Sykes, and the whole fucking empire down. And I'm going to honour his work, and you're going to get the fuck out of my face and out of my office.'

Cobb tried his best to hold Alan's piercing stare, but he broke quickly. Swallowing to mask his fear, Cobb shot a few glances around the room before taking three steps towards the door. Keen to try to assert what little authority he thought he still had, he grabbed his belt with both hands, readjusting it and pulling his back straight.

'Nothing like this ever happened before you both showed up.' Cobb reached out and yanked open the door. 'If you go looking for trouble and knock on the Devil's door, then you have to expect him to answer.'

Seething, Alan took a step towards Cobb.

'Trust me, the Riders will meet the Devil soon enough.'

Cobb twitched his upper lip and stepped out of the office, slamming the door behind him. The loud bang of the wood caused Alan to wince in pain, reaching a hand to the throbbing cut on his head. Alone in the office, he turned to the whiteboard, staring at all the evidence and the entire case he and Sinclair had been working on. As he did, he knew he should have been wondering about Sinclair's final moments, or where the hell Sykes had taken his body.

He should have been concerned about Sam and Alex, who had clearly been involved in a heavy car accident and were nowhere to be found.

But he didn't.

All he wondered, as he stared at the board, was why didn't Sykes shoot him as well?

———

Sykes knew it was a dangerous game he was playing.

As he rolled his motorcycle to a stop outside his apartment block, he took a moment to light a cigarette and take in the calming nicotine. With each inhale, he felt his nerves begin to dissipate, finding larger ebbs of conviction in the path he'd taken. Despite balancing delicately on the edge of Wyatt's trust threshold, Sykes knew that within twenty-four hours, none of that would matter anymore.

He wouldn't stroll into the Pit with Wyatt's severed head as a trophy, but he would command a similar respect.

While a large portion of the Riders' loyalty was towards Wyatt, the majority was with the badge.

With the code.

The Riders were a way of life, and for many of the riffraff who begged and pleaded at the bar to wear the patch, the belief in that badge would amplify with Wyatt gone.

Sykes felt nothing at the notion of betrayal.

Watching his own brethren murdered for his own gain was an unfortunate step on his way to the throne.

Besides, he'd caused the death of his own men before, and he'd never looked back.

As he took his final puff on the cigarette, he casually flicked the butt into the ether and dismounted his hog, adjusting the plump sports bag that was tied around his waist, ensuring nothing covered the proud Death Rider patch that was emblazoned on his vest. His twisted testicle still ached, and he cursed the idea of going to hospital to admit his emasculation by Wyatt. He headed upstairs, entered his apartment, and went straight to the fridge. As he pulled the cap off the beer and took a swig, Sykes stared at the large bag he'd dumped on the table.

It was a lot of money, enough to get away from everything and completely disappear. But he would forever be looking over his shoulder, and a life of fear is not something he could tolerate.

Besides, the moment he looked Wyatt dead in the eyes and told him his run was over would be worth more than the million dollars he'd stolen from the deal.

'Busy night?'

Wyatt's voice cut through the darkness of Sykes's apartment, startling the big man and causing him to knock into a chair.

'Jesus,' Sykes uttered. 'Bit dramatic, don't you think?'

Wyatt flicked on the table lamp beside his chair, illuminating himself and half the room in its glow. The open-plan kitchen, which backed onto the living room, was still bathed in shadows and Sykes stood his ground in the darkness. His eyes flashed to the bag.

'What's in the bag?' Wyatt asked sternly, his hands resting on his knees.

'Nothing.'

Wyatt slapped a little tune on his jeans and then stood

up, slowly walking around the sofa towards the table. Sykes sipped his beer, working through every anger management technique that had been fed to him over the years.

'See, Eddie. A little bird told me that someone hit the Vasquez drug deal down in Marion tonight. Two people were killed, one of them rumoured to be old Terry Sinclair. You know, that weasely bastard who keeps poking his nose in our business.'

'Is that so?' Sykes shrugged, taking another sip of his beer.

'It is indeed.' Wyatt approached the table, resting his hands on the back of one of the chairs. 'Mason arrived earlier today, looking for that son of a bitch Cooper, but he got on to our boys in the sheriff's department and they told him that no money was found at the scene. Isn't that strange?'

'Not really.' Sykes finished his beer and placed the bottle down on the wooden tabletop with a bang. 'You wouldn't hit a drop and leave empty-handed.'

'No, you wouldn't.' Wyatt nodded at the bag. 'So, what's that?'

'Fuck off, Trent,' Sykes spat. 'If you've come here to try to put a knife to my nuts again, you better be ready to do it properly this time.'

'Oh, I am,' Wyatt calmly responded, the fury building slowly in his voice. 'What's in the bag?'

'My fucking dirty laundry.' Sykes felt his fist clenching. 'Now get out of my flat, Trent, or…'

'Or what?' Wyatt's voice rose with venom, his eyes wide with anger. 'We go back a long way, Eddie. A fucking long way. When I found you, you were shaking down junkies to pay pimps for a sloppy back-alley blowjob. I gave you a fucking life you only ever dreamed of, and all I asked was for you to be loyal. No, to be honest with me. We've worked too hard for too long to start fucking up and hitting deals. Vasquez is a problem, and if you decided to strike first, he's going to be a hell of a lot more than that.'

'Whatever.' Sykes turned away from Wyatt, his hand slyly edging towards the bottle.

'And the shit you'll bring down on us from the DEA.' Wyatt stepped forward and wrapped his hand around Sykes's shoulder. 'Look at me when I'm talking to…'

The bottle struck Wyatt square in the temple, the glass shattering and slicing his face as he stumbled sideways, colliding with the kitchen counter before hitting the floor. With the bottle nothing more than a jagged shard, Sykes resisted the temptation to slash the man's throat.

Not like this.

The Riders could never know of the part he would play in Wyatt's death.

The only role he would play would be the avenging angel.

'Fuck you, Trent,' Sykes stammered, surprised by the sadness of his actions. For all his ambition, Sykes had been grateful to Wyatt until the gratitude had transformed to jealousy. 'If only you would have listened. Had grown a fucking pair and fought back, this would never have happened.'

Woozily, Wyatt tried to sit up, blinking the blood from his eye, and trying his best to gather his marbles.

'Wh-wh-what are you doing?' He eventually managed, pawing at the unit to try to pull himself up. Sykes lazily lifted his boot and pressed it against Wyatt's shoulder, pushing him back onto the glass-covered kitchen tiles. The glass crunched under the leather of Wyatt's jacket. Sykes tossed the glass shard across the room and then stood over Wyatt, who glared up at him with glazed eyes.

'You're right, Trent. There is a war coming. But you're wrong on one thing. I'm not the guy who caused it. I'm the guy who will end it.'

As he'd done so many times under Wyatt's command, Sykes threw a thunderous right hand downward, crushing his fist into Wyatt's skull and knocking him out cold. Wyatt's head rolled limply to the side, and Sykes stood staring down at his leader. Hatred and guilt danced through his mind, and he then calmly returned to the fridge and pulled out another beer.

As he sipped it, he kept one eye on Wyatt's motionless body. He pulled out his phone and keyed a message, which he sent to an anonymous contact, hoping they would be awake, even at such an ungodly time of the morning.

Got the money. Change of plan got Wyatt also. Still on for this afternoon?

Sykes took a few more anxious sips, and then headed to his storage cupboard for some cable ties. As he returned with them, his phone buzzed.

Good work.

With a cruel smile, Sykes rolled Wyatt over, bound his wrists and ankles together, and then toasted his fallen friend, and drank to his future as the leader of the Death Riders.

CHAPTER TWENTY-ONE

As the blurring around his vision began to fade, Sam looked out of the window and recognised the town of Dillon in the distance. Blinking to try to recalibrate his sight, he gritted his teeth at the sharp pain in his skull, while his jaw ached from its role as Edinson's punch bag.

He felt like shit.

But his situation was even worse.

With his hands still bound behind his back, he looked to the front of the Range Rover, where two of his captors were sitting. The driver, a plump man with tattooed forearms, stared straight ahead, his eyes focused on the road. The one in the passenger seat was an enforcer, there to make sure everything went to plan. The car hit a pothole, and everyone shook, and Sam rocked backwards onto his cast, the pain as fresh as the moment it had been snapped. Sam knew that from the moment he'd begun his fight back against the world of crime, he'd actively looked for trouble. Now, with his arm shattered by the Riders and being driven to his execution by Vasquez's men, he began to wonder if perhaps he was simply a magnet for it.

'He wakes.'

The heavy Mexican accent belonged to Raul, who sat a few feet from him against the other window in the back of the vehicle. Built in the mould of Vasquez, Raul wore a nice three-piece suit with an open collar, and his jet-black hair was heavy with product. He flashed Sam a pearly white grin, then mockingly waved the Glock 17 in his hand, a clear signal for Sam to stay still.

'Where's Alex?' Sam asked, looking back out of the window.

'She is safe.'

'Where're we going?'

'You, my friend, are going to the afterlife.' Raul chuckled. Sam nodded, trying to keep his body as still as possible. Unbeknownst to his captors, the cable tie binding his hand together had cut into the top layer of his cast. As Sam carefully lifted his left shoulder, he could feel it sliding through the material, slicing its way up the cast.

'What was Sykes doing at the drop?' Sam asked, locking his eyes on Raul and doing his best to conceal his shoulder movement.

'It is of no concern to you now.' Raul offered little, the gun resting casually on his lap. Sam flashed a glance at it. Raul's finger was not on the trigger.

Confidence or arrogance, Sam didn't care.

As he felt the cable tie slide over his fingers, he knew he would have one chance of escape. Ever since he had felt the cable begin to slice into the cast, Sam had been systematically grating the cast against the sharp plastic. In the few hours since, he had whittled enough of it away to feel the cable sliding down towards his fingers. With the cast removing the dip of his wrist, he found, with considerable discomfort, he had been able to manoeuvre his arm to the verge of freedom.

Now, he had to wait.

Pick the perfect moment.

Or he'd be killed.

'And Vasquez? Did he know?'

'You ask a lot of questions for a dead man.'

'I'm not dead yet.' Sam smiled, and after a few moments of confusion, Raul began to chuckle. The driver turned off the I-95 at the sign for Dillon, and the car cruised down the streets towards the town. The passenger, who had been silent the entire time, pointed to an old, abandoned truck stop and gave an order in Spanish.

'This will do,' Raul agreed, nodding to the rear-view mirror. Sam sat patiently as they rolled down the dirt road towards the abandoned building, the windows covered in graffiti-covered boards. Whatever sign which had proudly adorned the premises was gone, with the wiring hanging loosely from its fixtures.

The driver rounded the building, heading for the spot intended for Sam's grave. If they killed him this close to Dillon, the sheriff's department or cops would need to investigate and given the number of people who witnessed his interactions with the Riders, it wouldn't take them long to connect the dots to them.

Although his blood wouldn't be on their hands, his death would be pinned to them.

The car slowed almost to a stop, and Sam knew his window of opportunity, however small, was near. The driver killed the engine and the henchman in the passenger seat turned to Sam, a gun pointed directly at his head.

'Not in the car,' Raul yelled, raising his hand in disbelief. The man sighed and threw open his door, the humidity flooding into the vehicle and going to war with the air conditioning. As the henchman stomped around the car, Raul lifted the gun at Sam cockily.

'No hard feelings.'

As Sam heard the henchmen's hand grip the handle of his door, he launched into action. Revealing his hands were free, Sam shot them both up, snapping his grip onto Raul's wrist like a coiled snake. The element of surprise gave him a matter of seconds, and as expected, Raul squeezed the trigger in panic.

Sam had shifted Raul's aim to the window, and the Glock exploded with deadly intent, sending a bullet through the glass pane and blasting the henchmen in the chest. As the glass shattered over the man's fallen body, Sam pulled Raul in and drove his forehead into his face with as much force as he could muster. As his skull collided with Raul's nose, he could feel the cartilage implode, and a jet of warm blood splattered against him.

Raul was unconscious as he slumped back against the door of the car, and Sam whipped around, gun in hand, and pressed it against the driver's skull as he tried to intervene.

'Get out of the car,' Sam ordered. 'Slowly.'

The driver held his hands up in surrender and then fumbled back to the door. Sam stepped out at the same time as he did, and before the driver was fully out of the vehicle, Sam clubbed him with the butt of the pistol. The blow sent the driver sprawling next to his fallen passenger, who had both hands pressed against his chest, trying to stem the flow of blood that was pumping from his bullet wound. With the gun expertly held in his hands, Sam ducked his head into the driver's side of the car, clocking the keys still in the ignition. Ensuring the two men on the ground posed little threat, Sam kicked the handgun away from the bleeding henchman and then marched around the vehicle to the other door and heaved it open, allowing Raul's limp body to crumpled out and crash onto the dusty ground below. Sam slammed the door shut, returned to the driver's seat, and dropped in. The henchman tried to curse him, but with blood now dribbling from his mouth, Sam knew the man would be dead in moments.

He felt nothing.

All he knew now was that he needed to find Alex.

Find her and bring her back.

But he couldn't do it alone.

Sam slammed the door shut, threw the car into reverse, and navigated his way back around the building. He yanked the wheel and as the car skidded, he slipped it into first and seamlessly shot forward, shifting through the gears as he raced back to the road to Dillon. At some point, Raul would regain consciousness, but Sam was comfortable that he had enough time to get to his destination. As far as Vasquez was concerned, Sam would already be dead, and whatever the hell was going on would continue uninterrupted.

Sam would be happy to prove him wrong.

As he pulled into the car park of the sheriff's office, he could see a number of deputies rush to the window. In a sleepy town like Dillon, where the Riders were the law, they weren't used to the mayhem Sam had caused in the few days he'd spent there. A couple of them were already outside, hands to their holsters as Sam killed the engine and stepped out. The blood and bruising that stained his face put them on high alert, and they demanded he get on the ground.

Sam held his hands up in surrender, obliging as he got onto his knees.

A burly man with a moustache, along with a shiny sheriff's badge, stepped out of the office, trying his best to look in charge.

'Who the hell are you?' Sheriff Cobb demanded.

'He's here to see me.'

Cobb looked over his shoulder at Special Agent Alan, who strode out of the office with the confident swagger of a man in true command. Despite the scowl on Cobb's face, he ordered his men down, his deputies falling in line behind him as they scuttled back into their office. Alan approached Sam, offering him a hand up, which Sam gratefully accepted.

'You look like shit for a dead man.' Alan smirked.

'Likewise.'

'What the fuck happened?' Alan asked, scanning the surrounding streets. 'Where's Alex?'

'I don't know. But right now, I need two things. One, I need your help.'

Alan nodded.

'What else?'

'I need a cup of tea.'

Alan chuckled and shook his head, offering Sam his arm as support as they headed into the station. Sam took it, his body aching under the duress of the car accident and punishment Edinson had happily doled out. Despite their rocky start, whatever play was in motion had brought Alan and Sam together, and with Alan's vengeance and Sam's desperation to rescue Alex at the forefront of their next move, they needed each other.

They needed to figure out what was going on.

And they needed to know fast.

————

"Fuck!"

The scream of fury was followed by the sound of a strike, the unmistakable crack of a punch being thrown. Alex tightened her body in fear as outside the room she was being held in, she could feel Vasquez's rage.

It had been an hour since she'd last seen Sam, watching in pained terror as she was hauled from the room where they'd held him.

Had beaten him.

But as she heard the raised voices, she couldn't help but feel a small smirk fall across her lips.

Whatever they'd planned to do with Sam had failed.

She was sure of it.

She'd witnessed it first-hand all those months ago. First, in the underground bunker when Wallace had lured Sam into a trap. Sam had fought back; harder than any force she could imagine. During the scuffle she'd been shot, the scar still fresh across her thigh, but she'd watched as Sam engaged Blackridge's top mercenary, Buck, in a fight to the death.

Then months later, when she'd been used as bait to lure Sam out in the streets of Naples, Sam had fought back again.

Four members of Blackridge were left dead.

Whoever or whatever they threw at Sam, Alex was sure he could handle it.

He was built to survive.

Made for war.

The door to her room slammed open, and an irate Vasquez stepped in, followed by the scrawny, tattooed henchman who had leered at her since her incarceration. Whatever intentions sat behind his eyes; she was sure they were deeply troubling. Behind them, she could see another man dressed in a nice suit. Only his shirt was stained with blood. Judging from the bloody rag he held to his nose and the bruising around his nose, the blood belonged to him.

Vasquez stomped towards Alex; his eyes wide with anger.

'Your friend. Who is he?'

'What do you mean?'

The back of Vasquez's hand connected with Alex's cheek with such a velocity, it sent her sprawling off her chair. The pain was instant and caused her eyes to water.

'Sam Pope,' Vasquez spat. 'You tell me now, or I'll let Emilio have his way with you.'

Alex looked up at the vulgar man, who made his intention noticeably clear by grabbing his crotch. She pushed herself back up to her chair, collected the saliva in her mouth, and spat it out onto the floor.

'You have the Internet, right?' Alex smirked. 'Look him up.'

Vasquez ran his hand across his mouth, wiping away the froth that had grown with rage. Agitated, he pulled out his phone and tapped the screen. As the search returned its results, Alex smiled as Vasquez's eyes flickered with worry. It was only a split second, and despite his best efforts to hide it, he knew Alex had seen.

'Yeah. You boys are in trouble.'

'Shut up, you bitch,' Vasquez snapped. He turned to the man with the broken nose. 'We progress as before. If Pope shows up, I want you to put a bullet in his head. Do you hear me, Raul?'

Vasquez berated his right-hand man in Spanish. Although Alex didn't understand, she could infer that it wasn't a compliment. Vasquez turned and stomped from the room, closely followed by Raul who followed like an obedient puppy. Emilio lingered for a few more moments, blowing Alex a kiss, which sent a shiver down her spine. A shadow filled the room, and the hulking presence of Edinson filled the doorway. His eyes locked on the scrawny man.

Although Edinson didn't speak, the message was clear.

Emilio lowered his head, scuttling to the door and uneasily sliding around Edinson who made a point of standing in his way.

Once the man had got by, Edinson shot a final glance at Alex before slamming the door shut. Alex realised she was holding her breath and let out a deep sigh.

She'd made poor decisions her whole life. Most of them for the right reasons, but none that had ever landed her in as much peril as she was in now. Locked in an unknown location, a captive for a violent drug gang.

The threat of sexual assault hung heavy in the air.

The promise of death, almost an inevitability.

But instead of crying and giving up hope, she held onto the thought of her brother and sister. The idea of holding them close once more, this whole nightmare behind her.

Sam was still out there.

The man was built for survival. She had seen it first-hand, and until they threw his dead body in front of her, she knew he was still fighting.

Which meant there was a chance.

And that was enough.

———

Sam sipped the remnants of his tea and didn't even try to hide his disdain. For all the wonderful cups of coffee he'd sampled in the States, he'd never once been handed a nice cup of tea. Alan chuckled as he watched Sam gingerly put the mug down.

'That good, huh?'

'Lovely,' Sam lied.

'So, you have no idea where they're holding her?' Alan asked, leaning forward in his chair, his fingers pressed together.

'No. But whatever is happening is happening today.' Sam stretched out the ache in his spine. 'Sinclair really said nothing to you? This whole time.'

'Nothing.' Alan sat back, dejected. The mention of his former partner clearly hurt. 'I didn't even know Alex was his source.'

Sam pushed himself out of his chair and stepped to the window, his mind racing. None of it made sense.

None of it.

It was all too convenient.

Sinclair had planted Alex in the High Five, then within two weeks, Sykes insisted she try out at the Pit. He and Alan had mulled it over between them while Sam had persevered with his cup of tea. Alex had made it clear that Sykes had never approached her, never pursued a romantic tryst. Sam ran his hand through his hair, a feeling of helplessness coursing through him like a current.

Alex was out there somewhere.

Something big was about to go down.

And they had nothing.

'It just doesn't make sense,' Sam muttered through gritted teeth. 'All of this happens, and we have nothing. What are we not seeing?'

Before Alan could answer, a gentle knock echoed from the door and one of the secretaries entered. She smiled sheepishly at both men before handing Alan a file.

Alan flicked it open, thumbed some of the sheets of paper before tossing it onto the table in annoyance.

'Fuck.' He quickly turned and nodded his thanks to the secretary as she shut the door.

'What's that?'

'I asked Debbie to run your descriptions through the database of the guys you left up at the truck stop.' Alan shook his head and slumped forward. 'No matches.'

Alan's words jolted Sam awake, as if he'd just stepped on a nail.

'What did you just say?'

'The descriptions you gave us. Nothing. I mean, it was pretty vague.'

'No, after that.' Sam was already heading over to the messy table that displayed Sinclair's abundance of notes.

'No matches?'

Alan watched in confusion as Sam began shuffling through the paperwork. As he became more frantic, Sam started pulling out the drawers, tipping them onto the floor, their contents spilling in every direction. After the second drawer hit the ground, Sam's eyes lit up.

'Sam, what the fuck are you doing?'

As he bent down, Sam connected the dots. It had been staring him in the face the entire time.

Why Sinclair had kept Alex a secret from Alan.

How a trained marine like Sykes had shot twice at Sam and missed completely.

And why Sykes hadn't killed Alan.

He turned to Alan and tossed the small box of matches to him. Alan caught them, then looked at Sam in confusion.

'Do you still have the shirt you wore from last night?' Sam asked, his voice full of clarity. 'The one with Sinclair's blood on it.'

'Yeah.' Alan shrugged. 'Why?'

'You need someone to run a DNA check.'

Alan frowned, shaking his head as if banishing some cobwebs.

'I don't get where you're going with this.'

'Those matches. Where is that bar?'

Alan looked at the box. The match box was emblazoned with the logo of the Tiempo de Salsa bar.

'No idea.' Alan stared at Sam in confusion. 'Why?'

Sam's age-old habit of committing the smallest details to memory was suddenly his saving grace.

Sam reached over to the chair and lifted his blood and dust covered jacket and began to ease himself into it. Alan stood and followed suit, watching with interest as Sam lifted the Glock 17 he'd taken from Raul and tucked it into the back of his jeans. Compared to the cocky friend that

Sam had appeared to be a couple of nights ago, Alan was finally seeing the real Sam Pope.

A soldier.

A dangerous force who never knew when to quit.

A man of his word.

As Sam pulled open the door to the office, he looked back at Alan, his face as calm as his words were purposeful.

'Because Vasquez and Sykes had the same box.'

Sam marched through the door, heading for the exit. The dots connected in Alan's mind and he quickly followed, whipping the keys from his pocket as the two of them headed to his car ready to bring this all to an end.

CHAPTER TWENTY-TWO

No matter how hard he puffed on his cigarette, the nicotine refused to calm Sykes's nerves.

He hadn't slept since he'd sent the text message and had gone to work to ensure Wyatt was bound and gagged before hauling him out of the apartment, dumping him in the boot of the truck that he'd hired the day before. Fortunately for Sykes, the town of Dillon wasn't too active in the early hours of the morning, meaning he could move a motionless body without the fear of being spotted. Besides, the alleyway provided enough cover and there wasn't any CCTV monitoring his moves. The plan had always been to blindside his boss, but not this soon. He had almost an entire day before the meet, and the original plan was to meet at the Tiempo de Salsa to "clear the air".

Wyatt was to come alone. Based on the promise that Sykes would hand back his vest and drive off into the sunset.

That would have been enough bait for Wyatt to drop his guard, allowing Vasquez's men to move in.

But now, with a whole day to cover-up what had happened, Sykes was sweating. Knowing that Mason, a man who was dangerously loyal to Wyatt, was now at the Pit, things could get messy.

Sykes had spent the entire morning cleaning the apartment, disposing of every last shard of glass, cleansing the room of all evidence of his treachery.

It would all be worth it.

With Wyatt out of the way, and the Riders blamed for the raid on Vasquez's drop, a war would be declared. Sykes would take control of the Riders, nominate those he deemed feeble enough to be sacrificed to the charade, and eventually, when the dust settled, the others would fall in line.

Combined with Vasquez, the Riders would be *the* dominant drug empire in America, and when the time was right, Sykes would remove Vasquez from the equation.

Money.

Power.

Fear.

All the things Sykes craved were in touching distance, and all he had to do now was act natural.

After numerous cups of coffee and a long shower, Sykes decked himself proudly in his leather vest and jeans, his bandana pulled tightly to his skull and rumbled through the streets of Dillon to the Pit, the intimidating growl of his engine disturbing the peaceful town. As he dismounted his bike, he winced at the dull, aching numbness in his groin. He gritted his teeth and marched in, seeing Mason standing at the bar in conversation with another Rider. Upon seeing Sykes, Mason turned, agitation across his world-weary face.

'Jesus, Eddie. You look like crap.'

'You don't look great either, buddy.' Sykes pointed at the purple swelling that adorned Mason's head. 'Heard you got a pasting.'

Mason scowled, sizing up to Sykes, and as the only

member of the Riders who matched Sykes for size, a murmur of excitement spread through the few Riders in the bar. Donnie, who had accompanied Mason to Dillon watched in fascination, his face heavily plastered up from being introduced to the solid oak bar back in New York. Jay had stayed behind, his shattered knee rendering him useless for the next few months.

Sykes took a second to admire Cooper's handiwork, glad that the man had been taken care of by Vasquez.

'It seems you already dished out the receipt on my behalf,' Mason growled. 'I don't need you fighting for me.'

'Could have fooled me.' Sykes raised his finger to the young lady behind the bar, signalling for a late morning drink. 'So, where's Trent?'

Mason sighed and turned to the bar, resting his meaty forearms on the wood. For all intents and purposes, he'd bought Sykes's lie.

'No idea.' Mason shook his head. 'Few of the guys are worried. Unlike the boss to not show up. Especially with the cops asking questions.'

'What questions?' Sykes raised his eyebrows, lifting the fresh beer to his lips. 'About the shit down in Marion?'

'You heard about that?'

'A little.' Sykes shrugged. 'I did a little too much last night. Am a bit hazy today.'

Mason regarded Sykes with a quizzical eyebrow and then lifted his own beer.

'You look like you've been dragged through a bush backwards.' Mason gulped almost half the bottle in one. 'Maybe lay off the dust, eh?'

'Don't tell me what to do. That's not your place.'

A few of the other Riders turned away, not wanting to be caught staring at the growing tension between the more senior members. Mason chuckled.

'That's always been your problem, Eddie. Always

worried about how close your seat is to Trent. I bet you were happy as a pig in shit when I went to New York.' Mason flashed a glance to Sykes, who shrugged his agreement. 'But here's the kicker. I ain't here to nail that poncey little British bastard. Trent called me back because he thinks you're cooking something on the side. Man to man, I don't think you've got the balls for it. But seeing as how I trust Wyatt's judgment way more than I trust yours, I'm going to give you an hour to come up with a better excuse than you were high as a kite last night.'

Sykes slammed his beer down and leant in close, his lips a mere inch from Mason's ear.

'I'd be very careful if I were you.' Sykes warned, his words laced with imminent threat. '*Very* careful.'

Sykes downed the last of his beer and then gave Mason one final sneer before purposefully bumping him with his shoulder. As he strode past, Mason reached out, grabbing at Sykes, who shoved him away.

'I swear, Eddie, if I find out you've gone behind our backs, I won't wait for Trent to give me the order.'

'Yes, you will. You all will.' Sykes looked around the bar, taking his time to look everyone in the eye. 'No one around here has the stones to fight anymore. Everyone is too worried about their spot. When the change comes, get ready to fucking earn it.'

With that, Sykes stomped to the door, pushing his way past two members who were entering and cursing them as he did. As he flung his leg over the seat of his bike, he clenched his fists in frustration.

The whole intention was to throw them off his scent, to show his face and act like he was as concerned as they were. Knowing that Mason had been invited by Wyatt himself had triggered his temper, the one weakness that Wyatt had told Sykes would be his downfall.

The constant need to be superior.

Enraged, Sykes shot one final look back to the door where Mason stood, his arms folded across his leather vest and his eyes burning a hole through Sykes. The engine roared loudly, and Sykes pulled away onto the street.

They would be looking for Wyatt.

Soon they would knock on his door.

But it wouldn't matter.

Sykes would be gone, delivering the million dollars as a peace offering to Vasquez and Wyatt to his grave. That was the plan. At first, Sykes had been sceptical, but the more it had been laid out the easier it became.

Stage a Rider's hit on Vasquez's deal, giving Vasquez a valid reason to go to war with the Riders. Then, with Vasquez onside, Sykes would deliver him his money and Wyatt.

Vasquez would kill Wyatt.

Sykes would ascend to the throne.

A new partnership forged.

Then he would return, fit his hand snugly into his iron glove, and teach every single person who dared call themselves a Rider, a lesson in respect.

If they didn't offer it, then he would settle for fear.

Either way, Sykes was adamant that Mason would be used as the example of what happened when any of them stepped out of line.

Mason's loyalty would never be earned.

It would always remain with a dead man.

Sykes would be happy to reacquaint them.

———

Sam pressed his hands against the glass window, looking into the closed premises. Above the door where he stood, Tiempo de Salsa was nailed to the building in large, white letters, a playful font that promised its patrons a good time.

The outside was surrounded by a few benches and tables, all of them bolted to the ground.

A tiki bar was situated on the far end of the courtyard, the shutter down and the menu blank.

'Anything?' Alan asked, looking around the side of the building. Besides a few more benches, there was nothing but a tarmacked car park. Beyond that, a large, abandoned timber mill stood. A ghostly relic from a bygone era, which was previously the life source of the town.

Lake View had undergone the same gentrification as Dillon over the last few decades, moving away from the timber production that had previously funded most of the residences. Nowadays, the town was filled with quaint eateries, a few bars and a number of independent businesses. Like Dillon, it was a peaceful town. Although not the base of the Riders, as with Marion and the other towns that littered South Carolina, their presence was intense, and Sam wondered when the last time the Tiempo de Salsa even had a customer.

'No sign of anything.' Sam pulled away from the window and scouted the other side of the building.

Like Alan, he was greeted by the ghastly sight of the old factory, shielded by the large, metal sheets that comprised its fence. A condemned sign was tacked to the metal, desecrated by countless squiggles of graffiti. The humidity was high, and Sam had left his jacket in Alan's car, which they'd parked back in town before covering the half mile on foot.

Considering the ghostly surroundings, any hint of their approach would have been seen instantly, and Sam had already witnessed first-hand the punishment they would deal out.

'Maybe you were wrong?' Alan suggested, walking back to Sam, his white shirt sticky with sweat.

'Maybe.' Sam agreed, looking around for any hint of

life. 'But if you wanted to do some business out of anyone's line of sight…'

'This place is fucking perfect.'

Sam chuckled. Whether it was the lack of sleep or the severe reliance on pain killers, both men began laughing. The strangest things could build the strongest bonds, and the two ex-soldiers, from different sides of the law, had found that reason among an escalating drug war.

Nothing in Sam's life surprised him, but this certainly came close.

Alan's phone beeped, and he slid his hand around the gun fastened to his hip and slid the device from his pocket. He looked at the screen and shook his head. His teeth clenched.

'Fuck. You were right.'

'The shirt?'

Alan nodded, and Sam ran a hand through his hair. The blood that had pumped from Sinclair's stomach, the fatal wound that Alan had raced headfirst into danger to fix.

All of it was a hoax.

Sinclair wasn't dead. That much was clear.

But judging by the rage that caused Alan to shake, Sam realised that hit the agent harder than him. His fight had exposed countless police officers or high-ranking officials who broke the law. It usually put them in his crosshairs.

But to Alan, it was a betrayal.

It meant Sinclair was in on it.

It meant that the man who had mentored Alan had also been in cahoots with the man who had murdered his brother in cold blood.

Vengeance was a powerful drug, one that could propel a man to do seemingly crazy things. Sam was living proof of that fact, and he could see the fuse burning away on Alan's nobility.

'Hey, listen.' Sam stepped forward and put his clammy hand on Alan's shoulder. 'Don't let it beat you. Use it. Channel it. But don't lose focus here. Whatever the hell is going on, we'll bring it down. If Sinclair is involved, we bring him down, too. But let's not forget what we came here to do.'

Alan took a few deep breaths before shutting down his phone and sliding it away. He nodded, doing his best to swallow the betrayal and mask the heartache it had caused. It was for his own benefit more than Sam's, and Sam chose to ignore it.

Before Alan could respond, the sound of an engine roared, and both men turned to the highway they'd travelled to the derelict bar on. When they'd walked alongside it, they never witnessed one car or any semblance of life.

No one headed out this way without a reason.

Least of all a three-car motorcade, the sun beaming down on the black Range Rovers as they slowly came into view. The horizon line was blurred through the heat, and Sam and Alan moved quickly to the bushes that surrounded the tiki bar, shielding themselves from view. A few minutes later, the cars rolled by the bar, pulling into the car park. Numerous doors opened and shut, and they heard a volatile voice shout orders in Spanish. Amongst the yelling, they both heard the unmistakable clicking of a weapon being loaded.

'You smart son of a bitch,' Alan whispered. 'What's the plan?'

'I need you to stay here, keep an eye on things.' Sam peered through the bushes and caught sight of Vasquez. Dressed in an expensive suit, he barked orders at the man Sam had disarmed in the back of the car.

Beside them, the scrawny man still had a gun held to Alex, whose hands and mouth were layered with duct tape.

Sam felt his every muscle tighten. Every impulse urged him to rush headfirst towards them.

He had twelve in the clip and one in the chamber, and he could guarantee he was a better shot than them all.

The only problem was he had no idea how many others were in the other vehicles.

Giving away their position would leave himself, Alan, and Alex buried in an unmarked grave, left to rot under the boiling soil.

'You're leaving?' Alan barked; his eyebrows raised.

'They're heading to the abandoned mill.' Sam ignored the question. 'Whatever's going down here, we have time. I can get back to the car in five minutes, back to Dillon in twenty.'

Sam held open his hand. Alan sighed and passed him the keys. Despite the severe danger of their situation, Alan had no reason to doubt him.

Sam may have been a criminal. But he was a good man.

One of the few.

Sam closed his fist tight, then slid the keys into his back pocket. He peeked through the bushes again, watching as the hulking Edinson followed the last of the armed henchmen towards the factory.

'Coast's clear,' Sam whispered before sliding to the side of the bush. 'If I'm not back in an hour, call it in. If we can't play this our way, we still need to do whatever we can to get Alex out.'

'Understood,' Alan replied, with the authority of a marine. 'Where the fuck are you going, anyway?'

Sam flashed him a smile.

'To get back-up.'

CHAPTER TWENTY-THREE

Assuming command of the Riders was never something that Mason had prepared for. He'd been with Wyatt since the beginning of their journey and had been happy to stand to the side, carry out his orders, and enjoy the rewards they brought. He believed in the cause, in the brotherhood afforded to those who had lost their way, and the patch meant as much to him as he assumed a family would to a normal man.

But he never had eyes for the throne.

Sykes did. That much was abundantly clear, and he and Wyatt had spent many nights discussing the man's ambition over a cold beer. While Sykes had the killer instinct that made him such a useful weapon within their ranks, Wyatt knew he lacked the capacity to see the bigger picture. Mason agreed with that notion, often speculating how much trouble Sykes would eventually bring to their doorstep.

It appeared as though he was finding out.

The DEA were sniffing around and would likely press down further on them now that one of their own had been killed.

Vasquez wouldn't take a hit on his business lying down, and although the Riders would never back down from a fight, the man's reaction would be as brutal as it was immediate.

Factor in the unknown Brit who'd assaulted Mason in his own bar and the disappearance of Wyatt himself, and Mason knew somebody had to step up.

Sykes had gone AWOL.

His sudden fleeing was all the evidence Mason needed to pin the events on him.

Something big was coming their way, and he would be damned if he didn't face it with a gun in his hand, his mortality on the table, and the Rider's patch emblazoned on his back.

He'd dedicated his life to the cause. Giving it up for it would be no problem.

'What's the plan?' Donnie asked, speaking for the group as all eyes in the bar turned to the hulking Mason who was leant against the bar, trying to unravel the chaos.

'We find Wyatt,' Mason commanded. 'That's our number one priority. Call all the deputies and coppers who are on the take and get them to hunt down his bike. Get them to check CCTV. We need to know his last movements and we can work the rest out from there.'

'And Sykes?'

'Oh, he'll get what's coming to him. If he thinks he can abandon us when we need to stick together, then he knows what's waiting.' Mason cracked his knuckles. 'But whatever he's done or whatever he has instigated, it ain't going to disappear with him. So, let's try to find them quickly, because I got a feeling we're going to have some severely pissed off Mexicans knocking on our door.'

As the group of Riders murmured their agreement, the door to the bar opened and every head in the premises spun in its direction. Hands shot to their weapons, with a plethora of handguns lifted, aimed with deadly intent at the figure standing in the doorway. Mason's jaw dropped with shock, then a cruel smile formed among his beard.

'Well, this must be my lucky day.' Mason chuckled.

Sam walked into the bar, the brightness of the sun peeking in from the doorway casting a long shadow before him. Ignoring the firearms ready to put him down, he took a few steps towards Mason. He held his hands up in a way of surrender.

'We need to talk.'

Mason scoffed; his eyebrows raised in confusion.

'You are either the bravest or stupidest fucker I've ever come across.' Mason cracked his neck. 'Believe me, I've been around long enough for that to be an impressive title.'

'I didn't come here to cause any trouble…'

'Unfortunately, son, you already stamped your ticket when you got the jump on us a few days back.' Mason nodded to Donnie, who stood from his chair.

'Let's not do this again.' Sam warned, his hands still in the air. Mason looked at the dusty, battered cast that encased Sam's wrist.

'I see Sykes already gave you a warning.' He shook his head. 'It clearly didn't take.'

'Listen to me.' Sam's frustration grew. 'Whatever macho bullshit you need to get out of your system, save it. This is important. It's about Sykes.'

Mason's tough guy act slipped, and he stood to attention. He held up a hand to Donnie, halting the attack. Sam followed Mason's line of sight, the tension in his body relaxing. Mason scratched his thick beard and then nodded to the booth.

'You got two minutes,' Mason said through gritted teeth. 'If I ain't buying what you're selling, I'm going to put a bullet through your skull. Understood?'

'Loud and clear.'

Mason grunted and headed to the booth. Sam looked back at the other Riders, all of them on the edge of their seats, ready to lunge like a pack of dogs and tear him apart. Taking a deep breath, Sam followed Mason and slid in opposite. Mason gestured for Sam to begin, his body language telling Sam that it was a thankless task. But as soon as he began, Mason began to change. The air of disinterest evaporated, and his knuckles whitened.

Sam relayed everything to him. Who he actually was and why finding Alex was so important. The run-ins with Sinclair and Alan, and how they were transfixed on bringing down the Riders. How Sinclair had kept Alex's identity a secret and how he'd planted her within the Riders as a source of information.

When Sam questioned why Sykes was so insistent on Alex moving to the Pit, Mason shuffled uncomfortably, the truth beginning to take a stranglehold on his brain.

The assault by Sykes.

The drug deal that Sinclair had attended, seemingly executed by Sykes, but who's since gone missing.

No money at the scene.

Vasquez's capture and torture of Sam and the very real likelihood of not just a reaction from Vasquez, but a full-blown assault on the Riders.

The deal that Sam was convinced was happening as they spoke in an abandoned bar out of town.

Sam laid it all on the table, giving Mason time to digest it all. After a few minutes of eerie silence, Mason shook his head.

'I don't know. Too many coincidences to be fact.'

'Well then, get Wyatt,' Sam demanded. 'Maybe he'll listen to me.'

'We can't find him,' Mason admitted, shooting a quick, worried glance to the booth where their leader usually sat. 'No word since yesterday.'

'Another coincidence?' Sam raised his eyebrow. The comment drew a snarl from Mason.

'What the hell do you want from us?'

'I'm heading back to the Tiempo de Salsa. I'm getting Alex out of there and I'm going to make them pay for what they've put her through. I'll either get that done, or I'll die trying. I made that woman a promise and I intend to keep it.'

'What a hero.' Mason sneered.

'Tell me, if Wyatt is dead or worse, in on it, where do you think their next port of call is?' Mason's scowl told Sam they were on the same wavelength. 'You haven't got long to make up your mind. So do it quickly.'

Sam stepped out of the booth, leaving Mason to juggle a decision he never thought he would have to make. As one of Wyatt's trusted men, he'd always been a willing soldier. But he'd never had to give the orders.

Especially not one that could start a war.

Sam walked past a few Riders who stood rigid, unsure of whether to stop him or not. Just as Sam pushed open the door, Mason looked up from the booth and called after him.

'What are you going to do?'

Sam stopped and took a deep breath. The sun burst down through the open doorway and bathed him with a mixture of light and shadow.

'What I do best.'

Sam stepped out of the bar and headed back to Alan's car, leaving the Riders to decide their own fate.

His was already set in stone.

———

Sykes stood with his arms wide while Raul patted him down. As he approached the base of Sykes' spine, he felt the handgun.

'A little insurance policy.' Sykes chuckled. 'What happened to your face?'

Raul ignored him, removing the gun and then continuing the pat-down. Once he was happy with the situation, he stepped back. Sykes looked around the main forecourt of the abandoned mill. The impressive structure loomed large above them, with the heat bouncing off the dusty metal frame. The humidity hung heavy in the air, and Sykes could feel the sweat dripping down his spine.

They had agreed to meet at three, but Sykes intentionally kept them waiting for nearly an hour. A pathetic attempt at antagonisation, but he didn't want Vasquez to feel in control. By buckling to his demands immediately meant that Sykes would still be the second in command.

He may have the Riders, but he wouldn't have control.

As Raul stepped away from him, admiring the gun, Edinson slammed the trunk shut on the truck Sykes had hired. The hulking mute then reached down and easily lifted the bound body of Wyatt over his shoulder, carrying him with one arm like he was a toddler. Drenched in sweat, Wyatt tried to yell through the gag, but his muffled voice made little difference. As he brought him into the group, Edinson dropped him onto the solid concrete, the impact splitting open Wyatt's eyebrow. Fighting against his restraints, Wyatt rolled onto his back, his bloodied vision locking onto Sykes who stood proudly over him.

'Sorry, Trent.' Sykes smiled. 'Nothing personal.'

Sykes threw his boot forward, driving the steel cap straight into Wyatt's midsection, causing him to groan in pain. The impact of his boot seemed to unplug a rage within Sykes, and an avalanche of kicks exploded from him. As he hammered into the defenceless Wyatt, Sykes realised for how long he'd wanted to kill the man who had given him a purpose.

Given him a place in the world.

He'd failed as a soldier, his murderous temper costing the lives of many and his subsequent disappearance.

He'd failed as a human, falling down the rabbit hole of addiction, until Wyatt had pulled him up and given him a place by his side.

But Sykes had never been built to follow orders.

And with every boot he laid into the man's midriff, Sykes realised that the same fate would soon befall Vasquez.

'Enough.'

A voice boomed out from the other side of the court-yard. Everyone spun on the spot except Sykes, who squatted down and spat on the pained face of Wyatt. The exclamation point of his betrayal. Raul raised the gun at the hooded figure who was walking towards them, his hand raised in peace. Despite the gesture of goodwill, Raul kept the gun locked on him, nodding to Edinson to flank him. Emilio stood at the far end of the forecourt, covered in the shade afforded by the gigantic structure. Behind him was a door to an outhouse, where Alex had been locked inside.

'That's far enough,' Raul commanded, emphasising his point by steadying his arm. 'Drop the bag.'

'Let's all just calm down.' The man spoke calmly, the voice of experience. 'There is a deal to be made here and a partnership to forge. So how about we just lower the weapons, eh?'

After a few moments, Raul lowered his arm, removing his finger from the trigger. The man turned to Sykes and shook his head.

'I think he's had enough.'

Sykes shrugged and stepped away from Wyatt, who

214

was trying desperately to breathe through the pain. Raul approached the man, sceptical of the sudden intrusion.

'He's with me,' Sykes chimed in.

'We said come alone.'

'He did,' the man interrupted. 'Think of me as the middleman in this whole thing.'

Pulling back the hood, Sinclair nodded to Sykes, and then looked at Raul and smiled. Casually, he pulled his cigarettes from his pocket and lit one. As the smoke filtered from his mouth, he marched past Raul and approached Wyatt. As he peered over the fallen Rider, he smiled. More so at the shocked expression in the man's eyes than the pain he was in.

'I told you I'd get you, you son of a bitch.'

Sykes, having lit his own cigarette, pointed to Raul and repeated his question.

'What the fuck happened to your face?'

'There was an incident…'

'Incident?' Sinclair turned around. 'What incident? Do you have the girl?'

'Yes, she is fine.' Raul gestured over to Emilio. 'She is in there. Don't worry, nothing has happened to her. A few cuts from the crash, but that's all.'

'Good,' Sinclair barked, dropping his cigarette to the ground and extinguishing it under his boot. 'Keep it that way. I don't need her death or her rape on my conscience. Understood?'

Raul nodded, shooting a concerned look to Emilio who had made no secret of his intentions. Sinclair clocked him, noting that Alex's safety may not be as clear cut as he thought. Sykes stepped forward, flicking his cigarette at Raul who cursed him in Spanish.

'Hey, Fuckface. Answer my fucking question.' Sykes pointed at Raul. 'What happened to your face?'

'That British man. Pope. He did this.'

'Pope?' Sinclair asked with surprise. 'You mean Cooper?'

'He said his real name was Sam Pope.' Raul spat on the floor. 'Fucking cockroach. He did this and attacked our men. One of them is dead.'

'You killed him, right?' Sykes demanded. Silence. 'Right?'

Raul looked away, and Sykes's eyes bulged with fury. Before he could step forward, Sinclair threw an arm across his chest, holding him back. Loitering with malicious intent, Edinson kept his eye on the situation unfolding.

'If he had any sense, then he'd be long gone by now. No doubt the Riders want him, as well as my ex-partner. There is still a deal to be done here. So, let's get it sorted, shall we?'

As the voice of reason, Sinclair shot a glance to Raul and then to Sykes, hopeful that his words had defused the situation. Gritting his teeth, Sykes nodded his agreement, and Raul once again lowered the gun.

'Where is the money?' Raul asked.

'It's safe. I want to speak to Vasquez first.'

Sykes and Raul eyeballed each other once more, both of them aware that there wasn't room for both of them in the proposed new world. Sinclair sighed.

'Enough dick swinging. Where is Vasquez?'

'He's in the bar.' Raul pointed to the exit of the forecourt. 'He got tired of waiting and wanted a drink. He isn't happy with you, puta.'

'Go.' Sinclair turned to Sykes before he could react, and the unhinged biker glared at Raul before turning on his heel and heading back to the exit and the short walk down the dusty terrain to the abandoned bar.

It was time for him to take his rightful place.

. . .

Watching from the shrubbery, Alan pulled out his phone and keyed in a message to Sam. He'd seen Vasquez enter the bar over half an hour ago. Now, with Sykes moments away from starting the deal, Alan didn't fancy his chances of taking them all down himself.

He needed Sam back now.

Watching as Sykes pulled open the door to the bar and stepped inside, Alan kept low and made his way through the dying greenery to the back of the building.

While he was waiting for Sam to arrive, he wanted to get a better look at the situation and find out what exactly was going on.

Keeping low to the ground, Alan scurried up towards the mill, well aware that he was fast approaching a situation he had no way of coming back from.

CHAPTER TWENTY-FOUR

Sam rolled Alan's car back into the same parking spot where he'd picked it up and stepped out, the humidity covering the town of Lake View in an uncomfortable blanket. The air was thick and muggy, and Sam could feel the sweat trickling down his scar-covered back.

His body had been through the wars.

Explosions.

Knife wounds.

Bullet holes.

Now, with his face battered and bruised and his left wrist strapped in a dirty cast, he wondered how much longer it could keep going.

He was built to survive, but eventually, one bullet was going to hit where he couldn't recover.

Sam slammed the car door shut, adjusting his sticky T-shirt so it lapped over the handgun pressed against the small of his back. His pocket rumbled, and he pulled out the mobile phone, opening the message as he unlocked it.

It was Alan.

Sykes is here. Go time.

'Shit,' Sam uttered to himself, before he began to jog

the half mile out of town. As had been the case for his entire time in the States, there was no plan.

No way to know exactly how it would go down.

Only this time, he had back-up. A capable marine who had a vendetta that burnt as strongly as Sam's commitment to Alex.

Whatever awaited Sam when he got to the bar, he would face it head on. Alex had risked her life to save his. That night in Rome had replayed in his mind ever since he'd sat in the airport with Etheridge, saying goodbye to his good friend for what was likely to be the final time. Through the torrential rain, Alex had ignored the pain in her leg, the bullet wound blocked by the tourniquet Sam had created. She'd also ignored his plea for her to drive as far away as she could.

To get home to her family.

But she'd sacrificed her safety and her reunion to save Sam, showing up just in the nick of time to stop Sam's murderous ex-comrade, Mac, from murdering him.

They'd spent months lying low, with Alex doing her best to nurture Sam back to health.

Back to the fight.

All of it had been built on the promise that Sam would help her get back to her siblings, which Trevor Sims, the odious rat who ran Blackridge, had used to blackmail her.

As his feet pounded the earth, he kept that promise in his mind, knowing that whatever awaited him, he would fight it for her.

This wasn't his fight anymore.

But he would give his life to fight it on her behalf.

With the abandoned mill looming large in the distance, it cast a long shadow across the surrounding land, beckoning Sam to his conclusion.

———

As Alan approached the side panelling that surrounded the mill, he kept himself low to the ground. Halfway up the slight incline, he'd pulled his gun from the holster, sliding his expert finger over the trigger and making a silent commitment to himself that he wouldn't hesitate to pull it.

He had to restrain himself from taking aim at Sykes as he'd approached the bar, knowing that satisfying his vengeance would most likely cost Alex her life.

Her survival topped his need to see Sykes put down. Although his brother had been murdered in cold blood, Alan was still a DEA agent, sworn to protect and serve. Alex was an innocent pawn in a dangerous game, one that Alan was beginning to understand. Somehow, Sinclair was involved. The feeling of heartbreak at his death had been superseded by the betrayal of his lie.

Whatever his partner had done, there was no coming back from it.

That much was clear in Alan's mind. The desired outcome was the safe removal of Alex from the situation and Sinclair and Sykes in cuffs. The disbandment of two drug empires that would keep the streets clean and stop the catastrophic spread of addiction.

But Alan had seen the brutality of man during his time serving in the marines. He'd witnessed the cruel, unrelenting growth of the drug trade and the type of people who flourished within it.

There was no best-case scenario.

There would be bloodshed.

And the likelihood was that Alan wouldn't walk away from it the same as he walked in.

But walking away from it now wasn't an option, regardless of whether Sam made it back in time.

Alan shuffled quietly against the metal panels, welcoming the cooling shade they afforded. In the distance, he thought he could make out the shape of a man jogging.

Sam?

Alan refocused and edged his way to a gap created by the poor alignment of the fencing placed around the condemned building. The structure itself stood despite itself, and upon closer inspection, it looked like its foundations were creaking underneath its own acceptance of its fate. The building, covered in a thick layer of dust, wasn't long for the world and Alan wondered how long it had been on death row. As an eyesore at the end of the beaten track, it wasn't high on the list of priorities to remove.

The Tiempo de Salsa, a sad relic from a more fruitful time, most likely thriving under a different name during a period of unmitigated success for both businesses.

The reliance on the mill, which had caused it to thrive, eventually killed it.

The bar, too.

Now, it was a ghost, a tired old structure waiting for its fate as it rotted in the sweltering heat.

Peering through the fence, Alan's eye immediately locked onto the prone body of Wyatt on the ground, his hands and ankles bound, a gag strapped tightly to his face. By the way he winced, Alan could sense Wyatt's pain. Feeling little sympathy, Alan tried his best to see the rest of the forecourt. He caught a glimpse of a man in a suit, a gun resting in a hand that hung casually by his side.

Another person, just a hand, but the rest of his view was obscured.

Stepping back from the panel, Alan continued around the side of the building and approached an outhouse, the back wall of it separating the panels, and affording Alan a mucky window. Carefully, he cleared the muck with his forearm and peered in, dipping down quickly to ensure he wasn't seen. After a few moments, he poked his head up once more to peer in through the clearing he'd made.

Alex was slumped against the wall, her hands bound

behind her back, and tears trickled down her cheeks to the duct tape that held her mouth shut.

Instantly, Alan's quest for revenge felt insignificant. Despite the pure, visceral contempt which he held for Sykes, they both survived within the dangerous worlds they'd willingly entered.

Seeing Alex terrified and held hostage, reminded Alan that she was just an innocent young woman. One who, from Sam's explanation, was just trying to get back to her family.

Alan had to get inside to get her out. Instinctively, he tried to push the window open, drawing a shocked glance from Alex. Alan reached into his pocket and held his badge up to the window to reassure her, but she shook her head, a clear warning. She leant her head slightly to the door and Alan understood.

It was guarded.

Breaking the glass wasn't an option, and the only advantage he currently held was the element of surprise.

He took a few steps back and looked back to the heated horizon line.

The figure was closer to the bar now, dropping low to avoid detection, and Alan felt a small surge of hope.

Sam was there, approaching the bar to cut off the deal before Vasquez and Sykes were able to call for back-up. That meant Alan needed to know exactly what awaited them on the other side of the panels.

Along the side of the mill itself, he saw an old door that had clearly been jimmied open at its base. Most likely a junkie looking for a place to lose himself one last time, before the addiction claimed him. Using his considerable strength, Alan lodged himself in the gap, his back pressed against the door frame, and with every fibre of his being, he pressed his feet against the doorframe and shunted his entire weight against the door.

The lock shattered, and the door flew open, sending Alan sprawling onto the earth.

He stood, dusted himself down, retrieved his gun, and waited, finger on the trigger for any of Vasquez's men to investigate the sound.

Nothing.

Happy that the coast was clear, Alan headed into the dilapidated building, hoping it wouldn't collapse before he'd found his way to Alex.

————

'I never thought this day would come.'

Vasquez chuckled, lifting his glass of Scotch as he sat across the table from Sykes, who lifted his beer in response.

'Things change,' Sykes said coldly. 'You either need to embrace that or step aside. It was something Wyatt would never understand.'

'I heard such stories.' Vasquez spoke eloquently, his English as fluent as his Spanish. 'When we were expanding into America, the rumours were that the Riders would crash down on us like the wrath of God himself. But bit by bit, as we moved further and further out, this day did not come.'

'Believe me' – Sykes smiled – 'I pushed for it.'

Vasquez laughed again, reaching into his pocket and removing his gold-plated cigar case. It was a show of power and wealth, one which clearly appealed to Sykes, and Vasquez opened it and offered Sykes first pick. Greedily accepting the offer, Sykes took a cigar and then watched as Vasquez snapped the case shut, swiftly followed by him trimming the cigar with a gold clipper.

'You can expect ten shipments within the next month,' Vasquez began, tossing Sykes the clipper before striking a match. He allowed the flame to engulf the edge of the cigar, luxuriating in the fine flavour as the smoke billowed from his lips. 'I appreciate you need time to reorganise your men, but we cannot stop production. I need to know that won't be a problem.'

With a cocky swagger, Sykes sat back in his chair and let the thick, grey smoke flow from his mouth and combine with Vasquez's. A horrible tribute to their unholy union.

'Look at what I did to Wyatt.' Sykes smirked. 'If people don't fall in line, then I'll make them. Or I'll kill them. Simple.'

Vasquez raised his glass.

'I think we'll get along just fine.'

Sykes reciprocated by lifting his beer, trying his best to hide the smile that threatened to creep across his bearded face. While Vasquez was celebrating their union, Sykes was already wondering how far down the road they would have to travel together before he could realistically throw Vasquez to the wolves.

In Sykes's mind, this partnership was temporary.

A mere stepping stone until he was the dominant force atop an extraordinary empire.

But for now, as he toasted his new partner, he would share that infamy with the man across the table from him.

'I trust you have my money?' Vasquez stated casually.

'Yes, it's with Sinclair,' Sykes responded. 'I'm still on the fence about whether we kill him or not.'

'Meh. He is insignificant.' Vasquez waved his hand dismissively. 'Pay him his money and let him rot under the weight of his own guilt. If he comes back asking for me, my boys will put him to work.'

'Greed is a dangerous trait.'

'As we both know.' Vasquez smiled.

'Jose, as a gift for our partnership, I would like to offer you the opportunity of killing Wyatt.' Sykes shrugged. 'Let him look into your eyes so he knows his final act on this planet was falling to you.'

Vasquez took a long puff on his cigar, contemplating the offer.

'That is very kind. However, I would quite like to witness your commitment to this future. I am in the position I am in, Sykes, by being an incredibly careful man.'

'Not careful enough.'

Both men spun to the front door where Sam Pope was stood both hands wrapped around a gun that was pointed directly at them. Sykes, in a pathetic attempt to show defiance, reached into his jacket for his own gun, but Sam stepped forward. Despite the discomfort in his wrist that Sykes had taken great pleasure in shattering, Sam clung to the weapon in a cold, expert grip.

'Hands on the table,' Sam demanded, taking a few careful steps forward. Sykes grunted in fury and obliged, but Vasquez sat back in his chair, puffing on his cigar. Slowly, he began to clap.

'You are impressive. Like a cockroach who refuses to die.' Vasquez stopped applauding and his face turned into a twisted scowl. 'But you're signing your own death certificate with every second you point that at me.'

Sam ignored the threat.

He kept his finger calmly against the trigger.

'Who are you?' Sykes spat with frustration, his fist clenching with anger.

'Like I said to you before, I'm just passing through. Looking to catch-up with an old friend.' Sam took another step forward, the gun trained on two of the most powerful men in the drug trade. 'Now I've had a hell of a few days. I owe you both a lot of pain, but I'm willing to let that slide if you answer just one question. Where the hell is Alex?'

CHAPTER TWENTY-FIVE

Alex struggled against her restraints, a mixture of fear and frustration flooding her body as they refused to give. After a few minutes of twisting, the tape and cable ties began to cut into her skin, and she relented.

Defeated, she slumped back against the wall.

Considering she'd spent her entire adult life making bad decisions, she looked helplessly around the room, confirming that she'd outdone herself. All she'd ever wanted was to give her brother and sister the life their mother had never afforded her. Addiction had cruelly denied Alex a mother, and now her own poor judgment would snatch the idea of family from her siblings.

A tear formed in the corner of her eye and she shook it away, scolding herself for her own inner pity.

She'd made the decisions that led to this point.

Sam had warned her she was playing a dangerous game, but her desperation had blurred her judgment.

He'd abandoned her in Naples, heading back to the UK to put an end to Blackridge.

From what he'd told her, he'd succeeded, meaning she wouldn't need to spend her life looking over her shoulder.

But considering it was unlikely she would survive the day; it was scant consolation. The outhouse she was being held prisoner in had previously been an office, with a creaky desk and chair pressed against the far wall.

Possibly the security office?

It didn't matter.

It would likely be her final resting place.

Above the desk, a murky window offered a promise of sunlight, but the grime from years of abandonment kept the room dark. Alex was alone, locked in a shaded room with nothing but a bullet to the skull in her future.

Her only hope was Sam.

Having foiled Vasquez's attempt of an execution, he was still at large and knowing him as intimately as she did, Alex knew he would be knocking on every door to find her.

But they were in the middle of nowhere, hidden behind the metal barriers that locked the abandoned mill from the world.

Even though she knew Sam would walk through hell to make good on his promise to her, she held little hope he would ever find her.

She would die here.

Her brother and sister would remain in care, lost in a system that tries its best but one that would eventually chew them up and spit them into an adult life they were unprepared for.

Her mother would leave rehab, lose her fresh perspective, and turn to the needle once more.

The only comfort she held in her inevitable murder was that at least one person was fighting to save her.

One person cared enough to fight for her survival.

With a deep sigh, Alex rocked back against the wall, the breath leaving her body with the last remnants of hope.

A forearm pressed against the window.

She twisted her neck to look, and the thick, muscular arm wiped the muck away, clearing a smidge of glass to allow a beam of light to slice through the shadow like a knife.

Then Special Agent Joe Alan appeared, lifting his head up from under the windowsill, and peeked into the room.

Alex's heart skipped a beat.

She'd assumed him dead; her last memory was him lying at the mercy of Sykes among the anarchy of the night before. Alan nodded to her, and she shook her head, arching her neck to the door, hoping he heeded her warning.

The vile Emilio was outside the door, praying they let him have his way with her before they eradicated her from their plans.

Alan took the message and then disappeared, presumably to find another way to her.

Her heart sank.

For that brief moment, she'd felt a flicker of hope.

But the reality of the situation was bleak.

As the door slowly crept open, it got even worse.

She looked up, greeted by the crooked smile of Emilio who looked at her like a starving wolf circling an injured deer. Whatever was happening in the forecourt, it had clearly provided Emilio with the confidence that he wouldn't be disturbed.

'Are you ready, Mami?' he whispered, putting his gun down on the filing cabinet that stood next to the door. Alex's eyes widened with fear, and she once again struggled against her restraints. Blood trickled from her wrists, and Emilio's eyes flickered with arousal at her fear.

He walked slowly towards her, unbuckling his belt.

As he slid his jeans and boxer shorts to his knees, revealing his arousal, he lunged forward at her, his hands ripping at the buttons of her jeans as she struggled violently. A hard fist crashed into her cheek, knocking her backwards, and her brain shook from the impact. Struggling to regain her thoughts, she could feel her jeans being pulled down, the man's rough hands gripping her thighs.

Alex prayed for death.

A gunshot erupted in the room, the noise contained by the confined space, and it reverberated like a thunderclap.

Blood splattered the wall.

Emilio slumped to the side, his life escaping through the hole in the side of his skull.

Alex shook from the ordeal and the violent death of the man who had every intention of raping her. As she came to terms with what happened, she turned, and her eyes widened in shock.

Sinclair.

'I'm sorry, Alex.' His words were shrouded in sadness. 'It should never have come to this. I told them you were not to be harmed.'

Gently, Sinclair pulled her jeans back up, helping her to reclaim her dignity. Emilio lay half naked on the floor, slumped forward, his eyes wide open.

Drawn by the gunshot, Raul and Edinson appeared in the doorway, both shocked to stillness at the body of Emilio.

'What did you do?' Raul barked, his eyes drawn to Sinclair who stood, offering Alex an apologetic smile.

'The deal was she wouldn't be hurt,' Sinclair yelled with fury. 'That piece of shit was this close to raping the poor girl.'

'Jesus,' Raul uttered.

'Where the hell are Sykes and Vasquez?' Sinclair berated Raul. He turned to Edinson, who remained as stoic as always. 'Big guy, go and bring them back and let's get this deal done.'

Edinson turned and marched across the forecourt,

heading for the break in the panel that would lead him down towards the bar. As the hulking figure approached the exit, Sinclair stepped out of the office. Raul looked back one last time at the body of Emilio and then closed the door.

It didn't catch on the latch, and it slowly creaked open.

Alex had her opportunity.

Judging from the next sentence she heard from Sinclair, she needed to take it.

'Fuck,' Sinclair uttered in a violent whisper. 'She's seen my face.'

———

Alan crept slowly through the mill, angered by the layout. He'd hoped that the emergency door he'd broken into would lead him quickly to Alex, but instead it had been the gateway into a maze. The door opened into a narrow corridor that took him up a few flights of stairs before opening up onto one of the main production floors.

As he moved between the large pieces of archaic apparatus, he felt like he was in a museum that paid homage to bygone industries.

Each piece of equipment was tinted with thick orange rust. No one had operated anything within this building in years, and it saddened Alan at how quickly the world moves on.

A life without a smartphone or the Internet seemed impossible, but he could recall a time where the only phone he had was nailed to the wall of his family home.

Technology and the demands of human consumption had moved on quicker than humanity's capability to adapt, leaving behind generations of dissatisfied people who clung desperately to the 'good old days'.

Restoring his focus, Alan felt the cool steel of his gun in

his hand, reconnecting with the weapon. It had been a while since he'd pulled the trigger of a gun, but in his days as a marine, he was as deadly as they came.

A small part of him cursed himself for not taking his shot at Sykes as he'd approached the bar.

He could have pulled the trigger and ran, leaving Sykes to rot under the relentless sun and for Sam to deal with his own problem.

But it wasn't Sam's problem. It was an amalgamation of separate circumstances that had seen Alan's own partner manipulate a vulnerable woman into a drug war, and her own good deed pulling a viable saviour into the mix.

Sam was doing what was right.

Therefore, so was Alan.

His personal revenge was outweighed by Alex's safety, and as he glided between the defunct machinery, searching for a way to Alex, he hoped he wouldn't be too late. As he rounded one of the machines, he noticed one of Vasquez's men sweeping the area. Walking with clear boredom, the man lazily held a gun in his tattooed hand, a cigarette in the other.

Alan pressed himself against the large apparatus to shield him from view. As the man sauntered past, Alan slid around the side of the machine and swiftly draped his arm around the man's neck. Before the henchman could call for help, Alan slid his other hand over the man's mouth and locked his muscular arms in position, blocking off the man's air supply and lowering him to the ground.

As he squeezed the consciousness from the man's body, Alan left him prone on the ground and took his weapon.

Two weapons were better than one.

A gunshot echoed somewhere in the distance, the explosion bouncing through the abandoned mill and causing Alan to stop dead.

Alex?

Following the sound, Alan picked up the pace. He stopped briefly and pulled his phone from his pocket but there was no reception within the structure.

No way to contact Sam.

With just the two guns for support, Alan headed towards the door on the far side of the production floor, hoping it would bring him closer to Alex.

———

The unmistakable clap of a gunshot echoed weakly in the distance, and all three men turned their attention to the back window. Sam prayed that it wasn't Alex. That he wasn't too late.

Since his demand to be taken to her, Vasquez had become increasingly tiresome. Casually puffing his cigar, he was adamant in maintaining his air of control.

It was the opposite for Sykes. With his masculinity threatened by Sam, Sykes had responded with vitriol and had made several promises of a grim demise for Sam, and an even worse fate for Alex.

It was all for show.

Sam had pieced together much of what was happening. Sykes and Vasquez were planning a working partnership and Sykes, forever the attack dog for Wyatt, was keen to show Vasquez that he could wield the axe if need be.

He was desperate for parity with a man who had clear intentions to keep him one step behind.

'What was that?' Sykes spun in his chair, his eyes betraying his confidence. Sam and Vasquez maintained their composure, their lack of fear only adding to Sykes's increasing paranoia.

'What is it you hope to happen, Sam?' Vasquez asked,

extinguishing his cigar in the ashtray. 'How do you expect to walk away from this?'

'I don't,' Sam replied coldly. 'Just as long as she does.'

'Admirable.' Vasquez chuckled. 'Tell me, are you looking for work? We could use a man like you.'

'What are you doing?' Sykes turned to Vasquez, his fist slamming the table.

'It's called business,' Vasquez snapped back. 'There are times where you assess a situation and don't look for the immediate outcome. You look a few steps ahead.'

'First off, I don't think this partnership you guys are building is going to work. Just a feeling.' Sam kept the gun trained on Vasquez. 'Second, those are wise words but third, I'm not for hire.'

'That's a shame.' Vasquez sat back in his chair, nonchalantly twirling the cigar case on the table. 'Once you told me your name, we did some digging. Quite the life you've had, eh? Sam Pope, the man who brought down criminal empire after criminal empire. You would make an excellent trigger man.'

Sam shuddered at the notion. The truth and guilt of Project Hailstorm still clung tightly to his conscience and being reminded of the lives he'd ended threatened to derail his focus. Sam shook the vulgar memories from his mind, readjusted the gun in his hand, and looked at Vasquez.

'Make the call. Tell them to send Alex down here to me. Once I can see she is safe, then I'll put the gun down.'

'Fuck that,' Sykes roared, the veins popping on his neck. He turned to Vasquez, who maintained his calm. 'Order your men down here and let's kill this asshole.'

Vasquez raised his hand to silence Sykes, encouraging more anger from the treacherous biker. Vasquez glanced to the window and then back at Sam, a smirk across his face. Perturbed, Sam glanced to the window, seeing nothing but the derelict garden, which had once been a vibrant hub of social activity.

Sykes took his chance.

Lunging across the table, he shot his arm out to grab Sam's gun in a pathetic attempt to grasp control of the situation. Sam easily stepped aside, catching Sykes's wrist with his other hand, and yanked him hard against the table. Swiftly, Sam shot out of his chair and pinned his knee on the back of Sykes's wrist, twisting the hand upwards to the very edge of breaking point. He pinned Sykes's skull to the table with his gun.

'Do something,' Sykes mumbled to Vasquez, who watched in annoyance.

'Word of advice, Sykes. When you find yourself in a hole, you should quit digging.' Sam leant down on the wrist, causing Sykes to yelp in agony. With the gun firmly pressed against Sykes's head, Sam looked to Vasquez. 'Last chance, Vasquez. Make the call.'

With the situation escalating, Vasquez looked back and forth between both men. Sam had become an irritant that could derail the entire deal, and as he watched his new partner exude such vulnerability, Vasquez sighed. He pulled his phone from his pocket and lazily slid his fingers across the screen.

Then he stopped and looked Sam in the eye.

'I don't think I'll need to.'

Sam squinted in confusion, and Vasquez looked beyond him and over his shoulder. Sam turned, realising he was too late as Edinson's powerful fist collided with his jaw. With his knee on the table, Sam lost his balance, spiralling to the left, and crashed into another vacant table.

His gun spilled onto the floor.

Vasquez stood immediately, buttoning his jacket and looking at Sam with disgust.

'I offered you a way out of this,' he said coldly. 'A way

for both you and her. Sadly, you'll have to die knowing you made the wrong choice.'

Vasquez turned and marched back across the bar, heading for the back door and the conclusion of the deal. Sykes pushed himself from the table, massaging his wrist. He looked down at Sam who was slowly pushing himself to his knees, while Edinson waited, like a lion ready to claim its kill.

With Vasquez yanking open the door, Sykes followed, scolding himself for his rash judgment and for now following Vasquez's lead. He'd wanted to shed the skin of a subordinate but had quickly stumbled into the role.

Sam heard the door slam shut, wiped the blood from his split lip, and pushed himself to his feet.

Edinson stood, his face expressionless, but his eyes conveying the reality of the situation.

The bar was eerily silent.

His gun was somewhere in the room.

Sam took a breath, cracked his neck, and then clenched his fist.

CHAPTER TWENTY-SIX

There would come a time in Sam's life when he would look back on the path he took and the people he'd crossed. Every trigger he pulled and every life he'd ended. For each and every criminal he did battle with, he would try his best to work back from their death to the moment of justification to his cause.

That he was killing them out of necessity, not out of his own enjoyment.

As he stood ten feet from Edinson and shook the cobwebs from the clubbing blow that had signalled the behemoth's arrival, Sam knew he would have no such trouble if he survived.

Edinson was the only thing standing between him and Alex, and for her, he was willing to destroy a cathedral of blessings. He would gladly drill through the ground and choke the eternal life from Satan himself if it meant he removed her from the danger she was in.

Edinson's sturdy, stubble covered jaw twisted into a cruel smirk. The first emotion Sam had seen from the big man. With a body comparable to a granite wall, and ink covering every inch of his forearm, Sam knew his opponent was forged in a lawless prison, where only the strongest walk out with their heads high.

Whatever Edinson had done to be sent to such a place would have been beastly.

What he would have done to walk out would have been much worse.

Sam scanned the ground for his gun, but the scattered tables and chairs that littered the bar made it impossible to locate. There was no way other than to raise his fists and do what he did best.

Survive.

Not wanting to stand on ceremony anymore, Edinson stomped towards Sam, his bulging arms by his side and Sam threw up his fists and swung. With shocking agility, Edinson ducked down, the fist colliding with his shoulder.

Sam's hand shook on impact.

As he connected, Edinson lunged forward, drilling his shoulder into Sam's torso, stepping forward and shunting Sam across the table, sending him spinning across the wood and collapsing onto the floor below. Both impacts drove the wind from his body and Sam gasped for his breath, scurrying to his feet as Edinson circled the table, his eyes fixed on his victim.

Sam used the chair to haul himself to his feet, and in one motion, lifted it and swung. Edinson threw up his arm, the chair shattering against his bone and Sam followed it up with a vicious stamp to the knee. Edinson wobbled and dropped forward, and Sam jumped forward, swinging his hip and drilling a knee straight into the man's jaw.

The crack was audible, and Edinson slumped against the table. His eyes widened in shock.

Not pain.

But disbelief that Sam had floored him.

His jaw swung loosely, the blow from Sam breaking it clean, but the man showed little pain. Using the table for leverage, he pulled himself to his feet. Sam, taking the few moments to search for his gun, finally laid eyes on it, just as Edinson crushed his stomach with a thunderous right hook. Sam hunched forward and Edinson grabbed him by the throat with one meaty hand and his fingers crushed inwards. Sam instantly felt his airway close up and as he gasped for air and struck Edinson with flailing fists, he felt Edinson's hand press against his back.

In a sickening display of strength, Edinson hoisted Sam off his feet, and then drove him back first into the solid table. Sam collided painfully with the wood, his head snapping back and bouncing off the table. Woozily, he gasped for air but Edinson gripped the edge of the table with both hands and flipped it, sending Sam hurtling to the ground, the wood crashing down on his previously lacerated spine.

Sam yelled in agony, and then his focus snapped to the bar.

Resting against one of the stools was his gun.

With every fibre of his being, he began to drag himself towards the weapon, hoping Edinson would give him the split-second window he needed. There was no doubt in Sam's mind that hand to hand, he would die.

Edinson was a fighter, built and honed in the Devil's pit of a prison that he'd spent half of his adult life.

The man was a cold-blooded killer and judging from the punishment he was putting Sam through his intention was to make this as painful as possible.

The plan was clear.

Sam needed to get to the gun.

Otherwise, he would be beaten to death.

As he crawled within a few metres of the weapon, he felt a solid boot connect with his ribs, sending him rolling to the side. Another connected, his insides compressing under the vicious blow. With his stomach turning, Sam could feel the surge of vomit threatening to rush to the surface.

He suppressed it just as another boot drove towards him.

Sam rolled into it, clutching Edinson's foot with both hands, and he twisted with all his might.

He heard the bone snap.

The cartilage rupture.

Edinson collapsed to the ground like a tree falling in the forest, and the table nearby shook as he hit the deck. Sam let go of the man's broken ankle, shaking the pain from his own fractured wrist, which had absorbed most of the blow, and scrambled once more towards the gun.

He reached out with his fingers, the tips of them brushing the cool steel that would save his life.

Edinson's grip on his ankle was like a bear trap, and Sam felt himself hauled back across the wooden floor. He tried to throw a punch, but Edinson shook it off, slamming Sam's cast against the floor. Sam howled in agony.

He nearly passed out as Edinson crushed it against the floor under the full might of his fist.

Edinson then reintroduced Sam's cheek to his knuckle, cracking Sam with such velocity that a tooth shot across the floor, succeeded by a spray of blood.

Sam urged his body to move, willed himself to move away, but he couldn't. With his organs still rattled, his wrist a shattered wreck and his consciousness swirling, Sam felt the first cruel touch of death creeping towards him.

Another fist landed square against his jaw once more, rattling it horrifically and somehow not taking it clean off.

The room went blurry, and Sam stared up at the ceiling.

He'd tried.

That's all he'd ever done.

Try to fight back.

Try to put right the wrongs that the world turned a blind eye to.

Somewhere along the way, the world and the accepted reality of life had cruelly dealt Alex Stone a bad hand and had just expected her to cope.

Sam had tried to make that right.

Tried to get her back to where her heart had beckoned. He'd failed.

As he took a few deep, hard breaths, he gently rested his head back against the hardwood floor. The blurring in his vision had begun to subside, and he could see Edinson shuffling through the shattered remains of the chair Sam had struck him with. Whatever pain Sam had inflicted, it didn't show, and Edinson's eyes glistened as he lifted one of the broken legs, the snap of the wood providing a sharp edge.

With saliva and blood pooling from his broken jaw, the murderous giant dragged himself towards Sam, ignoring the searing pain of his snapped ankle.

He stopped next to Sam, flipped the wood around his hand and with both hands clutching it, he lifted it into the air, determined to drive his entire body weight behind the fatal plunge.

Sam shut his eyes, expecting death.

All he saw was his son.

Jamie.

His beautiful boy, who he'd fought to return to time and again. The catalyst for Sam's journey that had led him to this point.

Usually, every vision of his son was of his smile, a beaming grin that radiated love and innocence.

But here, stood in the darkness, his son stared back at him, his eyes wide.

Not with fear. With anger.

'Fight back, Dad.'

Sam's eyes opened, his son's words racing through his mind like a ghostly echo. In that split second, Sam's body absorbed and ignored the pain that was coursing through it like an unstoppable wave, and he saw the wooden stake raised high, ready to impale his chest and pin his heart to the wood below.

Sam lifted his feet, crunching his legs up, and in one push, he kicked them against Edinson's solid torso. The murderous henchmen didn't move, and he drove the stake downwards. But Sam used the momentum to roll backwards, the wooden stake slashing his calf as he dodged the killer blow.

He rolled through, his hand sliding over the gun, and he swung it up into his grip, planting one knee on the ground and his elbow on the other.

He pulled the sight to his eye.

Shut the other.

Sam had moved so quickly that Edinson had sprawled forward slightly as the wooden spike smashed against the ground.

As he looked up, he showed no fear.

Just acceptance at the fate the barrel of Sam's gun promised.

Sam pulled the trigger, his body controlling the kick-back from the pistol as he fired.

The bullet pierced Edinson's eye before ripping through the back of his skull with a majestic spray of claret.

He was dead before he hit the ground.

Sam stayed on his knee, lowering the gun and taking a deep breath.

The pain he'd temporarily removed from the equation returned with a vengeance, and every bit of him pleaded to stop.

Sam ignored it, pushing himself to his feet and

wobbling slightly as he stepped over the hulking corpse, his boot splashing in the man's blood as he headed towards the door.

Alex was still in trouble.

And he still had a promise to keep.

————

Raul had just finished hauling Emilio's corpse out into the forecourt when Vasquez stormed through the panel, followed closely by an anxious Sykes. Despite his dislike of Emilio, he still afforded the dead man the dignity of pulling his trousers up. He'd reached under the man's arms and dragged him back across the forecourt, and Vasquez's entrance startled him, causing him to release the dead man who clattered to the ground.

The man's gun hit the ground and bounced a few feet away.

'What the fuck happened?' Vasquez demanded, pointing at the hole in Emilio's head.

Before Raul could respond, Sinclair stepped forward.

'I killed him.'

'You want to tell me why?'

Sinclair looked beyond Vasquez to Sykes, noting the apprehension in the man. It caused his stomach to knot slightly. He needed Sykes to hold his nerve. Otherwise the entire deal would collapse, and the sacrifice of his career would have been for nothing. Greed had blurred his vision, but he needed Sykes to see straight.

'Because he was trying to rape, Alex,' Sinclair barked back defiantly. 'That was never part of the deal.'

Vasquez took a menacing step towards Sinclair and then turned to the prone body of Emilio and he spat on it.

'Fucking cockroach.' Vasquez smiled at Sinclair. 'You did me a favour.'

'What took you guys so long?' Sinclair asked.

'He's still alive,' Sykes yelled in fury. 'They didn't fucking kill him.'

'Who? The Brit?' Sykes turned to Vasquez. 'What the hell happened?'

'He is no longer a concern.' Vasquez chuckled. 'Edinson is taking care of him. That is the last we've seen of Sam Pope.'

Sinclair turned to Sykes, confusion on his face.

'Pope?'

'Yeah, apparently Vasquez got his real name out of him. Ran some checks. Everything he told us was bullshit.'

'Why do I recognise that name?' Sinclair said to himself more than anyone else.

'It is not important.' Vasquez snapped his fingers. 'He is a dead man now. Soon, his body will be rotting in the heat and no one will miss him. Now, I believe you have something that belongs to me?'

Sinclair looked the drug baron up and down before nodding. A tingle of excitement raced through his body as the moment had arrived. He'd stashed the money before he'd made his entrance, and now he would hand Vasquez a million dollars in cash. As the instigator and at times, mediator of this deal, he'd asked for half. A request Vasquez had been happy to grant.

Vasquez's empire, combined with the reach and sway of the Riders, was worth hundreds of millions.

Sinclair would retire with a cool half a million in the bank, as well as the life insurance and state pension he'd set up to be paid to a fake family member.

He would retire a rich man.

Although there was blood on his hands from today's events, it would be easy to wash off from his life of luxury.

Vasquez motioned for Raul to go with him, and as his right-hand man followed Sinclair to the money, Vasquez turned his attention to Wyatt. Lying prone on the floor a few feet from them, a cruel smile cracked across Vasquez's lips as he approached. Wyatt was bleeding from the eyebrow, the blood having trickled down and stained his gag red.

'Funny thing, isn't it? Power...' Vasquez began, squatting down next to his rival. 'For years, you were a god among men. They rode for you, they killed for you. They would die for you. To them, you were more than a man. You were a representation. A manifestation of what they wanted to become. Without you even seeing it coming, I snatched it from you. Your entire operation, it belongs to me. Your loyal dog, he is mine now and when he kills you, I just want you to remember how I could have done it myself. But I didn't think your death was worth a notch on my karma.'

Wyatt pushed himself up slightly, his murderous eyes locked on Vasquez. A sharp clap filled the air as Vasquez rocked Wyatt with the back of his hand, sending him back down to the ground. Wyatt pulled his arm up, the tape around his wrist giving out.

Ever since they'd dumped him on the ground, he'd been rubbing his wrists against the concrete. Not only had the tape begun to fray and loosen, but the thin layer of surrounding skin also belonging to his forearm and hand had been ground away. The blood had lubricated his wrist, and now, with his hand free, he had to pick his moment.

Wyatt wasn't afraid of death. Never had been.

He was afraid of dying without fighting back.

When the moment came, he was determined to take at least one of them with him.

Vasquez motioned to Sykes, who took a few steps towards Wyatt, his gun hanging by his side. Any nerves that Sam's intrusion had caused evaporated and replaced with a cruel and calculating snarl.

'End of the road, Trent,' Sykes quipped. 'I can't say I'll miss you.'

Just as Sykes went to raise the gun, an audible hum could be heard in the background. As it grew, second by second, the realisation began to flood over Sykes, the colour draining from his face.

Both he and Wyatt knew the sound.

Unmistakably, the growing roar was of numerous motorcycles. The Riders, heading towards the remote and abandoned mill, their engines heralding their arrival like a war horn being blown before battle.

Sykes took a few steps backwards, panicked in his movements, and before Vasquez could ask what was happening, Sykes turned and began to race towards the entrance to the mill. As he dashed across the courtyard, Vasquez yelled after him.

Sinclair, flanked by Raul, emerged from one of the other outhouses, both of them watching in bewilderment as Sykes threw the door to the mill open and disappeared into the building.

The roar of the engines began to echo around the building, and Sinclair felt his legs wobble.

Somehow, the Riders had found their location.

Had come for Wyatt.

Sykes had abandoned him, leaving him alone to face the consequences with a tyrannical drug lord and, unless they moved swiftly, a vengeful leader of a biker gang.

Vasquez turned to Sinclair, who felt Raul press the gun to the back of his skull.

'Give me my fucking money.'

CHAPTER TWENTY-SEVEN

As Alan ventured further into the mill, he could hear the distant murmur of voices. The sound lured him closer to the forecourt, and he walked slowly, the guns gripped tightly in his hands. He approached a window; the sun trying its best to battle through the thick layer of grime that smeared the glass. Alan rubbed his elbow against the glass, clearing his view, and he peered out.

Instantly, he felt sick.

Sinclair was alive.

Despite all the evidence, he'd hoped that he and Sam had been wrong. It was strange to pray for the death of a friend but watching Sinclair stroll across the forecourt with one of Vasquez's associates caused Alan to shake with anger. The betrayal, not only of Alan but of his brother's memory only reinforced his decision. He looked across the open space and watched as Vasquez squatted down over the prone body of Trent Wyatt.

His heart dropped.

Vasquez and Sykes were both there.

Which meant Sam hadn't made it.

Wyatt struggled to sit up, drawing a backhand from

Vasquez, who then stepped away. On cue, Sykes took a few steps towards Wyatt, his gun primed to finish their story and begin a new chapter.

Alan turned from the window and pressed his back against the wall. Taking a few deep breaths to accept his situation, Alan thought of his brother. Peter Alan had been his hero, his inspiration to follow his footsteps into the marines and to try to be half the soldier and man he was.

Alan hoped he'd done him proud. The dog tags that still hung around his neck bore Peter's name and rank.

The only way for Alan to survive now, with Sam out of the picture, was to hide.

To do nothing.

That wasn't an option.

Peter deserved more than to be killed by his own comrade, and the lack of justice Sykes faced couldn't be something Alan took to his grave. He scolded himself for his hypocrisy, having chastened Sam for the path he'd taken.

But he understood now.

There were some things that you couldn't let go of, and that would take you to places you couldn't get back from.

But Alan still needed to get to Alex. At least try to preserve the innocence of someone who had been drawn too far across the line. It was unlikely, but Alan would fight until the end.

Not as a DEA agent.

But as a marine.

Alan's concentration was broken by the raised voice of Vasquez, who yelled wildly at the sprinting Sykes, the large biker running in a blind panic towards the mill. Confused, Alan looked around the forecourt for answers, but then he heard it.

The roar of the motorcycle engines.

He shook his head.

'You son of a bitch.' He chuckled. Sam had managed to call in the cavalry. Below, he watched Sykes yank open the door to the mill, and underneath the platform he was standing on, he heard Sykes's footsteps approaching. The man was out of answers, searching desperately for a way out of the mess he'd created.

Alan wouldn't let him.

Begrudgingly, he put his faith in the Riders to deal with Vasquez, and Alan pushed himself from the wall and hurried to the stairwell, taking the steps three at a time. He stomped off the final step and sprinted as fast as he could onto the production floor just as Sykes sprinted into view.

Alan picked up the pace, leaning forward as he charged.

Sykes saw him at the final second, his eyes flickering with shock as Alan careered into him like a line-backer. The impact was room shaking, and Alan continued forward, using his momentum to carry the two of them into the metal railing, before they toppled over.

They crashed the eight feet down to the next floor of the mill; the landing causing both of them to gasp for air and Alan's guns to scatter across the metal floor. The large, metal panel they'd landed on was a machine winch, used to manoeuvre heavy machinery between the floors of the enormous structure. A few dusty pipes were stacked on one side, surrounded by loose chains and covered in a thick layer of rust. Both men caught their breath before pulling themselves to their feet. Realising the severity of his situation, Sykes smiled as he looked at the DEA agent, a man who had been working diligently to bring the Riders down.

A man of the law.

His only chance of making it out alive.

'Agent Alan.' Sykes smiled, lifting his wrists. 'I guess I'm under arrest, huh?'

Alan raised his hand to the dog tags that had sprung over the top of his shirt and he gripped them tightly.

'Not today.'

Alan charged forward at the surprised Sykes and rocked him with a vicious right to the side, before driving his knee upwards. Sykes managed to block the blow, pushing Alan away before catching him with a right hook. Alan stumbled back and Sykes threw another clubbing blow. As a highly skilled fighter, Alan ducked, allowing the tattooed arm to fall across his shoulder. He clutched it with both hands, pulled it forward, and arched his back into Sykes's body, flipping the man over his shoulder. Sykes crashed hard against the metal, causing a thin cloud of dust to rise up and the entire platform to shake. Alan planted his feet, keeping his balance as Sykes scrambled to his feet in exasperation.

'Hold on.' Sykes held his hand up. 'Look, there is a way out of this.'

Alan glared at Sykes; the once terrifying muscle of the Riders was now pathetically clutching at straws.

'Not for you,' Alan warned.

'You are a man of the law,' Sykes spat. 'It is your duty to arrest me. Serve and protect.'

'Your duty as a marine was to protect this country's interests. To serve with your brothers.'

Sykes laughed, his mocking chuckle echoing off the archaic structure.

'I haven't been a marine for a long time, son.'

'I know. Neither has my brother.' Alan's eyes were locked on Sykes with pure hatred burning within them. 'First Sergeant Peter Alan. A good soldier and an even better man. My brother. The man you killed all those years ago.'

Sykes's jovial face turned to a cruel, twisted scowl as he accepted there was no way out of the situation.

'Then allow me to send you to him.'

Sykes reached behind his leather vest, and his fingers gripped the handle of the bowie knife he'd attached to the back of his belt. Making a show of revealing the weapon he intended to end Alan's life with, he then pointed the blade at Alan and stepped towards him.

Alan awaited the attack, thinking of his brother before uttering the marine's motto under his breath.

'Semper Fi.'

Sykes slashed at Alan's throat, and Alan ducked, then blocked the return strike with his forearm, the blade just slashing the skin. He gritted his teeth, ignored the pain, and drove his knee into Sykes's hip, knocking him off balance.

With the fluidity of a Krav Maga expert, Alan drove his elbow into the side of Sykes's skull, sending him sprawling to his knees, the knife spilling from his hands. Sykes scanned the platform, his eyes locking on one of the guns Alan had dropped on their fall, and he scrambled towards it. His murderous fingers slid around it, and he spun on his knees to take aim.

Alan's boot connected with Sykes's wrist, and the gun flew from his grip. In one swift movement, he switched the momentum to his other leg and drove his knee into Sykes. His patella collided with the bridge of Sykes' nose, breaking it instantly, and Sykes rocked to the side, blood pumping from his shattered face.

The loud roar of the motorcycles rang through the building, and Sykes desperately clawed himself across the platform, his hands helplessly grabbing for the pipes to help support him.

The cocking of a gun caused him to stop.

Alan stood a few feet from him, the gun aimed squarely at Sykes' skull. Spitting out the blood that had trickled into his mouth, Sykes turned and slumped back against the poles, chuckling in the face of defeat.

'Go on. Do it,' Sykes spat, his teeth stained red. He fished under the white T-shirt he wore beneath the Riders emblazoned vest and pulled out his dog tags. He let them drop over his shirt and he looked at Alan. 'Kill a marine in cold blood. Trust me, it's fun.'

Alan felt his finger twitch, pressing against the trigger of the gun. Sykes was baiting him, not wanting to face the consequences that awaited him outside. With tears forming in his eyes, Sykes screamed.

'Just kill me.'

'I have.'

Alan lowered the gun and pulled the trigger, the bullet exploding forward and ripping through Sykes' shin. Sykes howled in anguish as the bone shattered and blood began to pump through the wound.

'Keep pressure on it,' Alan advised. 'And don't go anywhere.'

Sykes, cursing through the pain, called out after Alan as he reached up and grabbed the thick, metal chain that connected to the platform and the roof several floors above. Hand over hand, Alan began to haul himself up, reaching the ground floor level quickly.

As he pulled himself to his feet, Alan wiped the rust from his hands and ignored the vitriol the defeated Sykes shouted behind him.

He'd avenged his brother.

Sykes would either bleed out, or the Riders would deal with him. Now he needed to get to Alex, hoping he wasn't too late.

Just as he started towards the door, a gunshot echoed from outside, and he rushed forward, hoping he hadn't been answered.

'You think you can do this to me?' Vasquez yelled, his arms gesticulating wildly. 'You think you can take this from me?'

Sinclair was on his knees. The blow from Raul's gun had caught him on the back of the head, sending the world spinning and a trickle of blood to slither down his neck. Less than half a mile away, the motorcycles roared in unison.

It was over.

Vasquez turned to Raul; his eyes wide with frantic rage.

'Gather the rest of the men. I want all guns trained on those motherfuckers.' Raul nodded, turning on his heel and heading off towards the side entrance of the mill. 'And tell Edinson to get his ass back here.'

'It's over, Vasquez,' Sinclair said coldly. Vasquez struck Sinclair with a brutal clip with the back of his hand, the thick gold rings splitting the man's lip open.

'I am never over,' Vasquez spat. 'This is on you, you pathetic piece of a shit. You said you had Sykes primed, that this would be simple. Well, look at that motherfucker, running at the first sign of trouble.'

'We didn't account for...'

'For what?' Vasquez slapped Sinclair across the face. 'You said it was bulletproof.'

'For Sam,' Sinclair said through his gritted teeth. 'We didn't know that Sam Pope would show up looking for Alex.'

'Who was it that brought her into this, eh?' Vasquez pushed his finger into Sinclair's forehead. 'You were the one who said everything was in place. But now, we'll do things my way. Unlike you, Sinclair, I do not leave things to chance.'

Vasquez stomped across to the forecourt, and Sinclair

watched in horror as he pulled open the door to the outhouse and stepped inside. Moments later, he emerged, dragging Alex by her hair as she struggled against her restraints. Sinclair watched helplessly as Vasquez dumped her on the ground beside him.

'Alex, are you okay?' Sinclair asked, his voice pained with regret for her situation.

With her mouth taped, she looked at Sinclair with hatred. Vasquez circled them like a shark before pulling the gold-plated Glock from the holster within his jacket. Casually, he let it swing in his hand as he eyed them up.

The distant roar of the motorcycles had no effect on him. The noise had sent Sykes scurrying into the mill. But Vasquez had remained in place, refusing to back down from an impending fight. He'd built his entire empire of confronting violence with an unspeakable level of his own.

Now, as he held the gun in his hand, he was about to set his example.

'Her death is on you,' Vasquez said coldly, before staring into the terrified eyes of Alex Stone, his finger on the trigger.

Alex closed her eyes.

The gunshot was deafening.

With blood seeping down her face, Alex hit the ground. The roar of horror from Sinclair was drowned out by the ringing in her ears.

She opened her eyes, and Vasquez dropped to the floor beside her, his lifeless face a mere inch or two from her own. His blood, which had splattered across her, was pumping from the bullet wound that had ripped through the back of his skull and through his forehead. As his lifeless body twitched beside her, Alex screamed, her terror muffled by the duct tape. As she scrambled to the side, Wyatt stepped over the man he'd just killed and squatted down beside her, peeling back the duct tape.

He offered her a smile.

'You have some explaining to do.'

Alex looked at her saviour with trepidation, and he pulled out a pocketknife and cut through the tape that had bound her wrists together. Wyatt's own forearms were covered with blood, having disregarded his own pain threshold to escape. As he released Alex's ankles from her confines, he offered her a hand up, which she cautiously took. As he turned around, Sinclair held a gun to his face.

'Alex, with me.'

Wyatt sighed, showing little fear of Sinclair. Alex looked at the two men, confused. Whatever the hell was going on, her life was in imminent danger. What worried her was that Alan hadn't reappeared since she'd seen him snooping by the window.

What terrified her was the absence of Sam.

'What are you doing?' Wyatt asked Sinclair, clearly irritated.

'Alex, now,' Sinclair demanded. 'I'm walking out of here, with her, and with that money. If you make one move, Trent, I swear to god I will bury you.'

Wyatt shook his head and then pulled the trigger. A bullet blasted from his gun, straight through the top of Sinclair's foot. The disgraced agent crumpled to the ground, howling in agony as he reached for his foot, the wound already pumping blood onto the dusty concrete. Taking a cold, calculating step towards Sinclair, Wyatt ignored Alex's pleas, and he raised the gun once more, aiming it squarely at Sinclair.

'You made a serious error when you tried to cross me, son. A very serious error.'

'Drop the weapon.'

Alan's booming voice carried over the motorcycles, which were a few hundred yards away. Wyatt regarded Alan with respect, understanding that unlike Sinclair, Alan had the courage of his convictions. Considering that he'd emerged from where Sykes had disappeared, it didn't take Wyatt long to connect the dots.

'You really going to protect this piece of shit?' Wyatt asked Alan, who stepped a few more steps out from the mill.

'He is still an agent of the United States Drug Enforcement Agency. Killing him would leave you in a whole heap of shit, Wyatt. You know that.' Alan turned and looked at a hopeful Sinclair and took pleasure in dousing his optimism. 'Besides, he's under arrest.'

As Sinclair's face dropped, Wyatt smirked and tossed his gun onto the ground. He stepped back, holding his hands up to let Alan take control of the situation. Alan dipped his hand into his pocket, checking the signal on his phone.

It had returned.

He watched his screen in hope for a message from Sam, but it didn't arrive. All he received was the unmistakable feeling of a gun being pressed to the back of his head.

'Toss the phone, vato,' Raul hissed as he stepped out behind Alan. 'And the gun.'

Alan did as he was told, and Raul looked out to the forecourt and the chaos that had erupted in his absence. Sinclair was bleeding on the ground, begging for help. Alex stood with Wyatt, whose eyes darted to the weapon he'd foolishly discarded.

Vasquez lay dead on the ground between them all.

Raul felt his body shake. The vision of his cousin Jose, who had built an empire and a life beyond their wildest dreams, being shot and killed like a wild animal filled him with rage.

Raul was in charge now.

And, staring at the open, vacant eyes of his cousin's corpse, Raul promised him he would avenge his death with the same brutality with which they'd built their empire.

Starting with Alan.

Raul steadied his arm and pressed his finger to the trigger.

Alan accepted his fate.

Alex screamed in terror at the imminent death of the man who had risked his life to save her.

All of them were so transfixed by the situation before them that none of them had noticed Sam hobble through the gap of the panelled fence.

Ignoring the bodies that littered the forecourt, Sam watched Raul lift the gun to Alan, and he followed in turn. With his broken left hand supporting the gun, Sam drew the weapon to his eyeline and pulled the trigger.

The bullet erupted, followed by the loud clap as it exploded forward.

Before anyone had registered the gunshot, the bullet caught Raul in the throat, sending him spiralling to the ground, both hands uselessly clutching his neck as his life filtered out between his fingers in an unstoppable red wave.

Alan looked down at the fallen man in shock, then everyone diverted their attention across the forecourt.

Sam lowered his gun.

Alex was already racing towards him, her tear-stained face illuminated by the sheer joy that spread across it. Behind him, he heard the engines of the motorcycles shut down as the Riders dismounted their bikes.

Sam looked up at the sky, the heat of the sun pressing firmly against him.

For the first time in what had felt like forever, he finally felt like his fight was over.

CHAPTER TWENTY-EIGHT

Alex threw her arms around Sam. The euphoria of seeing him alive had taken over and the feeling of love was over-whelming. As she tightened her grip on him, he grunted with pain, and she quickly released her hold, checking him for injuries.

'I'm fine.' Sam smiled. 'A little sore.'

'You look like shit.'

'I feel it.' They both chuckled before Sam put a comforting hand on her shoulder. 'I told you I'd be back for you.'

Alex tilted her head to the side, resting her tear-stained cheek on the back of his hand. Limping, Sam took a few steps forward, and Alex joined him by the side, steadying him as they approached the chaotic scene before them. Behind them, the panels were shunted open, and over a dozen Death Riders marched into the forecourt, all of them proudly wearing their emblazoned vests, all of them carrying a multitude of firearms.

They had come to finish the war.

As they swarmed forward towards the mill, Wyatt gave them some instructions which Sam couldn't hear, but he got the message. The last of Vasquez's crew would be cowering inside the mill, outnumbered and leaderless.

Their surrender would be quick and easy.

As the group passed Sam, Mason stopped, dipping his sunglasses slightly to make eye contact, and he nodded a respectful ceasefire to Sam.

He'd led them to Wyatt and destroyed their upcoming opposition. To Mason, that made them even.

As the Riders stormed the mill, Mason greeted Wyatt with a brotherly hug. Sam stumbled slightly, the aftereffects of his brutal battle with Edinson taking over, and Alex held him steady as they continued. Sam noticed the dead body of Emilio lying face down in the dirt, a dark red pool outlining his skull, which was quickly drying in the sun.

As they approached the group, Sam looked down at the lifeless corpse of Vasquez, who's eyes were wide open and lifeless. The back of his skull had been blown apart, the remnants of which littered the surrounding dirt.

Wyatt had lit a cigarette, taking a long, satisfying puff. Alan stood, his hands on his hips, blood splattered slightly down his white shirt. As Sam joined them, Alan extended his hands.

'Thank you.' Alan glanced back at Raul's dead body. 'You saved my life.'

'Don't mention it,' Sam responded. Raul had bled out quickly, his hands down resting by his sides, and the hole in his neck had stopped gushing with blood. Sam turned his attention to Sinclair, who had fastened the sleeve of his own shirt around his foot, trying to stem the blood loss. He looked up at Sam in disgust, a desperate last stand before he faced the repercussions of his actions.

'You ruined everything,' Sinclair spat like a petulant child.

'What was the plan?' Sam demanded. Sinclair ignored him. 'Tell me.'

Sam raised his voice and stepped forward, crunching Sinclair's bullet ridden foot under his boot. Sinclair howled in agony.

'Fine. Get off,' Sinclair insisted, and Sam obliged. 'It was pretty easy, really. Build a trail of investigation into the Riders, skimming dangerously close to them. Sykes and Vasquez agreed for Sykes to hit the deal, make it look like I was shot and killed, the body taken from the scene.'

'So, you could disappear?' Sam leant on Alex for support, the blood from his battered eyebrow smeared across his face.

'Exactly. Vasquez has enough to launch an attack on the Riders, Sykes takes the throne, and a partnership is made.' Sinclair shook his head in disgust at his own actions. 'Everything planned meticulously. Everything planned and prepared for. Except you.'

'And Alex?' Sam demanded, the gun in his hand pointed squarely at Sinclair.

'Someone needed to corroborate it all. She was desperate, which gave me leverage. Sykes fast-tracked her to The Pit. We put the deal in place, and Alex would have been the witness to Sykes hitting the deal and putting a bullet in my head.'

Sam stamped forward once more, crunching Sinclair's damaged foot against the dirt. The disgraced agent rolled over in agony, screaming for mercy.

'It's because of people like you, that people like me exist in the first place.' Sam shook his head in disgust and put his arm around Alex. 'He's all yours, Joe.'

Sam nodded to Alan, shot Wyatt and Mason a cautious look, and then draped his arm over Alex's shoulder. They turned to walk away, not before Sinclair recomposed himself, a final stand before the pain got the better of him.

'Joe. Listen to me.' Sinclair scrambled towards his former partner. 'There is a way out of this. Arrest these men. They are wanted criminals. All the evidence is here. Dead rivals. Money. A deal gone wrong. We could be heroes, Joe. Think about it. Think about what it would do for your career.'

Wyatt chuckled and flicked his cigarette while Mason shook his head in disbelief. Sinclair reached out to Alan for support, but Alan took a step back.

The point was made clearly.

'Why did you do it?' Alan demanded. 'Thirty years, Terry. Thirty years of toeing the line, fighting the fight. Why now?'

'Because he's a greedy son of a bitch,' Wyatt chipped in.

'I'm not greedy,' Sinclair snarled. 'I just wanted what I deserved. Thirty years of dealing with scum like you. Criminals. Like. You. And what do I have to show for it, huh? What will it get me? A fucking golden watch and a state pension. I spent my life putting people like you where they belong, and I sacrificed everything to do it. This was my way out. A way to move on, live in comfort and enjoy whatever is left of my life.'

Mason couldn't contain his amusement, and he squatted down next to Sinclair, who flinched.

'Do you know what the rest of your life looks like, pal?' Mason smirked. 'What do you think happens to crooked cops in prison?'

The realisation caused the colour to drain from Sinclair's face, and he couldn't hold the tears back any longer. Feebly, he turned to Alan once more, pressed his two hands together and sobbed.

'Please, Joe. Just kill me.' Sinclair was distraught. 'At least do that for me.'

Alan stared down at his mentor and a man he thought of as his friend. The Riders were right. Sinclair would be tormented in prison, most likely to spend his sentence in solitary for his own safety. The man had thrown away a long and respected career, his legacy and every fibre of his freedom for a payday. It saddened him, and as Alan looked into the man's desperate gaze, Alan could feel his finger twitch.

'Don't do it, Joe.' All of them turned their heads to Sam, who had stopped a few steps away. He'd watched Alan toy with the idea in his head. 'If you do it, there's no going back. Different paths, remember?'

The words hit home, and Alan slid the gun into his holster, much to the dismay of Sinclair who slumped onto his side. Behind them all, the Riders began to filter out of the mill, the remaining members of Vasquez's crew with their hands on their heads and their mortality clearly on their minds. Donnie emerged, dragging a bound and gagged Sykes through the dirt, the man howling through the cloth as they paid little attention to his shattered shin.

Wyatt and Mason stared unblinkingly at him, and the fear in Sykes's eyes was palpable. Lighting another cigarette, Wyatt turned to Alan and blew smoke into the sunshine.

'Sykes is coming with us. The rest are for you. Hell of a bust.' Wyatt nodded his respect to Alan. 'Did you do that to Sykes?'

'You're damn right I did,' Alan confirmed proudly. 'Pretty sure I don't want to know what you plan to do with him, do I?'

'No, Agent Alan.' Wyatt turned with a smile. 'No, you don't.'

As the Riders filtered towards the exit, Sam shuffled slowly alongside Alex, watching with amazement as the scene concluded around him. Whether the outcome was for the greater good or not, didn't concern him.

All that mattered was Alex was safe.

He clung to her for support, adding a little extra squeeze of happiness that he'd made it in time.

———

It had taken a while, but Alan had managed to haul Sinclair to the exit, and he stepped out through the metal panels that the Riders had prised open and slumped Sinclair down against the metal. The combination of blood loss and realisation of his actions had taken its toll, and Sinclair rolled lazily to the side.

Alan checked his former partner's pulse, getting just enough of a reading to declare him alive. Behind him, the Riders watched on. Perched in a row on their motorcycles, it was an intimidating sight, and one that would have filled Alan with fear a few days before.

But somewhere along the way, through the extraordinary events that had unfolded, a budding mutual respect had been forged.

He was aware of Wyatt's code. What he'd instilled throughout the brotherhood and Alan's fight alongside Sam clearly resonated with Wyatt.

They hadn't fought for greed or for power.

They had sacrificed everything to save Alex, a young woman who had been manipulated by the system and thrust into a world she didn't belong. One of the Riders had willingly given up his bike, which Wyatt was now perched on, watching with interest as Alan surveyed the scene.

On the ground before them, four of Vasquez's men were bound and gagged.

A gift from the Riders.

Sykes was sitting on the back of Donnie's bike, their spines held together by a thick chain.

There was no escape in sight, and considering the

audacity of his moves against Wyatt, along with the physical assault, Alan didn't expect Sykes's death to be quick.

Alan felt nothing for the man.

For years, he'd been driven by vengeance but watching the man whimper on the back of the motorcycle, he couldn't even muster pity for him. Face to face, Alan had beaten the man, reduced him to a pathetic shell of his former self. He'd stopped him from seizing the power he'd craved and left him battered and bloodied in the ocean for the sharks to circle.

Alan had avenged his brother. He could finally lay that hunger to rest. As the humidity dropped in the air, the sky began to fill with clouds, extinguishing the thumping heat, and Alan welcomed the cool breeze that danced around him. He reached into his pocket and pulled out his phone, shooting a glance at Wyatt.

'You boys should probably get going if I'm going to call this in.'

In unison, the engines roared to life, their thunderous rumbling echoing proudly around the dilapidated war zone. As the bikes slowly turned and rolled down the incline, Alan beckoned Wyatt over. Wyatt rolled his bike forward, and Alan whispered his request into his ear. Wyatt chuckled, nodded, and then turned to leave.

Alan called after him one last time.

'Hey, Wyatt. You didn't happen to see where the bag of money went, did you?'

Wyatt shot Alan a playful grin.

'What money?'

His engine growled as he shot forward, coasting past the other riders and taking his rightful place at the front of the pack. As they skirted around the bar and joined the main road, Alan watched in amazement as they passed the stumbling figure of Sam, still leaning on Alex for support.

In a show of respect, Wyatt raised his fist in the air to salute him, followed by the other riders.

Alan shook his head in disbelief.

He'd laid to rest the ghosts of his past, uncovered his partner's betrayal, and was about to call in the biggest bust of his career.

Wyatt had seen the death of his biggest rival, rooted out the treacherous breach within his ranks, and was most likely a million dollars richer.

But Sam, all he'd wanted, was to get to Alex. To keep her safe and to help her get back to her family.

He'd given everything.

Risked everything.

Just to keep his promise.

As Alan pressed the call button on his phone and drew it to his ear, he watched as Sam and Alex continued their stammered walk back to town and Alan knew he would do everything in his power to help Sam keep his word.

CHAPTER TWENTY-NINE

The creaking of the chains provided a sharp and repetitive noise to focus on. They hung from the roof of the bike garage, bolted to the concrete, and were usually used for one of the Riders to winch their bike above the ground, allowing them access to the machinery underneath. The majority of the Riders were keen mechanics, and a few of them had opened the Motor Gun Shop a few years back.

With Wyatt's blessing, of course.

Everything went through Wyatt.

Every decision, every step forward. All of it passing across his booth for his approval.

For many years, Sykes had been happy with his place by Wyatt's side.

He wanted for nothing. Drank every day and hung out with like-minded people. He had access to all the cocaine and women he wanted.

All Wyatt demanded in return was loyalty.

Loyalty and respect.

It had never been too much of an ask, but Sykes was internally programmed to fight against orders. It's why he failed at school, why he failed at being a soldier, and why he failed at being a human.

Both concepts were things Sykes had craved, but had never been able to earn. In response to that, he deplored anyone who commanded both, and it had always been a matter of when, not if he would try to take Wyatt's place.

He'd tried.

And he'd failed.

Two days had passed since Alan put a bullet through his shin and left Sykes to a fate worse than death.

Two days with minimal food and water.

Two days of listening to the creaking of the chains that reached down from the ceiling and clung to his wrists, his shoulders numb through their elevation.

Two days of pure torture.

A single spotlight had been trained on him from the far corner of the room, the bright LED bulb making it impossible for Sykes to sleep. That, along with searing agony of mutilation.

His right eye was the first thing that Wyatt removed, an on the nose reference to the old saying,

An eye for an eye.

Sykes had howled in agony as Wyatt had carved it out with a sharp, serrated blade. After that, Wyatt had left Sykes in the dangerously capable hands of Tony Mason. The man had previously settled on a cushy job in the other bar. Until Sykes's betrayal had relit the fire within him, and the man who Sykes had replaced as the Riders' problem solver, had returned to happily settle this one.

Over the course of the next twenty-four hours, Mason had systematically begun to strip Sykes of his identity. The first thing he stripped from Sykes were any tattoos of the Riders patch. Unfortunately for the burly traitor, he had four tattoos, which Mason seared from his skin with a blow torch. Then came the fingerprints, which he took off with a handheld circular saw. To stem the flow of blood, Mason roasted a metal screw fixture over a blowtorch, and with every knuckle he sliced through, Mason quickly followed it up with the red-hot metal.

The heat melted the skin together, cauterising the wound and ensuring Sykes stayed alive.

Despite his pleas for death, every time it seemed as if the pain was sending Sykes to a more comfortable state of consciousness, Mason zapped him with a taser, jolting his body back to life and causing Sykes to excrete beyond his control.

Mason ignored it, his focus primarily on reducing Sykes down to the husk of a man that he'd turned out to be.

Mason only needed to ensure that the fingerprints were removed, not that his work was particularly tidy, and over the course of an afternoon, he'd cut through ten fingers with varying care.

Some of them were still intact, with Mason perfectly slicing the tip off like a waiter de-foaming a pint of lager.

Some of the fingers had been butchered entirely.

As the sun began to set on his second day of torture, Sykes was a broken man. Frail from the lack of sustenance and weakened by his inability to sleep. The pain had pulsed through his body for nearly forty-eight hours, and he was broken.

His eye socket was a bloody chasm, the dried edges turning a dangerous dark green colour.

His hands were a mishmash of jagged bone and blood splatter.

His shirtless torso was riddled with bruises and burn marks.

The underwear he'd been afforded to hide his modesty had been soiled countless times, with the inside of his legs covered in urine and faeces.

As Wyatt approached him, he appreciated the sterling work that Mason had done in chipping Sykes away. When your most violent attack dog bites your hand, you need to put it down.

Not retrain it.

Not provide it with a second chance.

Wyatt had given Sykes fair warning, but the man had let greed and ego dictate his thoughts. Terrible choices, fuelled by his obsession with status. And for those, he would pay the ultimate price, one which Sykes would have approved of from any other angle.

Two days of brutal torture had been enough.

The man was a wreck.

He would die a pathetic man who had soiled himself in fear and panic. A treacherous man, who lacked the nobility that Wyatt demanded from his Riders. They may have been criminals, but they had a code.

A brotherhood.

They were family, and the moves Sykes had made, the vicious contempt he'd held for Wyatt when he was bound and gagged on the floor of the forecourt, meant there was no other way.

As he stood a few feet from Sykes, Wyatt reached out with his gloved hand and rested it on his shoulder.

Years spent together.

Ripped apart by greed.

'It's over, brother,' Wyatt offered kindly. Sykes struggled, but raised his head, his lone eye wet with tears. He nodded his acceptance. Behind them both, the thick, dominant smell of gasoline filled the air as Mason sloshed the gas canister around the garage. As he finished, he hurled the metal can into the shadows and walked back over to the two men.

'Ready?' Mason asked.

'Yeah, one last thing.' Wyatt pushed Sykes's mouth

open and inserted a cotton wool bud. With little care, he swabbed in and around Sykes' mouth before removing it, letting his jaw slam shut, his teeth snapping as they collided. 'Take his teeth.'

Sykes's head lifted again in horror as Wyatt stepped away, enclosing the cotton swab in a ziplock bag. Sykes howled in terror as Mason approached him, mockingly clicking together a pair of pliers.

Wyatt waited outside, enjoying a relaxing cigarette as the blood-curdling cries of anguish echoed around the vicinity. They were a long way from help, and even if a police car happened to approach, Wyatt would send them on their way.

Ten minutes and a couple more cigarettes later, Mason emerged, casually strolling from the garage with his blood covered hands grasping a plastic bag, which jingled as he swung it. Judging from the blood seeping through the plastic, it contained all of Sykes's teeth.

Everything that could have been done to identify him had been stripped of him.

Sykes was nothing.

Just a shell of a man waiting for death. Mason sat on his bike and turned to Wyatt, who stared into the dark shadows that were on the other side of the doorway.

'Do you want to do the honours, or should I?' Mason asked. Wyatt took a drag on his cigarette and then flicked it into the shadow. The orange flicker was immediate, and beyond the flames, they heard the pained cries of Sykes. To drown them out, Wyatt roared his bike to life, and he rolled away from the garage. Mason followed, and as they drove down the dusty side-track back towards civilisation, the fire blazed, eradicating Sykes from the earth.

———

'You going to miss this place?' Sam asked, looking up at The Pit from the bench outside. Having rested up for a couple of days at the motel, a Rider had stopped by to invite Sam to the bar that afternoon. Although the invitation sounded like it wasn't mandatory, Sam didn't feel like taking his chances. Alan and Alex had also stayed at the motel. All of them decided they could do with a rest after the ordeal. Alan had to report into the office on numerous occasions, providing statements and evidence to back up the very real claim that Sinclair had tried to use his position to instigate a drug war, while bribing the guilty party for half a million dollars.

It would be the easiest sentencing ever, and Alan had received several handshakes from those higher up.

Multiple promises of doors opening and the promise of a bright future ahead.

Politely thanking them all, Alan had spent two days soul searching. While being a soldier and working for the government had fulfilled him, he didn't want to follow in the footsteps of Sinclair.

A man so lost in the filth and darkness of the job that stepping over the line was the best option.

Also, watching Sam's relentless quest to save Alex, regardless of his own or the state's rules, had shown him that there were other ways to help. Maybe not by following the same path as Sam, but Alan knew he needed to clear his mind.

Alex had helped.

After the first night, and a few beers, they'd shared a few secret kisses. Unsure how Sam would react, both of them were caught off guard when he called them lovebirds at breakfast. Assuming the role of Alex's big brother, Sam threatened Alan with an *'ass whoopin'* if he didn't treat her right, which drew a few chuckles and empty threats from both of them.

Whatever it was between them, both Alan and Alex looked excited by the prospect.

Sam turned to Alex, awaiting her response, and she sipped her beer casually.

'Not really.' She looked around at a few of the bikers who were conversing nearby. 'The guys were not that bad.'

'And you, Joe?' Sam turned to Alan. 'You staying on to bring these guys down or what?'

Alan smiled sheepishly. His hand was on the table, his fingers interlinked with Alex's. He lifted his Scotch and took a sip.

'I think I have a few ends to tie up here and then a lot of things I need to figure out.'

'Cheers to that.' Sam held up his beer, and the three of them drew their drinks together.

'What about you?' Alan asked, and Sam sat back and took a second. He hadn't really thought about the next step. For so long, all he'd known was the pain of his son's death, followed by the relentless need to fight back against a system that neglected so many.

He smiled and then recoiled; his face still heavy with bruising from Edinson's assault.

'I think I'm going to go home.' Sam shrugged. Before Alan could answer, two motorbikes shot around the corner, their engines echoing down the high street as they approached the bar. Wyatt and Mason pulled their bikes to a stop just outside the bar, causing a few of the Riders to scramble inside, no doubt to give everyone the heads up. Wyatt dismounted and strode confidently towards the table, where all three of them turned to face him.

'Afternoon ya'll.' Wyatt smirked, lifting a cigarette to his mouth. As he fumbled in his pockets, he removed the ziplock bag with the cotton swab and tossed it across the bench to Alan. 'Here. Catch.'

Sam raised his stitched eyebrow in confusion at Alan.

'Side project.' Alan shrugged, turning back to Wyatt. 'So, what now?'

'I think we'll clean up the mess. Drive the last of Vasquez's empire south of the border.' Wyatt took a long puff. 'We won't stop our business, but we'll sure as shit shut down whatever they'd built. That going to be a problem?'

'I don't know.' Alan sipped his Scotch. 'Still figuring out my next move.'

'Hell, if you want a jacket and a hog, let me know.' Wyatt chuckled. 'Same goes for you too, Sam.'

'Thanks, but I'm good.' Sam chuckled. 'I think it's time I went home. Been a rough week.'

'Well, if you ever change your mind.' Wyatt held his hand out, and Sam took it, shaking it firmly. The man was a criminal, but Sam wasn't exactly a saint. But most importantly, the man had saved Alex's life, and for that, he would be eternally grateful. Sam turned, only for a rock-solid fist to catch him square in the gut, causing him to hunch over and gasp for air. Mason stepped back, chuckling, as Wyatt signalled to Alan to calm down.

'We're even, now.' Mason scoffed, before heading into the bar, to his new-found role as Wyatt's number two. Wyatt patted Sam on the back before saluting to Alan and Alex. Alex stepped forward and wrapped her arms around him. Awkwardly, Wyatt patted her on the back, telling her to get gone. Alex then moved to Sam, who held his hand up to satisfy her concern.

Alan clicked the fob on his keyring, and the Range Rover beeped, unlocking from the other side of the street.

'Let's get out of here,' Alan stated powerfully, shooting one final look back at The Pit. He turned to Alex, his fingers interlocking with hers. 'Get you back to your family.'

Alex squeezed his hand and as they headed to the car Sam watched them, a smile spreading across his face.

His war had taken him to the darkest corners of the earth, and face to face with some of its worst inhabitants.

Watching a bond grow between two people he liked was a small pleasantry in a world of pain.

Hopefully, reuniting Alex with her family would feel even better.

They all clambered into Alan's car, and momentarily, they all felt a lull in energy. The exhaustion of the last week hung heavy in the car, and after a few moments, Alan turned the key, pulled away from the curb, and the three of them headed out of Dillon, leaving the town and the Riders behind them.

CHAPTER THIRTY

On the drive back to New York, Alan had stopped for gas and a batch of coffees, and then asked Alex or Sam to drive. Alex, understanding the pain coursing through Sam's body, stepped up, glad to be behind the wheel of a car once more. As she'd sipped her coffee, she glanced into the rear-view mirror at Sam, who dozed in the back seat.

It dawned on her, studying the cuts and bruises that adorned his face, just how much he'd given for her.

He'd travelled halfway across the globe to find her. He tracked her down to a backwater town in an entirely different state, and he'd fought for her.

Sam was like a magnet, incapable of moving away from something that doesn't feel right.

Now, watching him sleep, Alex felt a warm smile spread across her face. She'd experienced a lot of disappointment in her life. From her non-existent father to her drug-addled mother, Alex's hand had been a dud since day one. But through her sheer perseverance, she'd forged a decent pathway for her brother and sister to travel. She'd done everything she possibly could, whether she strayed across the line of the law, to keep them on track to a better life.

And through it all, the only guarantee she had was herself.

Her street smarts.

Her sheer refusal to accept defeat.

Until now. Sam had gone as far as he possibly could to get her back to her siblings, and with Alan deep in conversation with the necessary bureaus, she'd never been closer.

Three hours into the drive, Alan finally made the right call and as he hung the phone up, he gently rested his hand on Alex's knee. It had taken some considerable sway, and Alan had leveraged his current standing among the senior members of his department, but he'd pulled the required strings.

Doors had been opened.

Joel and Nattie were coming home.

Alex felt her hands shake as he told her the news, and at the next service stop, they switched seats. Sam, well rested, took the wheel, affording Alan and Alex some time in the back of the Range Rover. Half an hour later, and Sam glanced into the rear-view mirror to see them both asleep, with Alex cuddled into Alan's hulking frame.

A smile curled across his lips. Whether it would develop further once he'd headed home, Sam wasn't sure. But he certainly approved.

As the miles passed and the hours ticked by, they rode through Virginia and after passing through Richmond, cruising up the I-95. On the approach to Washington D.C, they whizzed past The Marsh Motel in Fredericksburg, and Sam wondered if Tammy had made it far enough away from her abusive partner.

Sam hoped she had. He'd done as much as he could to give her every chance.

A few hours later, they were passing through Philadelphia, with Alan and Sam in a deep discussion about the likelihood of Wyatt and the Riders reining in their drug business. Alan was hopeful, but with his career aspirations possibly elsewhere, he was unlikely to ever know. Sam was less enthused, noting that men who acquire money and power don't tend to be willing to let it go.

With no opposition from the DEA or Vasquez, Wyatt had complete control. He was level-headed, but he was still a cold and calculating criminal.

But he'd saved Alex's life.

For that, Sam would be eternally grateful.

As they approached New York, Alan made another phone call, directing Sam to a government building on the outskirts of Brooklyn. They crossed over the Verrazzano-Narrows Bridge and carried on down through Sunset Park until Alan directed them to the New York City Administration for Children's Services in Crown Heights.

As they made their way through the building, Sam noticed Alex shaking, and he clasped her hand to keep her calm. Alan approached the desk, spoke authoritatively with the senior member of staff, and then disappeared with them into the offices behind. Alex watched on anxiously from the waiting room.

The door opened on the other side of the corridor.

Alex turned, releasing Sam's hand immediately, and then broke into a sprint. Everything turned to a blur to her. The posters on the wall, the notices tacked to the corkboard. Any of the other people watching or dealing with their own issues.

All of them melted away as she ran to them.

Nattie and Joel.

Her brother and sister's initial confusion dissolved and their bright, white smiles lured Alex towards them, and they quickly bounded towards her, the three of them colliding together, which drew a gasp from Alex. To feel her hands around them, to smell their hair. She was weeping uncontrollably, squeezing them as tight as she could. Nattie complained, trying to maintain her teenage cool, but the reunion clearly meant the same to her. Joel however, nuzzled his head into Alex's side, refusing to let her go.

Alex had no idea where they'd been or what they'd been through since she'd been gone.

They would have no idea of the road she'd taken to return.

But now she had them, and as she squeezed them as tightly as possible, she knew she'd walk through hell to stay by their side.

As the three siblings held each other, Alan approached Sam with a warm smile on his face.

'Worth it?' Alan asked.

'She is.' Sam nodded. 'If you're thinking of sticking around, remember that.'

'I will. She's an incredible woman.' Alan gently rested his hand on Sam's shoulder. 'I've got the ball rolling for her to adopt them. I've called in a few favours, but it should take a week or so.'

'Thanks, Joe.' Sam extended his hand. 'For everything.'

'You not sticking around?'

Sam shook his head. He'd long since cried out the majority of his emotions when Jamie had died, but Alan thought he could see Sam holding back a tear or two.

'It's time for me to go home, I think. Face whatever's waiting for me.'

Alan took Sam's hand and shook it firmly. His eyes lit up with excitement.

'I imagine it will be an obituary.' Alan chuckled. 'I had Wyatt bring me a DNA sample from Sykes. Considering the job, they did on that piece of shit, I'd imagine the only identifier they would leave would be a DNA check. Wyatt took the swab. I called in the last of my favours and wouldn't you know it, it looks like Sam Pope perished in a fire in South Carolina.'

Sam's mouth hung open in shock. Alan laughed, and Sam realised he was still shaking the man's hand.

'You did that?' Sam scoffed. 'Why?'

'I don't know. Seemed like the right thing to do.' Alan shot a glance to Alex, who was squatted down, talking to her brother. 'You went through hell to get Alex her life back. I figured I could give you the gift of death. Give you a fresh start.'

Sam shook his head in disbelief. From the hostility when they first met to the final handshake, Sam had grown to see Alan as more than just an ally. He was a good man who, despite his obsession with revenge, still put Alex's safety first.

Joe Alan was a good man.

Sam was proud to call him his friend.

'Thank you,' Sam finally stammered. 'Tell Alex to check the bag in the car.'

'You're not going to say goodbye?'

'It's easier this way,' Sam said firmly, his voice cracking slightly. With that, he patted Alan on the shoulder and turned, marching with purpose towards the exit. A few steps from the door, he heard the growing rumble of footsteps racing behind him and he turned just in time to catch Alex, who had raced after him. She collided with him, squeezing as hard as she could and ignoring any groan of pain he might offer.

Sam didn't.

He just closed his eyes, savouring the moment and the love that existed between the two of them. After a few moments, Alex took a step back, wiping the tears from her cheeks and offering Sam a big smile.

'Thank you, Sam. You saved my life.'

Sam reached out, wiping the final tear from her eye. 'Now we're even.'

He gently stroked her cheek and then watched as Alan walked across with Nattie and Joel, the two of them looking at Sam with understandable apprehension.

'Take care, guys,' Sam offered, reaching for the door.

'One last question, Sam,' Joe said. 'How much money did Wyatt really walk away with?'

Sam pressed his back against the door and smiled.

'About seven hundred and fifty grand.'

Alan shook his head.

'I thought you didn't do this for the money?'

Sam winked at Alex before pressing his weight back against the door, opening it to reveal a warm blast of sunshine.

'I didn't.'

With that, Sam stepped out of the building and merged with the tremendous footfall that accompanied most streets in Brooklyn. After a few further hugs, Alex and Alan led Nattie and Joel to his car, where Alan would drop them back to their apartment block. On the ride over, Alan and Alex arranged a date for the following week. He had an awful lot of paperwork to get through, but his heart was pulling him closer to New York and further from the DEA.

There was something about Alex.

Something that felt right.

As Nattie and Joel thanked him for the lift and exited the car onto the sidewalk, Alex leant in, planted a passionate kiss on his lips, and told him not to be a fool.

It left Alan grinning like a Cheshire cat.

Alex opened the trunk and pulled out her bag, along with her siblings' belongings.

She recognised Sam's sports bag from his room at the motel. There was a note attached to it.

'Alex. Give them the life you've worked so hard for.'

Alex unzipped the bag, peered in, and immediately closed it. Acting as casually as possible, she removed the bag, closed the trunk and then slapped the car, indicating to Alan he could leave. Alan did with a friendly toot of his horn, and Alex felt a tinge of excitement about seeing him next week.

There was something about Joe Alan.

Something that felt right.

But then and there, in that moment, all she could think about was getting her brother and sister back in their flat, sorting through their belongings and ordering them a pizza.

It was time to give them the life she'd worked so hard for.

And later that night, when she counted out the two hundred and fifty grand Sam had left for her, she could feel her hand shaking.

There was no way of thanking Sam for what he'd done.

He'd not only rescued her from death's clutches, but he'd rescued them all.

They were together.

With a chance of building a proper life together.

As she watched Nattie and Joel bicker over slices of pizza, she felt the tears of happiness sweep over her lashes.

She didn't brush them away.

They were a reminder of just how lucky she was, that above all things, Sam Pope was a man of his word.

———

That morning started just like any other.

Leon had risen from his bed early, making himself a coffee and watching the streets of the Bronx come to life, the sunrise like a call to action for the early risers. Businesses opened, and the traffic filtered through the streets, filling Leon with the usual sense of pride for his local community. Today was going to be a difficult day to navigate.

He had a meeting with a financial adviser at the local bank, hoping to get some support for the increasing pile of bills with which his pensions were unable to cover.

The very real possibility of leaving the apartment, where he'd spent decades with Lizzy, building a life he'd clung to lovingly ever since she'd passed away.

As he finished his coffee, he caught a glimpse of himself in the reflection of a photo, his tired, withered face ruining the radiant look of love from their wedding day.

He felt like a failure.

'Sorry, Lizzy,' he said softly, lifting the photo of their love and gently running his wrinkled fingers across her image. 'I guess I couldn't do it on my own.'

Leon clutched the photo to his chest, but his ears picked up the thundering feet in the hallway outside his apartment. The excitable footsteps had been missing for a while and he rushed to the door, pulling it open to see Nattie and Joel excitedly running up and down the corridor. Joel had his scooter and was trying to pull off a neat trick way beyond his skill level.

Leon felt his body shake.

He thought they'd gone.

It had been over a week, nearly two, since he'd accosted Alex's British friend in their apartment, before sending him on to the High Five where she worked. He hadn't heard anything since, although there were rumours that someone had mugged the bar and given the proprietors a bit of a beating. But as his eyes twinkled with pride at watching the two kids playing the stairwell, his stomach flipped as Alex stepped from the apartment, offering him a wide smile.

'Alex,' he exclaimed, and she stepped across the corridor to embrace him. 'Boy, am I glad to see you.'

'Likewise.' Alex squeezed his frail body.

'Are you back for good?'

'Maybe.' Alex shrugged. 'We're hoping to move Mum into a permanent facility and then we'll see from there.'

Leon clutched her hand tightly.

'If you ever need anything, you know you can always knock.'

'I know.' Alex smiled. She then startled. 'Oh, I have something for you.'

Alex handed Leon an envelope, with his name crudely scrawled across the top.

'What's this?' Leon raised his thick white eyebrows.

'It's from a mutual friend.' Alex smiled. 'Right, we better go. I'll see you soon.'

Leon waved his goodbyes, then closed the door. Already the day felt different. The positivity exuding from Alex was a breath of fresh air, and Leon felt ten years younger. With a confused exhale, he opened the envelope, his eyes widening with disbelief.

He stumbled slightly, catching his balance on the door frame.

The envelope dropped to the floor, with hundreds of notes spilling out. He wouldn't know it until he later countered it, but there was thirty thousand dollars in total.

A lot of money.

And a note.

You're a good man, Leon. Never be afraid to accept help. JC.

Jonathan Cooper.

Leon would never know that wasn't the ex-soldier's real name, but he would forever be grateful for his kindness.

With a spring in his step, Leon offered a loving glance to the photo of his beloved wife, and then went about his day, a flicker of positivity telling him that maybe the world wasn't as bad as his years of loneliness had had him believe.

Despite how hard life could hit at times, there were good people out there.

Good people doing the right thing.

EPILOGUE

It had been a long time since Sam had walked through London without looking over his shoulder. His 'death' had made it back to the government and before long, the papers had got wind of the story.

The vigilante, who had escaped prison, had found himself in the middle of a drug war in America, which had cost him his life. Alan had gone above and beyond to make the story stick, even sharing CCTV footage of Sam's assault on the High Five bar, along with the attack Sykes had dished out in the car park of his motel.

It all fed the narrative, and the papers took great joy in filling in the blanks.

But for now, he was a dead man, and that offered a liberty he hadn't experienced in a long time.

Thanks to Etheridge's generosity, Sam had spent a few days resting in New York, booking himself into a high-end hotel that offered spa facilities. Not one for pampering, Sam took full advantage of the massage services, with the masseuse commenting on the war-torn state of his body. Sam spun them a lie about being in a car accident, chuckling at the reality of what he'd been through.

He'd been to war.

For the last year or so, he'd been to war. Countless people had died, numerous criminal organisations reduced to dust.

Along the way, he'd lost people.

Good people.

But he'd kept his last promise to Alex, and now it was over.

The fight was over.

Knowing that, combined with effectively being a ghost, gave Sam the warmest feeling in a long time. Before he'd returned to the UK, he'd visited a salon, having his brown hair highlighted blond and neatened around the edges. He grew out his beard, trimming down only the neck to present it as deliberate.

Sam had never been one for style, beyond a military haircut and a beard trimmer.

But while he might have been reported dead, he still needed to look different. Blond highlights would do for now.

As he strode through Bethnal Green, the sunshine hit him, warming his body, and he felt the traditional British need to visit a beer garden. Maybe that would be the next port of call? As he rounded the corner, he could see the kids filtering out of the Bethnal Green Youth Centre. A diverse group of kids, with different ages, races, and genders all bonding under the wonderful, shared experience the centre offered. Sam waited across the street, watching with a warm smile as Theo's legacy, his dedication to helping the local community had been taken on.

Theo's death still hung heavy around Sam's neck.

He was sure it would until the day he died.

But the youth centre had been a passion project for Theo, and ever since Adrian Pearce had retired from the Met, it had been his, too. Sam could feel the smile spread across his face as he watched Pearce lock up the building, retirement clearly working for him. Dressed in chinos, trainers, and a white polo shirt, Pearce looked plenty younger than his fifty years of age, the only tell being his grey hair and beard, which stood out against his dark skin.

Without the toll of investigating bent coppers, Pearce looked fit as a fiddle. And as he turned away from the locked door, he stopped, his eyes wide with surprise as Sam walked across the road.

'Well, well, well,' Pearce finally said. 'This is a surprise.'

'How are you, Adrian?' Sam offered with a warm grin. The sun shrouded them with a warm glow, and the idea of the beer garden grew in temptation.

'Not bad. You?' Adrian pointed at him. 'You're looking well for a dead guy.'

Sam chuckled.

'You heard?'

'I did.' Pearce stepped forward and thrust his arms out. 'I didn't believe it for a second.'

Sam stepped in, and the two men hugged. Just as he had with Alan during his fight for Alex's survival, Sam had built this unbreakable bond with Pearce by their shared need to do the right thing.

For both of them, it was a compulsion, and the sad reality was by doing so, they'd alienated everyone.

'I need a job,' Sam eventually said. 'I don't need to be paid or anything. I just want to be a part of what you and Theo have built.'

'Good, because the pay is terrible.' Pearce joked before patting Sam on the shoulder. 'Come on, I'll buy you a beer. You can tell me what prison was like.'

Laughing out loud, Sam followed Pearce through the sun, ready to start his first day as a free man, without the need to set the world straight.

As they sat in the beer garden, Sam raised the beer to his lips and savoured the chill in the heat.

He appreciated the company of Pearce.

Sam had accepted where his life was. Who and what he'd lost. The things he'd done.

What he'd tried to be.

A good man.

A man of his word.

And as he settled down, ready to enjoy the rest of his life and the possibilities it held, he realised he was finally content.

The fight was over.

GET EXCLUSIVE ROBERT ENRIGHT MATERIAL

Hey there,

I really hope you enjoyed the book and hopefully, you will want to continue following Sam Pope's war on crime. If so, then why not sign up to my reader group? I send out regular updates, polls and special offers as well as some cool free stuff. Sound good?

Well, if you do sign up to the reader group I'll send you FREE copies of THE RIGHT REASON and RAIN-FALL, two thrilling Sam Pope prequel novellas. (RRP: 1.99)

You can get your FREE books by signing up at www.robertenright.co.uk

SAM POPE NOVELS

For more information about the Sam Pope series and other books by Robert Enright, please visit:

www.robertenright.co.uk

ABOUT THE AUTHOR

Robert lives in Buckinghamshire with his family, writing books and dreaming of getting a dog.

For more information:
www.robertenright.co.uk
robert@robertenright.co.uk

You can also connect with Robert on Social Media:

 facebook.com/robenrightauthor
 x.com/REnright_Author
 instagram.com/robenrightauthor

Cover by The Cover Collection

Edited by Emma Mitchell

Proof Read by Lou Dixon

Printed in Great Britain
by Amazon